THE FUTURE HISTORY OF THE GRAIL BOOK TWO

WAR
FOR THE
GREEN LAND

LANCELOT

J.G. FOLLANSBEE

I0565864

THE FUTURE HISTORY OF THE GRAIL

OF THE GRAIL

Book 2: War for the Green Land

A novel

by J.G. Follansbee

©2020 Joseph G. Follansbee / Fyddeye Media
All rights reserved.
Print ISBN: 978-1-7354656-8-5
E-book ISBN: 978-1-7354656-1-6
Seattle, Wash., USA
Cover art by Christian Bentulan
http://coversbychristian.com/
Edited by Melanie Austin
https://seattle-editing.com/
Proofread by Edith Follansbee

CHAPTER 1:
PRISONER OF WAR

Sir Percival Rathkeale scraped morsels of oat gruel from the bottom of a bowl and fed them to a wounded man. Like miniature vultures, flies circled the putrefying wound on the man's leg. The insects had found plenty of illness and death to feed upon in the weeks since Percival watched thousands of his fellow Viridians die at the River Colum.

The flap of the tent flew open, and a centurion in his crested helmet and red ochre fatigues barged in. "I'm looking for someone named Rathkeale."

Percival stood up, his heavily muscled shoulders filling his blood-stained shirt. "That's Sir Percival to you."

Fire in his eyes, the centurion held himself back. The name tape said "Cantwell." He held the rank of tribune. That meant he was on the general staff. "You're wanted."

"By whom and why?"

Tribune Cantwell spoke in a thick accent. "None of your fucking business. I'm to fetch you, that's all."

"Are you sending me home?" Percival doubted Cantwell understood sarcasm, even if it contained a hint of desperation. Some Viridian families had ransomed relatives. His mother might try to ransom him.

Cantwell grinned. "You've got the least chance of getting out of here alive, Rathkeale."

"I'd like to finish feeding these warriors." Percival gestured to the dozens of injured, some moaning, some motionless.

Cantwell slapped away the bowl in Percival's hand. "You're

done. Are you coming or do you want to join them?"

Breaking Cantwell's gaze, Percival told the Viridian soldier at his feet, "I'll come back and change your dressing, if this nice man lets me."

Cantwell grabbed Percival by the back of the neck and pushed him through the tent opening. Percival stumbled into the mud, but he checked his urge to fight back. For all he knew, the Lucian was taking him to the execution grounds.

Cantwell pointed Percival to the makeshift gate at the end of a lane between two areas of lean-tos, salvaged field tents, and milling prisoners in rags. Camp smoke drifted into the cloudy sky. Surveillance cameras on tall poles followed their movements. The captives watched Percival with a mixture of pity and fear. He recognized a few. They had left the hospital, thanks in part to Percival's ministrations, and they nodded in respect. Percival found it hard to return their gratitude, for he felt more like a coward than a nurse. After all, hadn't he run from the battle like a frightened dog?

Cantwell waved at the guards, who opened the gate, letting the prisoner and his escort through. They walked toward the gallows, where crows tore at the faces of three Viridian bodies. An electric cart waited to take the corpses to the incineration pit. Percival's mouth went dry. Was he next? He could not think of any transgression. No Lucian officer or guard had warned him of anything.

His racing mind flashed to the battle. Screams of dying men, women, and horses filled his ears. On the field, he met blow for blow from each opponent, once slicing open a man's belly, spilling intestines like they were macabre sausages. Percival killed three Lucians, including an officer. Were the Lucians about to take their revenge?

He blinked in relief as Cantwell led him past the gallows to another tent. Four legionnaires guarded the pavilion, and Percival noticed the sigil of Dardarius, the Lucian's commanding general, on their breast armor. The legionnaires belonged to Dardarius' personal guard.

"You there, in the tent," Cantwell bellowed. "I found your lackey." The Lucian pushed Percival forward. He raised the flap.

Inside, the windowless walls danced with shadows. A single lamp illuminated the face of a man. Arturus, dressed in the sack cloth tunic worn by ordinary Lucian slaves, stood tall, but with a slight tremble. The king's eyes glistened in the weak light.

Disbelieving his own eyes, Percival fell to one knee. "Majesty."

Arturus stepped forward and placed his hands on Percival's upper arms, urging the knight to rise. The monarch of Viridiae studied Percival as if he hadn't seen him for a thousand years. He embraced Percival as he might a lost brother. "Sir Percival, I cannot tell you what a blessing from Gaia it is to see you again."

"Likewise, Your Majesty, but—" Percival could not find the words to express his surprise and delight. With Arturus came hope. "We heard nothing. The Lucians would never answer our questions. There were rumors, but ..." He couldn't finish the sentence.

"I wouldn't blame you if you thought I was dead." Arturus collected himself. "For a while, I thought I was dead, despite Dardarius' promises."

"Promises?"

Arturus gestured to a pair of chairs next to a table with bread, cheese, and wine. "I'm a hostage, surety for my country's good behavior and a trade for Merlin."

Merlin? Why Merlin? How could he be more important than the king? "Have they hurt you, sire?" Percival's hands warmed with anger to think that Merlin was more important than the king. "The last time I saw you, you were in chains in front of Dardarius."

"No. I'm more fortunate than others." He glanced in the direction of the gallows.

"Majesty, what is happening? More prisoners die every day. Ten thousand surrendered. It's been two weeks. There's five or six thousand now. There's no food and water and we're living in our own shit. We can't take much more. I've been working in the hospital. We have one doctor, and she's overwhelmed."

"I suspect Dardarius is consolidating his gains in Viridiae before taking us back to Lucana."

"Us?"

Worry creased Arturus' forehead, as if he was imagining the next days and weeks. "Dardarius wants to treat me according to my rank." Arturus chuckled to hide embarrassment. "He has a certain practical honor when he isn't killing people. I asked to have an aide attend me. I asked for you."

Percival startled. Of all Viridiae's soldiers, including men and women of far greater influence than he, Arturus had chosen him.

"I didn't forget the day of the battle. All of us saw the inevitable and ran for our lives, but you said you'd stay beside me. You were the only one, Percival. Did you know that? That took bravery, because if there was anyone the Lucians wanted dead, it was me. Anyone around me would've died too. As it turns out, they really wanted Merlin."

"Why?"

"He has knowledge they want, and it's connected to the stolen Grail, but I don't know the details."

Percival hadn't thought much about the Grail since the battle, feeling his quest to find it was as much a failure as his performance at the River Colum.

"What about Camelot, my lord? We hear rumors it's destroyed. We didn't believe them."

Arturus fingered his plastic tumbler of wine. "The walls still stand, but Dardarius is preparing a final assault."

"Our people will defend it to the last man and woman."

"No, they won't."

Percival's mouth gaped. In the space of two minutes, he'd found the king he thought was dead, and learned that Camelot with its nine towers and tree-lined streets would soon be a pile of ashes. His heart thumped at so much loss in so short a time.

Arturus saw his distress and grasped his arm. "Listen to me, Percival. There's information in what the Lucians haven't told me."

"I don't understand."

"Have you seen or heard from Mordred? Anything from Lancelot, Galahad, or Bors?"

The mention of Lancelot brought back a moment from the battle. She was surrounded by a dozen mounted Lucians. Her war cry was so powerful, Lucian ears leaked blood. Arms and heads flew off with each swipe of her sword Arondight. Percival never saw a scratch on her, but like the other knights listed by Arturus, she vanished in the awe-inspiring chaos of flesh and mud.

"We've seen no bodies, and they're not among the prisoners or the wounded."

Arturus smiled. "Dardarius would've told me if my leading commanders were dead or captured. I'm willing to bet that most or all of them escaped. I just hope they made it back to Camelot and save as many people as they can before the Lucians wreck the place." Arturus paused. "I know you have a special connection to your sister, Dindrane. Can you tell me anything?"

Percival had sensed nothing since last seeing Dee in Camelot a lifetime ago.

"I'm truly sorry about that. I hope she's safe."

"If Mordred and the others are alive, would they try to rescue us?"

"That would be stupid, and Galahad is not an idiot. I left him in command after Mordred tried to depose me, but the people admire Mordred. They'll give him the benefit of the doubt, particularly now. He won't attack for the time being, given our losses."

"What about us?"

Arturus rubbed his chin. "Tell me more about our brethren."

"The Lucians have separated the wealthy from the less-so. Some have already been ransomed. The prisoners who haven't fallen sick are losing hope. Everyone is frightened."

Arturus folded his hands, as if praying. "Things are going to get worse before they get better, far worse. I know that I will be taken to Lucana's capitol as a hostage. You will be with me. The dead and perhaps dying will be left here. Maybe those most likely to pay ransom. Those who can walk will go with us. Those that survive will be enslaved."

Percival thought of the wounded man whom he had fed morsels of gruel. What was the point of saving his life if he was to become a slave? The knight's emotions descended into despair, as he counted all the things he had lost in the past days. He'd lost his country, his sense of self-worth, and his sense of honor. The only thing he'd recovered was his king, who happened to be his only friend. If they could survive whatever was coming, maybe there was a chance at seeing home again.

CHAPTER 2: CONQUEROR OF CAMELOT

Robert Dardarius Juventa, commander of the Sixth, Seventh, and Eleventh Legions of the Army of Lucanus, tapped the gold hilt of his sword, a sign of unhappiness. He'd fought his way through Viridiae, taken his enemy's capital, and he expected to earn a huge windfall from ransom distributions and servitude contracts once he got his prisoners to market. But the main prize eluded him. In his pavilion, its fabric woven with images of horses, armor and weapons, he addressed Arturus.

"One last time, where is Merlin?"

"I don't know."

The king of Viridiae held his spine as straight as he could, given the chains around his neck, waist, wrists and ankles. Robert had him trussed up for the benefit of the cameras. He had to remind people back home that he was a conqueror. The footage would also find its way to the remnants of Viridiae's government as a warning against resistance.

"You disappoint me, Your Majesty. There's no point in lying. It's beneath you."

"I wouldn't tell you if I knew."

The propagandists in psychological operations would edit out Arturus' recalcitrant answers. His image was the important thing. The king appeared physically drained, even sick, with his stringy hair and sallow complexion. You'd never guess he was the inheritor of the legendary Arturii dynasty. Perhaps the story about the Viridian Grail was true. As long as it remained lost to Viridiae, the king and his land would sicken and eventually die.

Robert had no time for folklore. His empress, Vetrania, wanted answers. When he reported his victory to her, the first question out of her mouth was the same one he asked of Arturus.

"You haven't introduced me to your companion."

"Forgive me. This is my aide-de-camp, Sir Percival Rathkeale."

"Ah, I remember the request. Step forward, Sir Percival."

In his early twenties with flaming red hair, the man wore a bloodied shirt.

"Do you know where Merlin is, sir?"

"I'm sorry, but I don't know."

Percival had the same air of defiance as Arturus, but while the king carried himself as a king should, Percival exuded a bitterness that led to misjudgments. Robert didn't understand why Arturus might choose an impulsive child as his companion for the coming ordeal.

"You're one of the Knights of the Round Table, I take it. One whose patriotic goal is to find the Grail. I have news for you, son. We have the Grail. It's sitting in a lab at our best university, right in the heart of Lucana. All we need is Merlin to make it work."

"You stole the Grail from us. Why would I betray Merlin to you?"

"Easy, lad."

Arturus shivered as he restrained his aide. Robert couldn't afford Arturus' death from the disease sweeping through the prisoner-of-war camp. That's one reason he isolated him. Thousands had died since the battle on the River Colum. Disease always killed more soldiers than wounds.

Robert moved a camp chair next to Arturus. who sat, his chains clinking. "Forgive my lack of manners, my lord. It's not often that I interrogate an enemy superior to me in rank. I've killed or captured plenty of generals and governors, but never a king, and an elected one at that. It's like having the whole nation standing in front of you. Sitting, in this case."

Robert signaled to his nephew, Tribune Adrian Dardarius Cantwell, his most junior aide. "A cloak for King Arturus. And get him some food and water."

Adrian reached for a woolen cloak, and Percival stepped forward, ready to perform his role. Adrian practically hissed at Percival, and in an instant, Percival's anger transformed into hate. General Dardarius had seen it many times before in the halls of the capitol. Strangers one moment, mortal enemies the next, usually over something trivial.

Winning the first confrontation with his new nemesis, Adrian draped the cloak over Arturus' shoulders and loosened the cuffs on his hands. Robert was unconcerned about Arturus' potential threat to his person. If the king laid a hand on him, he'd slaughter every prisoner. Arturus knew it as an unspoken truth.

He didn't touch the bread and wine placed next to him.

The air was thick with hate and frustration. For his part, Robert cursed his country's sage-scientists and engineers. If they had succeeded in unlocking the Grail's secrets, he wouldn't be standing here. Lucanan agents, with the accidental help of the Viridian Gawain, did a brilliant job of stealing the Grail and bringing it home to Lucanus. One of the 12 Great Machines that controlled the earth's climate lay at the northeastern edge of the Lucian Empire, but the Grail device at its core showed signs of failing. The sage-scientists couldn't fix it, so Vetrania pilfered the one belonging to her neighbor. She also decided to expropriate the only man who could make it work, Merlin, Arturus' chief science adviser. She ordered Robert to find Merlin. From a military standpoint, his surprise two-pronged attack on Viridiae had succeeded beyond his wildest dreams. But Merlin was nowhere to be found.

"I can understand, Your Majesty, why you wouldn't want to give up Merlin. He's been called the most brilliant man since the Dissolution. A valuable asset, perhaps more than the Grail itself."

Arturus stared ahead, the shock of the past days like a mask. Robert had seen that look on hundreds of his own men and women over the years. A lifetime of soldiery never eased his feeling of responsibility, even in an enemy's face. Arturus had special reason for his trauma. He was completely unprepared for his defeat. Robert almost felt guilty as his legions killed thousands of his people at the River Colum and he was about to raze its capital.

"What's he worth to you?"

Arturus cast his eyes down, but said nothing.

"What if I offered to return all of your territory in exchange for Merlin?" Robert had no authorization from Vetrania to make such as offer, but she was far away and he liked to gamble.

Arturus' lethargy reversed itself, though his laugh was weak as a child's. "Lucanus and Viridiae have been enemies for generations. My grandfather united quarreling neighbors into a force that stopped your cancerous expansionism. We've had a peace of sorts for a hundred years. You wreck that peace and expect me to betray the man who's taught me everything? How could I live with myself? How would history remember me?"

"As someone who won back his country at the cost of a single man."

"Even if you lived up to your bargain, you'd be leaving behind a husk of a country, ready for reconquest whenever you felt like it."

Arturus was right. Robert might honor such an agreement, but Vetrania wouldn't. That's the kind of thing that irritated Robert about Vetrania. He admired the Arturii, including the third dynast who had thrown every man and woman he had, even boys with pitchforks, at his veteran infantry and cavalry. Vetrania could not understand such a thing. She called it a foolish waste. He saw it as the last defense of a noble way of life.

What's more, Arturus spurred his own doubts about Lucana's future and whether its constant wars would end in its destruction. In his weakest moments, he wondered if a change was warranted that favored his view, that peace, not war, was the path to ultimate victory. He took that thought and locked it in a box placed in the deepest corner of his soul. Under the current regime, the thought was treasonous.

Robert rubbed his freshly shaven jaw. "Perhaps we can strike another kind of bargain, Majesty. Perhaps your people will deliver Merlin to us willingly. Maybe the man will give himself up."

Arturus glanced sidelong at his captor.

"Have you ever been to Lucana, Majesty? It's a beautiful city, perhaps more than Camelot. I'd like you to be my guest."

Arturus straightened himself, even as he gazed at the food on its silver plate. "I wish to be treated like any other prisoner of war."

"Don't be ridiculous. You're a sitting monarch. I'm an honorable man who believes in the ancient traditions of hospitality. You'll live in my house, eat my food, drink my wine, and teach me all you know about Viridiae."

"While you bargain my life for Merlin's help?"

"It's a fair trade, I think."

"I don't have a choice."

"No, you don't, of course, but I'm prepared to show my good faith by halting hostilities after Camelot is ours. Half a loaf— you, that is—is better than none. I'll get the other half in good time."

"How do I tell my people about this?"

"You won't. Instead, I'll send a message and token. We will release a prisoner." Robert addressed his nephew Adrian. "Go to the stockade. Bring me someone, perhaps a page."

Adrian returned with a boy about thirteen and threw him at Robert's feet.

Percival tensed, ready to attack Adrian if it weren't for the pila pointed at him by Robert's guards.

"Not so rough, Tribune." Robert chuckled. "Make a nice present of the boy. Send it when I give you the signal."

Adrian leered, as if acknowledging a secret message. He dragged the screaming child away. Arturus' eyes followed the youth, as if seeing himself in him.

Robert raised his voice so that more of the Lucians in his tent could hear. "King Arturus is now my personal guest. Treat him well. We will be spending a great deal of time together."

In his heart of hearts, Robert wondered how long he could keep Arturus alive.

CHAPTER 3: DEE AND HER VISION

Camelot had played its last card, and it had lost. Flames leaped from its nine towers. Time to escape. Time to survive. But Dee wasn't ready to abandon her city. Not yet. She breathed in and breathed out. She closed her eyes, letting her training as a novice theurgist assert itself. She would be like the haystack rocks on the coast, the waves of her people's despair breaking over her with no effect. Terror would not break her spirit, just as the invaders would not break her country.

"Dee! Dindrane Rathkeale!"

Mordred's voice. He approached her on his warhorse, tall in his blood-spattered black cloak, surrounded by a few officers.

"Dee, you have to leave the city." Lord Mordred Lothian, Camelot's last prime minister, dismounted. "Lucian legionnaires are everywhere."

An aide begged Mordred to follow him through the gate. Mordred ignored him, locking his gaze on Dee. "If something happened to you ..."

Dee understood his meaning. He loved her, and he wanted her safe. She did not share the feeling. Not today, at least. Other days, she wanted nothing more than to be near him. She couldn't decide. For the moment, she pushed past him. "I have to get the tapestry."

"The work is lost, Dee. Everything here is lost."

"I have to see for myself."

"Half the palace is destroyed."

Dee wanted to ask about the hall, but she didn't want to hear the answer.

Mordred reached for Dee's arm. "You're in danger, Dee."

Dee removed a dagger she wore for self-protection. "Don't touch me." Mordred had commissioned the light tapestry after seeing her work in a gallery. She owed him something, but she wouldn't back down now.

Mordred's aide drew his sword, but Mordred waved him off. "I can't force you to leave, Dee, but I can't protect you."

In fact, she wanted Mordred to protect her. She imagined falling into his arms and letting him take her to safety.

"We don't have the soldiers or knights to defend Camelot any more, much less one person. We've lost this battle."

Dee flashed to the new video of a captured Arturus. She cried when the camera focused on the grief-stricken face of the monarch. The propagandists would twist the scene to their own benefit. For all she knew, he had defied his captors. But it was hard to fake the look of an exhausted and humiliated man who seemed to ask himself, am I the last king of Viridiae? The scene included a hard-edged man identified as General Dardarius. The narrator crowed at how the legions had destroyed the Viridian forces like a man kills a cockroach with his boot.

Propaganda works best when it tells most of the truth.

Dee also recognized her brother, Percival. Before the invasion, Dee had killed assassins sent by Morgause, Mordred's mother, allowing Percival to escape to Camelot and stop an attempted coup by Mordred. She'd killed the assassins—hired trolls—from five kilometers distant, a theurgic feat rare as snow in summer.

"I can't go with you, Mordred, not after your mother Morgause tried to kill Percival."

"Dee, we can't fight about this now. The Lucians are going to destroy Viridiae, not just Camelot, if we don't find a way to stop them. Your brother and I fought side-by-side against the Lucians at the river. He set aside our differences to defend the country with me. Can't you do the same?"

Whistling military drones in the skies above argued his case. "I'll get out of the city somehow, Mordred, but I have to get the tapestry."

An explosion interrupted the conversation. The aide pleaded with his commander. "Look for me in the west, Dee. I'll protect you and your art work. I know how important it is to you and the country. Promise me you'll leave as soon as you can."

Dee lowered the dagger. Mordred mounted his horse, and after glancing back at her, galloped through the gate.

Had she made another mistake? Had she given up the chance to survive the sack of Camelot? What would happen to her if she was captured by the Lucians? Even in the chaos around her, she forced herself to breathe in and breathe out, but her heart would not slow.

No one guarded the palace. She expected enemy legionnaires in their red ochre helmets, but found none. Loose papers, electronic tablets, and furniture lay scattered in the long corridor leading to the great hall's arched entrance. Percival had fought Mordred here, striking him with a javelin and stopping the prime minister's attempt to depose Arturus. Then came word of the Empire's invasion, and Arturus forgave Mordred. Saving the nation from the Lucian horde mattered more.

When Dee entered the audience hall, her huge light tapestry still shone, the projectors drawing power from batteries. Covering more than half the length of wall above the side aisle, the work was largely unfinished, but the cartoons, sketches, and studies reassured her. The bright colors and subtle animations hinted at her vision of Viridiae's apotheosis when knights found the missing Grail, brought it home, and made the nation whole.

She paused the work, believing she would again stand before the epic canvas, directing the lasers and mirrors into a story of the Grail that would survive the Lucian assault. Taking another breath and exhaling, she set to work shutting down the light projectors, packing them into their carrying case with the controlling tablet, stuffing the case in her pack, and hoisting it all on her back. No one disturbed her.

A distant explosion rocked the city. Bits of plaster rained on Dee. The shock waves came from the west, and she feared for

Mordred if he was still at the city gate.

She raced out of the hall into the palace square. Shouts of Lucian centurions echoed in the open space. Fright overcame her discipline, and she sprinted down the long processional street to the city gate. She half-hoped Mordred had come back for her, but he wasn't there. Was he killed in the blast and his body carried off? For a second, she thought she was the last one in the city, because the gate was empty, its doors blown off its hinges. The Lucians had attacked it, but she saw no bodies or blood. The orange rays of the setting sun caromed off the blackened stone and bronze, giving the gate the appearance of a gaping wound.

Dee might be the last Viridian in Camelot, but she wasn't alone. Several Lucian officers, marked by the crests on their helmets, loitered by a guardhouse. Fearful of discovery, Dee ducked into an abandoned pastry shop, praying the Lucians would leave so she could escape.

Another officer appeared, and the others saluted him. Even at this distance, his eyes signaled an indifference to anyone's pain but his own, if he felt any pain at all. Gaia in Heaven, it was General Dardarius. In the video, he wore a tailored, embroidered uniform, complete with peaked cap, waving the baton of a field marshal. Here, he was in simple, if clean fatigues. Though she couldn't make out the conversation, she had the impression he was looking for something or someone.

"And I thought all the pretty girls had gone."

Dee wheeled around. A stocky, muscled Lucian legionnaire, short sword in hand, at the shop's rear entrance, confronted her.

"I was just leaving."

"I'll bet you were." Seeing no threat, the legionnaire sheathed his sword. "You'll have to stay, I'm afraid."

Dee eyed the store entrance. The legionnaire followed her gaze and jumped faster than Dee might've expected, blocking the way. She moved toward the rear entrance, but he stepped forward, cornering her behind a display case of vegan truffles.

The legionnaire glanced at the sweets, and then at Dee. "Tasty."

Dee gulped. "Let me go."

"Why? I need a new house slave, and Viridian girls make the best kind, so they say."

"I'll scream."

"No one will hear you. No Viridian, anyway. My comrades will think I'm having some fun, and leave us alone. Nice of them, eh?"

Dee tried her best to get past the man, but he taunted her in a macabre dance, staying just out of reach.

"What's that you're carrying?"

The backpack weighed on Dee's back like a ton of stones. "My belongings. My art supplies."

"You're an artist. I've struck gold. You can decorate my house. My friends' houses too. I'll hire you out. You'll make me rich." He lunged for Dee, laughing and leering.

She backed up, but ran out of room.

"Don't be shy. Let's get to know each other."

Dee had practiced swordsmanship with Percival when they lived on their mother's land next to the King's Forest. Neither had formal training. They relied on online videos and books, but they played hard. Trapped by the centurion, Dee recognized her advantage. She feinted to the left, as if she wanted to run by the legionnaire. He followed, and she shifted right, slipping her hand into her sleeve. She removed the dagger, the one she pulled on Mordred, and slashed the centurion's cheek. Surprised, he yelped, raising his hand to his face, already dripping blood. Dee shoved him out of the way, running out the rear entrance of the shop. He roared after her, but she knew where the alley exited close to the gate.

She turned the corner, expecting to see the Lucian commander and his officers, but the gate was vacant. They hadn't bothered to post guards.

Her attacker spotted her and bellowed in anger. Despite the weight on her back, she was smaller, more maneuverable, and she knew the ground. She bolted through the gate, and slipped down a trail that she'd taken in better days to a favorite diner with the best noodles she'd ever eaten. Memories of onion and sage came to her. Would she ever taste the miso again? After ten minutes of hard running, sharp turns, and doubling-back, she lost the legionnaire. The streets of the lower city outside the walls were dead silent. Camelot was empty, except for its enemies.

Dee stared at the burning citadel, the nine stone towers blackened, the wooden roofs collapsed. A standard flew from one of the burned-out towers. Even though its device was too small to see, she knew it was the eagle and laurel of the Lucian Empire. Despite the destruction, and her brush with slavery, a sense of freedom calmed her as she ran west down an empty road. She had survived, at least today. And she was happy, because she had a vision of Viridiae's return on her back.

CHAPTER 4: DARDARIUS' PROPOSAL

Dee walked into an argument among men and women with swords and pistols. A rider from Lord Mordred's camp had found her among the refugees streaming out of Camelot. As she waited in the field tent for her escort to announce her, the soldiers whom she thought were fighting for Viridiae fought with each other.

"Ambush them here." Sir Alan Christopher Bors de Gannes jabbed his finger at a point on a large map west of Camelot. "Cut the column in two and block the road with their stinking Lucian corpses."

"It's a plan I'd expect from a one-armed farmer." Dame Lancelot du Lac crossed her arms. "Exactly what do we attack with? A squad of pigs from your farm?"

"Why don't you go and fight them yourself? You don't need us, O champion of champions, winner of tournaments large and petty." Bors sneered, believing he'd hit a soft spot.

Lancelot's hand itched toward his war blade Arondight.

To Dee, their words fell like blows. Other than the video images of Arturus in Lucian propaganda, and her brief glimpse of Percival, she'd seen nothing of any other survivors. She thrilled to see that Camelot's best warriors had escaped the slaughter at the River Colum and in Camelot, though they were all careworn and bloody.

Here they were, squabbling like children.

It must felt like this a thousand years ago, during the Dissolution, when the world fell apart.

Sir Galahad du Lac-Corbenic intervened in Bors and Lancelot's spat. "Intelligence reports a second column here. The Lucians are following their standard doctrine. Attacking one column would only delay their offensive and cost us troops we don't have. We need another way to defend the refugee columns."

Lancelot and the others were terrified and desperate. They had no answers for stopping an attack on defenseless civilians. Growing up, Dee had heard stories of Lucian atrocities.

The three soldiers sought out Mordred. He back was turned, as if he couldn't stand the bickering. She wanted to go to him, but now was not the time. "We don't have a choice." Mordred's voice was deep basso, soft, and grave. "We'll have to abandon the refugee column."

"Are you insane, Mordred?" Bors hissed. "Are you giving up? Are you going to let these Lucian animals run riot over us? And you thought you'd do a better job as king than Arturus."

Mordred, prime minister of Viridiae until Arturus dismissed him, turned on his heel. His face hard as iron, he addressed Bors directly, though his words were meant for everyone in the tent. "If we attack and fail, the Lucians might slaughter our people. If we leave them alone, acting as a rear guard, they might leave our people alone. It's not as though we haven't inflicted our own casualties. And we don't know what they really want. Why attack Viridiae now?"

Perhaps they were only interested in theft, murder and conquest, as she'd always been taught. Dee's thoughts turned to the precious cargo in her backpack. Precious to her, at least.

"If it's all the same to you, Bors, I'd like to fight for a living population, instead of a pile of corpses." Mordred's gaze shifted to Dee, and his eyes softened. "My dear, you came." He stretched out his hand, inviting her to his side.

After she greeted each of the knights, Lancelot offered a tender hug.

"Have you heard anything from your brother?" Lancelot said.

"Nothing. I was hoping you might have."

"I last saw him alive when we were cut off from each other at the river. Then there was the video. I think you'd sense it if he'd died since. Those special powers of yours."

Dee wiped away tears. Dee and her brother shared a bond few siblings claimed. For Dee, the bond was enhanced by a genetic mutation handed down generations before by pre-Dissolution science.

Bors took a breath. "With all due respect, Mordred, we have a duty to fight."

Mordred lifted his voice to be heard. "We will fight when the time is right. For now, we withdraw. We heal and gather our strength again."

Dee felt her confidence returning.

"We are on our own ground." Mordred lay his hand on his sword hilt. "The people are frightened, but they're willing to struggle for return of their country. If we are lucky and smart, we might be able to get Arturus back."

Dee wished Mordred had mentioned Percival, but she kept silent.

Galahad nodded in agreement with Mordred. Lancelot and Bors exchanged glances.

"Above all, we need allies. Lancelot, I propose you and Guinevere make your way across our northern border and contact the petty states along Lucana's northern border. They hate the Lucians as much as we do. Convince them to join us."

The mention of Guinevere caught Lancelot short. The queen was also implicated in the plot against Arturus, but the king had sent her back to her people in Cameliard. Everyone also knew Lancelot and Guinevere were lovers.

"Galahad and Bors, you travel to the Hot Lands to the south. See if the coastal cities will break their isolationist policies and fight with us. They must see Lucanan expansionism as a threat."

"What will you do, Mordred?" Bors said.

"Run a guerrilla war, for the time being anyhow. If we can gain the allies we need, and if we act together, we can attack Lucana as one. The empress and her generals, including Dardarius, will have to pull their troops back to defend their own borders. That's when we retake our country and teach the Lucians a lesson."

Dee's heart swelled. Maybe they had a chance to win, though it might take months or years. She studied Mordred's strong face and marked his determination, as well as the flecks of doubt. A piece of him was unsure, but he was willing to risk failure, which would likely mean his own death. She decided she'd be with him to the end, if it came to that.

"Agreed?" Mordred said.

One by one, the knights assented.

A man-at-arms lifted the tent flap. "Sir, a patrol brought in a Lucian messenger with a white flag. He gave us this and asked for safe passage back." The soldier set a wooden box in front of Galahad. "We've swept it as much as we can. We don't have x-ray equipment, but the dogs didn't react. The envelope is addressed to the general staff."

Galahad removed two pieces of paper from the envelope, which was imprinted with the golden image of a laurel wreath and the initials "SPDL," which stood for "Senatui ac Populo de Lucia" in the Lucian language used for formal documents.

"One of the letters is signed by Arturus," Galahad said. "He's agreed to be a hostage. He instructs us not to attack Lucian columns, even if there's a chance to rescue him. In return, the Lucians will treat him and the remaining five thousand Viridian prisoners humanely."

"It's a Lucian trick," Bors said. "Did Arturus really sign it?"

Galahad studied the signature. "If it's fake, it's a good fake."

"That settles that," Lancelot said. "We stay away from the Lucians for now."

"The other letter?" Mordred said.

Galahad read silently. "It's from Dardarius. He's repeating his pledge. He also wants something: Merlin."

Mordred was incredulous. "Why?"

"He doesn't say, but he says he'll trade Merlin for Arturus. It must be something to do with the Grail." Galahad read further. "He's also sent a gift encouraging us to meet his demands."

Galahad set the letter down, and peered into the box. The stench of death filled Dee's nostrils. She was almost used it to by now. In a corner was a rumpled cloth wrapped around something round. Gingerly, despite the soldier's assurance that it wasn't a booby trap, Galahad removed the object and unwrapped it. Blood stains appeared and then a face.

The "gift" was the head of a boy about twelve or thirteen. Dee retched and turned away.

"Lucian cocksuckers," Bors said. "I recognize him. He was from a family next door to my farm."

"This is a typical Lucian warning," Mordred said. "This could've been Arturus' head. This is what we're up against."

It could've been Percival's head. The flicker of hope fanned earlier by Mordred dimmed in Dee's heart. Mordred was right to order a withdrawal, but she wondered if her people would ever have the strength to defeat a nation that murdered innocents without a second thought.

CHAPTER 5: ESCAPE ATTEMPT

A squad of legionaries stormed through the prisoner-of-war camp before dawn. The soldiers rousted everyone out of their tents or lean-tos, ordered them to gather their belongings, and to form up in ranks. An overnight rain had soaked the torn-up ground, turning every square centimeter into a slippery mess. Within ten minutes, legionaries prodded the five thousand or so prisoners through the main gate.

The surprise orders magnified Percival's frustration. The Lucians had confiscated all their personal coms, cutting the prisoners off from the outside world. They wouldn't supply paper and pencils for letters, and no messages arrived from Camelot. They rarely had any idea what was happening.

It was easy to feel that Viridiae had abandoned the prisoners. The only thing that gave insight into the outside world's attitude were the disappearances. A prisoner might be called out and vanish into the Lucian camp. When they executed prisoners, the Lucians always displayed the bodies as lessons. They dumped prisoners dead from disease or hunger into mass graves, where they could be glimpsed. But the disappeared never returned, dead or alive. Rumors persisted that these prisoners had gone home after their families paid backbreaking ransoms.

The only ransom Dardarius would accept for Arturus was Merlin.

"What about the infirmary?" Percival asked Tribune Cantwell, who was supervising the move.

"If any of your Viridian slackers can get out under their own power, they can join the march."

"And if they can't?"

"Let the vultures enjoy a feast."

All might not be lost for those left behind. Perhaps the Viridians who lurked in the hills behind the camp would help them. The entire Lucian force was pulling up stakes, though Percival knew at least one legion had departed westward days previous, probably to attack Camelot.

"Where are we going?"

"Transietum, and then to Lucana."

Transietum was the terminus of Lucanus' northern railway. "That's almost 500 kilometers from here. Where are the transport trucks?"

"Are you serious, Viridian?"

Percival tamped down his growing anger. "If you didn't starve us or beat us, we might be able to walk ten kilometers, but not 500."

"Don't worry, my friend." Cantwell mocked Percival with a softer tone. "I'll keep you alive until you get to the rail head. A dead prisoner isn't worth much on the labor market in Lucana."

By labor market, Cantwell meant the servitude market, where prisoners and criminals signed contracts to work ten years or more. "You expect me to hand over my life to a Lucanan factory?"

"And I expect you to be grateful for it."

Percival could practically hear the coins jingling in Cantwell's pockets. They were the cut he and his uncle, Robert Dardarius, would earn from brokering the contracts.

The departure meant he had to revise his plan to escape. He'd scouted for opportunities since the day of his capture, but nothing had presented itself. The march might create the disruption he needed to steal away. For the moment, he helped a few of the healthier prisoners in the infirmary onto the two hand-drawn carts allowed the hospital. An electric cart carrying four legionaries sped past him, splashing mud on his already caked tunic.

By midday, a rough column of prisoners headed east, headed

by Arturus, with Percival at his side. They followed the north bank of the river, flanked by legionaries on foot and horseback. Dardarius offered Arturus a cart, but the king refused.

By the end of the day, a pattern set in. Wounded or injured prisoners who could not carry on or persuade others to help them were treated as refuse. Legionaries speared them or shot them where they fell, taking any valuables. Viridians who raised objections faced verbal and physical abuse, and the prisoners learned to keep quiet. Some whispered that servitude was preferable to death. Perhaps if they behaved themselves and worked hard, they might buy their own freedom and return home.

Percival knew better. Veterans of past wars with Lucanus told of captives taken to the remotest parts of the empire, only to be sold to slavers who transported them across the Eastern Ocean to Africa or the lands of the Red Sovereigns. He'd rather die than never see Dee or his mother again. He sometimes thought of Lina Catalpec, the girl in the art gallery. He was a Knight of the Round Table, he'd fight for his freedom, and he'd see them all again.

He did not know how he would tell Arturus of his plans. At the end of the first day one of the march, he sat quietly with Arturus in the tent set aside for the monarch and his aide.

"Majesty, I'm leaving tonight."

Arturus paused while finishing a bowl of watery oat gruel. "I understand."

"I think this is the best moment, while the Lucians are still sorting out their plans for the march, and we're near the mountains, where we have places to hide. When we reach the desert, escape will be much harder."

"Seem reasonable."

"Two men are going with me."

"Strength in numbers. Good."

Arturus seemed less than enthusiastic. "I feel it's my duty, sire."

"Of course it is."

"You don't seem impressed."

"You expect me to be impressed with doing your duty?"

"Aren't you going to order me to stay with you?"

"Why would I do that?"

Arturus' attitude confused Percival. The knight expected his sovereign to at least raise an objection along the lines of "too dangerous" or "you're needed here." Instead, Arturus appeared almost uncaring about Percival's departure. "Do you want me to go?"

"No, I don't, but it's not for me to say. I will miss you, Percival, and I'm afraid for you, but I won't keep you from trying."

"Come with me."

Arturus' laugh came from his mostly empty belly. "What would that look like to our comrades?"

"That you can still fight. That you can tie up enemy soldiers with a search. That you can defy Dardarius."

"What happens when I'm recaptured?"

"You won't be. You'll have friends who'll help."

Arturus looked thoughtful. "Even though I'm a prisoner, I'm still king and commander to five thousand of my people. I can't walk out on that. You don't have that kind of burden."

"You won't object?"

"Like I said, it's not really my decision to make. Even if I did object, I think you'd eventually disobey me. You've done it before, when you joined the expedition to Koda. I wouldn't blame you if you did."

They remained silent for a while, bathed in streaks of light from battery-powered lamps. Percival's heart quickened, anticipating the night ahead. "I will tell everyone back home what a great man you are."

Arturus grinned. "Just tell them not to give up, even if they think I'm dead."

They rose to their feet together and embraced.

"Go with my blessing and Gaia's protection, Sir Percival."

Percival bowed his head in thanks, and lifted the tent flap, disappearing into the night.

* * *

Percival met his companions Eli and Sil at the edge of camp after midnight. Eli was another volunteer nurse in the infirmary. Sil had come in for treatment for a festering wound after the battle on the River Colum.

They padded through the sleeping camp, doing their best to avoid notice. A sieve had fewer holes than the camp's perimeter, and the Lucian guards were equally as tired as the prisoners. Clutching crusts of bread hoarded from the evening meal, they slipped away, pledging to stay together until they reached a friendly town or farm.

They headed for the nearest cover, a wooded area a hundred meters from the main camp. An overcast made visibility nil, but they could hear rustling in the brush. Percival imagined night creatures waiting for the marchers to break camp the next morning, when the animals could scour the leavings for food.

Once in a while, he heard voices. Other prisoners had the same idea. He almost laughed at the notion that no prisoners would remain to be sold by the time the Lucians reached Transietum.

The baying of dogs sent a shiver through Percival. He hadn't seen any dogs among the Lucians in camp. Had they hired local Lucian sympathizers? It wasn't uncommon, especially on the eastern border, where some ranchers resented Camelot's edicts. The barking escalated. Percival resisted the urge to run. He could barely see his feet in the darkness, and one slip could mean a broken ankle or leg.

Eli gave in to his panic. He'd found a thin path through the woods, and ran. A few seconds later, Percival heard the pounding of horse's hooves and a scream. He knew Eli was dead.

Sil had disappeared long ago. So much for sticking together.

Percival found himself in a clearing. Looking up, enough moonlight filtered through the clouds to turn the branches of hemlock and fir into silhouettes. The dogs' excitement surrounded Percival; he was flanked by searchers and he had nowhere to hide. Blood pounded in his ears. Perceiving activity to his left, he moved to the right and heard the heavy breathing of a winded horse. He was trapped.

Bright white lights blinded him. He raised his arms as a shield, expecting a sword blow or the pain of a pila's stab.

"Sir Percival, I'm disappointed in you."

Tribune Cantwell's voice. Percival dropped his arms and squinted, wishing his eyes would adjust faster and confirm his fears.

"I knew you'd run, but I didn't expect it to be so easy to find you."

Cantwell sat on his warhorse. A drone with floodlights hovered over him, back-lighting his helmeted face, so that his voice was disembodied, like a ghost. Another cavalry rider and a legionnaire arrived with Sil in custody.

"You need to pick your friends better, Percival. My informant has been very helpful."

Percival realized what happened. The Lucians watched all the prisoners as best they could, but Cantwell put extra eyes on him, in part because he was a prominent knight, and he was close to Arturus. An escape by Percival would look bad in Lucanus. Percival regarded Sil as he might an infected boil.

"Don't blame your companion, Percival. I threatened to take his skin off in strips if he didn't report every time you take a shit. Fear is quite a motivator, don't you think?"

Cantwell dismounted and approached Percival, who squinted against the lights. The Lucian punched him in the cheek with his gloved fist. The knight collapsed to the ground, stunned and humiliated.

"Don't ever try to escape again, or I'll cut your throat."

Cantwell pulled Percival to his feet and tied his hands behind his back with a leather thong. He looped a rope around Percival's neck and tied the other end to the pommel of his saddle. Percival felt like a limp rag, totally powerless. The overcast had broken, and a half-moon cast thin light over the forest. Cantwell half-walked, half-dragged Percival back to the camp. By the time they reached camp, the rope had rubbed Percival's skin to bleeding.

Percival spotted Eli's body, thrown into a pit with five others.

Cantwell released Percival in front of Arturus' tent. He glanced at the rope burn. "Put some of this on the burn." Cantwell handed him a vial of ointment. "I wouldn't want your little scratch to get infected."

"Why do you care about my health?"

"I don't, but Dardarius does, and I answer to him."

Percival vowed Cantwell would answer for his crimes against his comrades. He'd find a way to take care of Sil as well.

"You Viridians are such idiots. You could've walked out of here today yourself. Instead, you're going to have loads of fun over the next few weeks."

"What are you talking about?"

"Your mother appealed directly to Dardarius."

"What?"

"She hocked all her property for your ransom. She was ready to deliver cash. Then you ran and blew your chance. Wouldn't look good for my uncle to hand over a prominent escapee at the standard rates, especially someone like Sir Percival Rathkeale, would it? Your ransom price just tripled."

The news shocked Percival. Nothing had reached his ears. Eleanor must've had a direct line to Dardarius.

Then he remembered the stories his mother told of her friendship with Arturus. Had he known about the ransom offer, and said nothing to him? Had he kept quiet, knowing Percival would likely be recaptured and brought back alive? That might explain his nonchalant attitude about his escape plan.

Arturus greeted Percival as warmly as he would a son. Percival was relieved to see his king again, but he held back returning Arturus' embrace.

"What is it, Percival?"

"Why didn't you tell me, sire?"

Arturus didn't answer. Instead, his shoulders slumped a little more than usual, as if a new burden had fallen upon them. "I can't order you to stay, Percival, but I can't let you go. You are right that we have to continue the fight, but we're overwhelmed. A single escape is nothing, and a ransom only makes the Lucians stronger and Viridiae weaker. When I heard your plans, I gambled that you would be recaptured alive. I'm glad that it paid off. Believe me, we'll get home again, but it has to be on our terms, not the Lucians'."

Percival willed himself to accept Arturus' judgment, but he left the man upset and confused.

CHAPTER 6: RECRUITING GUINEVERE

Dee traveled next to a smoldering fire. That's how she regarded her escort and companion, Dame Lancelot, as they approached the fortified estate. The knight reminded Dee of the blackened landscape in the aftermath of a forest fire on the edge of her mother's land. Smoke puffed from the earth, as if it were resting up for another burn. Dee and Lancelot had left Mordred's base camp a few days before on a mission to find allies. As they chatted before the hearths of country roadhouses along the way, Dee sensed a burning anger, its edge honed by the kind of sharp, deep hurt only a lover can inflict.

Like Lancelot, the owner of the estate was also Dee's friend, but the crenelated walls, imposing gate, and patrolling surveillance drones at Cameliard gave the buildings the menace of a prison, not a home. In the early evening chill, the security lights illuminated the gate with an icy glare, magnifying Dee's trepidation. The house's occupant, however, had invited Dee, though the expected welcome didn't dampen her anxiety.

Dee worried how Queen Guinevere, Cameliard's mistress, might receive Lancelot. Evidence implicated the queen in an interrupted conspiracy to depose Arturus, and he had banished her to Cameliard just before the battle at the River Colum. Lancelot had fought Mordred in the Great Audience Hall—the site for Dee's commission—when she discovered the plot. She'd come close to dying at his hands, if Percival hadn't intervened at the last moment.

Lancelot went to Guinevere afterward, but the queen sent her away. In the wake of that parting, Lancelot's mood soured. After the battle, she came back with a new measure of tension, perhaps because of Arturus' capture. The king was Lancelot's best friend, betrayed by friends and lost to enemies. Was Guinevere the former or the latter?

On the road to Cameliard, Lancelot treated Dee warmly, asking after the health of Dee's mother and listening as Dee complained of missing her brother and her art practice. Dee marveled at Lancelot's dedication to the warriors' craft. She took time out at every stop to exercise her skills with sword, shield, and single-shot pistol. In front of Cameliard's main gate, Lancelot leaned forward as if to spur her animal to a gallop and attack it. She surveyed the ground ahead and relaxed, perhaps deciding that a frontal assault was imprudent.

Would Guinevere and Lancelot make peace for the good of Viridiae?

Uniformed guards in black and gold livery checked Dee and Lancelot's identification against their tablets and opened the outer and inner gates. The visitors dismounted, leaving their horses to a groom. A chauffeur invited them to enter an electric car. The drive to the main house took two or three minutes over a winding gravel drive, and in the fading light, the mansion loomed over a broad lawn. Less stark lighting along a flight of stairs led to a door carved with the Cameliard's crest in the form of a stylized puma.

A butler opened the door to the foyer, where another servant took Dee and Lancelot's wraps. The entrance hall impressed Dee, with its bright, but not glaring chandelier. Modest, yet exquisite 2-D paintings and 3-D light tapestries decorated the walls. Many depicted ancestors whose faces suggested a thousand secrets. Behind the décor and the efficient care of the staff, Dee sensed a thousand eyes on her. The house was alive with surveillance, something Dee expected from the most powerful woman in

Viridiae.

The queen called Dee's name and stretched out her hands in greeting. Before the war, Guinevere had championed Dee as an artist, helping her get the commission in the Great Audience Hall. The memory clouded Dee's attitude, but the feeling was swept away by Guinevere's warm cheek-to-cheek embrace. Radiant in a modest navy house dress, Guinevere was happy, even relieved, to see a friend from Camelot.

Guinevere's expression grew formal as she greeted Lancelot, as if raising a defense. Lancelot bowed to kiss the queen's signet ring. Dee could read the tug of war between anger and love in Lancelot's round face.

"Dame Lancelot," the queen said, "I didn't expect to see you so soon after our losses."

"Lord Mordred asked me to accompany Ms Rathkeale."

Like all powerful people, Guinevere dissembled as a way to protect their knowledge. Morded informed Guinevere of Dee's mission, and it was impossible to imagine that the queen didn't know of Dee's escort. On the one hand it was silly, but Guinevere —and Lancelot, for that matter—were skilled at maintaining fictions. For years, they kept their relationship secret, or at least discreet, which almost made Dee laugh, because all the world knew. It was known, but not discussed. People thought Arturus knew as well, but he never hinted at it. He had to participate in the lie. In a political sense, Guinevere was his greatest ally, because her family controlled the biggest single chunk of land and wealth in the country. Arturus couldn't afford to alienate her. Even as he loved her as a husband, he allowed Guinevere a private life separate from his, as long as it didn't impinge on his rule. That agreement nearly broke down with Mordred's attempted coup. The Lucian invasion changed everything. How long could Arturus ignore the affair?

Guinevere invited the visitors to an adjoining room for tea and snacks. "I would've thought, Lancelot, that you'd be helping Sir Galahad plan our resistance."

"Before Arturus was captured, he made Galahad overall commander, as you know, my lady. Mordred has taken over the political aspect of our resistance, something Galahad is glad to hand over, I think."

"Which brings us to Dee's visit."

During her briefing by Mordred's staff, Dee learned of his strategy, but she nearly asked to be relieved of the responsibilities he gave her. Dee was a minor figure in court life, the daughter of a noblewoman who rarely set foot in Camelot. Mordred trusted her, but she felt out of her depth. Just two years out of university, she'd only lived in Camelot since age 15, when Arturus invited her and Percival to become part of his household. Politics was not Dee's strength.

A shadow crossed Dee's face with thoughts of her brother. Guinevere noticed. "Do you want to rest before we discuss business, Dee?"

Dee straightened her back. Mordred had given her a mission, and the part of Dee that loved Mordred as a man didn't want to disappoint him. "No, my lady. We don't have a lot of time."

Dee and Lancelot explained the tactical situation, including Dardarius' demand for Merlin in exchange for Arturus. Guinevere listened intently, though Dee understood that she probably knew the outlines, if not the details, of Viridiae's predicament. Like everyone, Guinevere monitored the news nets, and she had her own sources at court.

"In short, my lady," Dee continued, "my lord Mordred is asking you and Dame Lancelot to request help from our friends in the north and east on Lucana's border. In exchange, we will relieve pressure on their borders by harassing the Lucians, forcing them to redeploy troops elsewhere. When the time is right, all the allies will attack Lucana at once. We hope that will cause our enemy to withdraw from Viridiae."

"What about the Hot Lands to the south and east?" Guinevere said.

"Galahad and Bors are planning an expedition to the area," Dee said.

Lancelot leaned in. "Because of the harsh climate, it's sparsely populated, but we don't want problems at our back door, so to speak."

"And the cities on the southwestern coast?"

"They're watchful, but the fighting is distant to them," Dee said. "They're taking a hands-off attitude."

"That's odd. If Lucana succeeds in conquering Viridiae, Gaia forbid, the cities would have a hostile neighbor to their north. I can't believe they don't care."

Dee shrugged. "That's what I've been told, my lady."

"It's our belief," Lancelot added, "that Empress Vetrania is less interested in conquest than capturing Merlin. Once she has him, she will pay less attention to Viridiae, allowing us to take back what is ours."

Guinevere gazed out a window. The evening had turned to night. Pinpricks of light in the distance suggested the edge of her estate. "Are you planning to hand Viridiae's most important sage-scientist to our enemies?"

Dee and Lancelot glanced at each other. "Viridiae must have its elected king back," Lancelot said. "Our people love him. His loss might break their spirit."

"Arguably, Merlin has more value than Arturus," Guinevere said.

The statement shocked Dee at first. She realized, however, that Guinevere, as a leader, needed to subsume her personal feelings for her husband against the costs of giving up the country's best scientific mind.

Dee said, "We're given to understand that Merlin has volunteered to go to Lucana."

"I might add, though I don't know specifically, that Merlin has a reputation as a trickster. Rumors are already swirling that he has something up his sleeve." Lancelot grinned, as if sending a coded message. "We're certain he'd never deliberately help the Lucians with whatever it is they need."

"Do we know why they want Merlin?"

"It might have something to do with the stolen Grail," Dee said. "He's the world's leading expert on the Great Machines, and one of them runs in Lucana's northeast province. It might be failing, just like ours."

"Gaia preserve us if more of the Great Machines are failing. They're the only good things left to us from the pre-Dissolution world. Without them, what would happen to the climate?"

Neither woman answered. Dee knew it was a rhetorical question, because the answer was clear. A thousand years ago, the Great Machines were the last effort by the Old Civilization to stop catastrophic climate change. The scheme worked, until the last decade or so, when the devices began to fail. The Grail was a critical piece of hardware, and Merlin had been struggling to understand how it worked, at least until it vanished and turned up on the island of Koda. The Lucians had stolen the Grail belonging to Viridiae's machine. Did that mean the Lucian version was broken? No one knew.

"My lady, will you help us?" Dee said.

"Well, that goes without saying, doesn't it? What kind of queen would I be if I didn't volunteer? In fact, I am already packed for a long, difficult journey."

Dee laughed and clapped her hands. "We didn't doubt you would, but hearing you say it makes me happy."

"And what does Dame Lancelot think?" Guinevere showed a hint of anxiety.

"If we can convince just one of the ten provinces to help us, I'll be thrilled."

Lancelot's smile doubled Dee's confidence.

Guinevere said, "Did Mordred have a strategy?"

"Other than approaching a strong military power, he had nothing to suggest," Dee said. "He thought you would know best."

"Say what you will about that man's ambition, he knows how to delegate. I suggest we focus on the Ontaríi. I have well-placed relations in Villefroide's navy. Lucian ships harass them to distraction. I think we'll find many sympathetic ears."

* * *

Guinevere promised an early start, and when a servant showed Dee her room, she found a hot meal of lentil soup and fresh country bread on a side table. Dee caught up on the war news via her tablet. Though Camelot the physical place was destroyed, it still existed in the minds of Viridians and on the net.

She had no news of Percival. The strength of their connection depended on distance. The further away he was, the weaker her awareness of his health and well-being. Occasionally, like a sound wave that travels across the still waters of a wide lake, she felt his spirit, and it gave her hope that he was alive, if not necessarily well. The connection had never faded to nothing, which would signal his death, she believed. The connection, however weak, gave her hope.

The soup, a mug of mulled Napene wine, and a fire in the hearth urged her to the bed and its piles of quilts. Dee thought she could sleep for days.

A couple of hours into her slumber, however, an argument awoke her. The oak paneling on Dee's wall muffled the mixture of shouts and pleas, but the voices belonged to two women. Guessing who they were, Dee resisted the urge to eavesdrop. She'd heard her share of lovers' fights while living in a group house near Camelot University, and she avoided the spats because they were so juvenile. Here, though, the queen of Viridiae and the country's greatest knight quarreled. In a moment of anxiety, she imagined Lancelot drawing her sword and doing something unspeakable, until she remembered that Lancelot had left her weapon with her horse, which was taken by the groom. That said, she'd likely have a dagger. So would Guinevere.

The argument intensified, and Dee, wide awake, could no longer resist listening in. Guinevere assigned Lancelot a room down the hall from Dee. The young woman donned a cotton robe, opened her door with the stealth of an assassin, and tiptoed down the carpeted hall. Dimmed electric lights showed the way. In an instant, the shouts exploded when Lancelot's door flew open and Guinevere stormed out. Dee ducked behind a plush chair and tried to make herself as small as possible.

"I've had enough of your moralizing, Lancelot. Life is more complicated than you think."

Dee couldn't see Guinevere, but she could hear the trembling in her voice. She'd been crying. Heavy steps signaled her departure. Other heavy steps followed: Lancelot's.

"Everything is politics and intrigue to you," Lancelot shouted. "I'll stab your back if you stab mine. That's your motto."

"You're oversimplifying again. Everything is black and white to you."

"You're either loyal to your king or you're loyal to yourself. You were going to marry Mordred, weren't you?"

"I told you, only if Arturus gave up the throne. And only if Arturus granted the divorce."

Dee stopped herself from gasping. Hearing about the conspiracy directly from the queen's mouth made Dee shudder, as well as fearful. What if her eavesdropping were discovered?

"We should keep our voices down," Guinevere said, as if hearing Dee's thoughts. "Dee is discreet, but she's no fool."

"You've made me feel like a fool." Lancelot's voice lost some of its emotion, a mixture of hurt and fright. "Why? I just want to understand. I love Arturus like a brother. I'd fight every Lucian soldier single-handed if it meant freeing him and the country. But I love you as well. How can I be loyal to my elected king and to the love of my life who tried to take what the people gave him? It's driving me crazy!"

Dee's heart went out to Lancelot. The knight had 15 or more years on Dee, but she sounded like one of Dee's peers, at least when it came to matters of the heart.

"This isn't easy for me either," Guinevere said. "When I think of you, my whole body quivers, like someone has plucked a bow. But I'm also the leader of my own people. Cameliard is more than this building and estate. It's almost a third of Viridiae, and I have a claim to lead my country as much as the Arturii. I can't ignore that."

"Must you do it by stealth? Must you take it with a traitor like

Mordred?"

Dee imagined Lancelot's other dilemma: She needed to follow or at least tolerate Mordred, because he had the political skills to keep Viridiae together. Dee had seen how ordinary people expected him to restore their country.

"I will do what I need to do, Lancelot, and if that means dealing with Mordred, I will. In the meantime, I will go with you to Ontari:io and earn the Ontarii's trust and an alliance against the Lucians."

A silence fell between Guinevere and Lancelot. Dee would not risk a peek at the lovers, but she heard a rustle of clothing, and she imagined them reaching out to each other and embracing. After a moment, she heard Lancelot's door close, and the murmurs of conversation. They may not have reconciled, but the verbal brawl was over. If they were like other fighting couples, they'd make peace in the most intimate way.

Dee made her way back to her bed, a little embarrassed at her brazen invasion of Guinevere and Lancelot's privacy. But she was also heartened by it. The two may have a profound disagreement about the future of Viridiae, but they would make a persuasive team before the leaders at Villafroide. Dee hoped that when the war ended, she would not have to choose between them.

CHAPTER 7:
THE MARCH TO
TRANSIETUM

Robert Dardarius' thoughts drifted to the prisoner's column. For ten days, he'd rode his campaign horse Maxima at the head of two legions toward the rail head at Transietum. A kilometer behind his column, thousands of Viridian prisoners walked, shuffled, or stumbled, and often died. At first, the escape and death rates among the Viridian prisoners held at an acceptable level, but the chart accompanying the latest report showed a steady rise in the death rate likely to raise eyebrows in Lucana.

He reigned in his horse and beckoned two of his personal guard to follow. At a fast trot, he approached the ragged line of prisoners, but his concern for their well-being paled in comparison to his worry over what might happen when he returned to the capital. When Empress Vetrania called him to the Regia and appointed him to head a surprise invasion of Viridiae to find Merlin, he accepted the command, as he was bound by oath to do. But he understood the true reason for selecting him; she wanted him out of Lucana. Would she welcome him? Or would she find a way to eliminate him before he set foot within the city's walls?

As he pondered the problem, a detachment of cavalry soldiers snapped to attention. Robert focused on two prisoners a few paces behind the cavalrymen. Arturus trudged forward, Percival a half-step behind, puffs of dust kicked up with every footfall. In the burning heat, surrounded by greasewood scrub and rattlesnakes, dirt caked their sweating faces and old bloodstains marred clothes barely covering their bodies.

Though Robert wore his standard-issue ocher fatigues and helmet with the crest announcing his rank, he felt as if he wore the formal wear required of royal weddings and annual openings of the Senate in comparison to Arturus. A twinge of embarrassment colored his solemnity when the Viridian king met his gaze. The captive's look suggested stubborn persistence rather than prideful defiance. Robert considered again offering his personal powered litter, but he wouldn't insult or embarrass the king.

He couldn't afford to lose Arturus to dehydration or disease either. He was Robert's best chance to lure Merlin to Lucanus and complete his mission.

What then? Would Vetrania really complete the trade, assuming the de facto Viridian leader, Lord Mordred Lothian, agreed to the exchange? He'd said nothing since the column left camp. Or would the empress, famous for duplicity and capriciousness, renege on it once Merlin was in hand? What would happen to Arturus then?

An idea formed in Robert's mind. Perhaps the captive monarch could be more valuable than he first appeared. Arturus was a hostage, and the Viridians were aggressive enough to attempt a rescue. At first glance, such a move was reckless in the extreme. On the other hand, a large multi-pronged attack by the remnants of Viridiae's army allied with Lucanus' enemies could destabilize Vetrania's hold on power, giving Robert the chance to advance his clan's interests, and his own. He had no idea if this was what Mordred had in mind, but if he were Mordred, he'd do his best to make it happen.

Robert spurred Maxima down the column. The animal snorted at the acrid smell of suppurating wounds. Many of the prisoners stared at their captor with murder in their eyes, while others ignored him in their minute-by-minute quest to stay alive. Legionaries gave prisoners sips of water, whipping those who took more than their share or who gave their share to another. The soldiers were responsible for keeping their charges alive, if they could. Corpses rotting next to the trail testified to individual failures.

The sound of a galloping horse distracted Robert. Tribune Cantwell stopped and saluted his commander. "Sir, I'm honored by your visit, but I hadn't prepared for an inspection."

"You should always expect an inspection, Tribune. Didn't they teach you that at the war college?"

Adrian Cantwell blanched. "Forgive me, sir. I shall form the prisoners in ranks immediately and—"

"Relax, Adrian. I'm only here for a moment. I wanted to see you."

The tribune's face regained its color. "How can I serve you, General?"

Robert liked his nephew, whom he thought was the most intelligent of his sister Maia's children. Adrian fought like a demon during the border attacks and at the River Colum, and he'd shown a good head as an administrator, taking on the thankless job of managing the prisoners. "I thought it was time we talked. I've read your daily reports. Very thorough."

"Thank you, sir."

"Are you sure of these numbers, Adrian?"

The earnest junior officer lowered his eyes. "I've checked them myself against the field reports, sir. They show no sign of getting better."

"A thousand dead in the past week. That's almost 150 a day."

"It's this unexpected heat, sir. And most of these Viridians are average civilians. They have no training or endurance."

Robert huffed. "At this rate, we won't get enough prisoners to the rail head to make shipping them to the brokers in Lucana worthwhile."

Adrian remained silent.

"Come to my tent tonight, and we'll discuss it."

Adrian raised his head and saluted.

That evening, Adrian sat at a camp chair next to Robert.

"What do you think we should do about the attrition rate, Tribune?"

"Sir, I..." Adrian's voice trailed off.

"You can speak freely, Adrian. Nothing you say will leave this room."

The promise reassured Adrian. "General, if we increased the water ration, just a little bit. And the food ration. A few hundred calories might make the difference between losing all and losing half our captives."

"You talk about the prisoners as if they were cattle, not human beings."

Adrian was taken aback. "They're Viridians, sir. Our enemies."

"Our enemies, yes. But they are not animals."

Adrian glanced at the table, then at the flagon of Napene wine. Robert poured two goblets, and handed one to Adrian. "Let me tell you what I saw today, nephew."

Adrian drank from the goblet. "Yes, uncle?"

"Arturus was at the head of the prisoners. Not only is he a king and proud, he's ill, something long-term and wasting."

"Should I force him to take the car?"

"Gaia's breath, no. Adrian, he's a man to be admired. He knows what leadership means. I can tell his people love him. It's what separates humans from most of the animal kingdom, even if he is Viridian."

"Sir, doesn't that also make him dangerous?"

Robert smiled and patted his nephew's arm. "Your mother told me you were perceptive."

"I'm blessed to have her as my mother."

"I will write to her and tell her that you have made your family proud. Tell me, Adrian, what do you think of life in the capital these days?"

"If you're asking if I miss home, I do."

"I miss it as well, but I was thinking about the political situation. Your mother has no doubt expressed her views."

Adrian laughed. "Just about every day, sir, either in long letters or texts. She is..." Adrian's voice trailed off.

"I promise our conversation is only between us as family, Adrian."

Adrian cleared his throat. "She is disgusted with the empress, sir. Her corruption and incompetence grow by the day. That's what Mother says."

"And what do you think?"

"I'm an officer, sir. I don't get involved in politics."

"That's the correct answer, Adrian, but you're off duty. I'm your uncle and head of our clan. Tell me what you think."

Adrian hesitated, as if searching for the right words. "I think it's long past time for a new leader."

Robert sighed. He traced his finger around the edge of the goblet. "Your reticence is wise, Tribune. How does a man achieve the apparently impossible, such as bringing a change that benefits the entire community, the whole nation? I'll tell you how. He waits, until an opportunity presents itself."

Adrian leaned back in his seat. "Do you see such an opportunity, uncle?"

"The germ of one. I'm not quite sure whether it's a real opportunity, or the wishful thinking of a middle-aged soldier too close to retirement. In the meantime, I have another problem, one I hope you can help me solve."

"I'll do my best."

Robert nodded. "Adrian, do you know what happens to captured chieftains when they are brought to Lucana?"

"Of course, sir. We must show our enemies that the gods will be revenged on those who defy them, or us."

"Arturus cannot be that sacrifice."

Adrian breathed hard. "If he is not given to the gods, what of the empress?"

"Exactly. She and I need Arturus to get Merlin, but the people have expectations, and she must meet them."

"What do you want me to do?"

"Find me a sacrifice, one that will appease the gods. And Vetrania."

Adrian looked doubtful. "My mother said serving you would

mean making choices I'd rather not make. She said I'd have to do things ordinary people refuse to do."

"This is why I'm proud of Maia and her son. I know you won't fail me." Robert drank deep from the goblet, finishing it. "I've invited a king to dinner. Watch and learn."

Robert signaled the guard outside the tent and he poured more wine for Adrian. When Arturus entered the tent, followed by Percival, both Lucians stood.

Daradarius had not seen Arturus up close since the beginning of the march to Transietum. He invited both Viridians—some might say ordered—to bathe and change into clean undergarments and workingman's tunics before arriving. But the rushed cleanup did little to modify Arturus' gaunt appearance. Percival fared better, but only because he was younger and stronger. Neither wore shoes. Thorns and rocks had left pink scars and more recent cuts. Robert imagined the bookmakers in Lucana laying odds against their survival to the rail head, if not the capital. He wouldn't bet against those odds.

"Your Majesty, it's a pleasure to see you again." Robert put out his hand, but Arturus stared at it for a moment before taking it. Arturus' grip hinted at past strength. Robert extended his hand to Percival, but the man leered at it as if it were poisonous. Adrian glared at Percival in contempt.

Arturus said, "Please forgive Sir Percival. The last few days have placed great strain on him."

"Of course, sir." Dadarius gestured at Adrian. "I believe you know Tribune Cantwell, a member of my staff, and my nephew."

"I wish we could know each other under better circumstances, Tribune."

Percival kept his eyes on Adrian, as if waiting for a chance to strike. For his part, Adrian relaxed, knowing he had nothing to fear from the knight.

Robert invited them to sit at a table set with camp-style plates and forks, but no knives. A steward brought in a platter of dried fruits, nuts, fresh loaves of coarse bread, and reconstituted powdered butter. Robert poured wine into four goblets. "I hope you don't mind simple fare, Your Majesty. I prefer to eat the same food as my soldiers."

"An admirable trait, sir."

"However, I have a weakness for good wine. This is the last bottle from my private stock. I hope you like it."

"I'm honored."

Arturus reached for the goblet, his fingers trembling. Robert pitied the king's decline. Arturus eyed the food, but did not reach for it.

"Please eat, sir. And Sir Percival as well. I'll be shamed if you refuse." Robert surprised himself with his half-pleading request. "I'll have my steward bring another platter for you to take to your fellows."

Adrian cast a glance at his uncle in rebuke, despite his request to better feed the prisoners.

Steadying his hand, Arturus took a slice of bread and slowly buttered it. Percival followed the king's lead, holding back from a desire to swallow the food as if it were the last on earth.

Placing a slice of bread on his plate, along with dried apples and a few Brazil nuts, Robert chewed before swallowing another mouthful of wine. "I saw you at the head of the prisoners' column today, sir. I hope my officers take your example as a lesson."

"Encouragement is all I have left to give my people, General."

"Understandable. I felt as if I should know you better. I'm a curious man, and I had never been to Viridiae before."

"And on your first visit, you destroyed it," Percival snapped.

"No, Percival." Arturus held up his hand. "We are General Dardarius' guests tonight. Let us remember our manners."

Dardarius ignored Percival's slight, though Adrian itched to respond. "I've been reading about your family history, sir. The Arturii have an amazing past, particularly your grandfather, Arturus I. Did you know that my ancestor, who was also of the Dardarian clan, fought your grandfather's army at Widow's Crossing?"

Arturus' eyes glittered. "My grandfather defeated the Fifth Legion, led by your grandfather, sending them running like frightened dogs."

Percival smirked. Adrian kept still.

Robert did not rise to Arturus' bait. "Even the greatest armies suffer defeats, Lucanus' armies included. I honor your grandfather, sir." The general raised his goblet and drank the remaining drops.

Arturus sipped from his goblet.

"I would like to ask about one story I came across, Majesty. It's referred to as the 'Sword and the Stones'. Is it true Merlin taught your grandfather how to forge swords from simple stones."

"There are several versions of the story, General. Not all are accurate."

"Please, tell me the correct version. I'm certain you know the truth."

It might have been the food and drink, or perhaps the proud remembrance of family lore, but Arturus set his goblet down, and began the tale.

CHAPTER 8: THE SWORD FROM THE STONES

Arturus Strong-Arm pounded the glowing curl of metal, each strike sending a tremble through his dense muscles to his broad shoulders, his thick neck, and his round black-bearded face. Trained for combat with mace and shield, he turned his checked frustration into horseshoes, farm tools, and iron décor for the rich rustics with whom he shared his exile. If the wind was right, his country's enemies to the east heard the incessant clanging, though the Lucians hadn't raided the locals in a hundred years.

Day-by-day, however, Lucana treated its border with Viridiae like an inconvenient fence.

Under a maple tree, Arturus' friend Merlin leaned over an electronic book. Late spring sunlight filtered through the translucent green leaves. Arturus' rhythmic hammer interrupted Merlin's concentration.

"Can you give it a rest for two minutes?"

Arturus ignored the request. Merlin pushed up his spectacles and marked his place. Next to the tablet was a fist-sized, gray-black, pitted stone. Standing at the smithy's open double-door, Merlin waved his arms to get Arturus' attention.

Arturus pushed back his hearing protection and lifted his safety glasses. "What's the matter?"

Silently, Merlin pointed to the book, then to his eyes.

"Go read somewhere else." Arturus slipped his gear back on and resumed pounding. After a moment, however, he stopped and set down his blacksmith's hammer. Merlin had the intellectual appetite of a whale. He probably wanted to share a useless, but interesting factoid. "Quiet enough for you now?"

Arturus and Merlin had known each other since they were babies. Merlin's mother was a lady-in-waiting to Igraine, Arturus' mother. Both only children, they were as close as any brothers.

"Thanks," Merlin said, without conviction. "You know I have sensitive ears."

When Arturus' father, Uther, exiled him after an incident in the Greater Viridian Council, Merlin offered to go along to keep Arturus out of further trouble. They were between semesters at university, in any case.

"You're the dumbest person I've ever known, Merlin. You bitch about your ears, but you hang around the forge while I bang away at one thing or another. Go inside and read your book."

"If you don't want me around, I can go back to Camelot. I don't have to be here."

Arturus regretted what he'd said. He liked having Merlin around, and Merlin didn't have a lot of other friends. If Merlin went home, they'd both be miserable. Arturus brought a jug and two cups to Merlin's table. He poured icy water into both cups. "Sorry, Merlin. I get into these moods and I say shit."

Merlin gave him a look that was half-rebuke and half-forgiveness.

"Maybe you should've stopped me from saying the shit I said at the Council meeting."

"You had a point."

"You think so?"

"But you didn't have to insult your father in public. He's the king, in case you didn't know."

Thoughts about the Council raised Arturus' temperature. As the crown prince, Arturus was automatically a member, along with the leaders of Viridiae, the smaller, but influential Cameliard, the independent city of Perditon, and a half-dozen other principalities that constituted the Confederation of Greater Viridiae. Over the past year, the Lucians had launched four incursions. The Viridian military had beaten back each incursion, though losses were mounting, and Lucanus was a huge nation that spanned half the continent.

"We cannot risk provoking Lucana," Uther said at the last Council meeting, referring to Lucanus' capital. "The emperor's ambassador assures us that he prefers peace."

"Diplomatic obfuscation," declared Leodegrance, the Duke of Cameliard. "Lucana sees our weakness, and it's licking its chops."

"Do you want a war on your hands, Cameliard?"

"I want us to stop squabbling and defend ourselves."

Arturus agreed with Cameliard, and it was getting hard to hold his tongue out of respect for his father. He'd given an interview to a news chan, expressing sympathy for Cameliard's view. Uther went apoplectic, but Arturus believed the danger was far worse than Uther thought.

"Perditon has already called up its reserves." The mayor was a balding man in a business suit. "But we cannot fight Lucanus alone. We need leadership from Viridiae. You have the biggest military in our confederation."

"We should provide better leadership." The words came out of Arturus' mouth before he had a chance to stop himself.

"Well," Cameliard said. "At least one member of the royal family has sense."

Uther glared at his son.

"Please, sir," Cameliard goaded. "Tell us more."

Too late, Arturus realized he'd stepped in it. On the other hand, his disagreement with his father was well-known. "Lucana craves expansion above all things. The emperor wants our resources. It wants Perditon's manufacturing. It wants Cameliard's productive land. It wants Viridiae's inventiveness and educated populace. If we continue to argue among ourselves, it may get all these things without firing a shot. We need to unite and fight as one. That's the only way to stop them." Arturus resumed his seat.

"Well said, Prince Arturus." Cameliard tapped the table in polite applause. A few of the other members, including Perditon's mayor, joined him. The others remained still.

Uther looked as if he was ready to explode, but he kept his composure. "My son is young. He's proven himself on the battlefield, but he has not even finished university. He knows little of the world beyond arms."

"I fear, Father, that others at this table know more than you."

Silence fell over the audience like a stone. Even Cameliard's jaw slackened. Arturus cursed himself for his impetuousness. But his father was wrong. Viridiae had to lead a defense against the Lucians. In the worst case, it might have to strike first to prevent a disaster that could cost thousands of lives and centuries of progress since the Dissolution, when the world fell apart.

Uther touched the table with his gavel. "I believe a short break is warranted." The mild words belied his rage. "I will speak with my son privately."

Arturus took a breath, preparing himself for another lecture, delivered with shouting. He never expected what he got.

In Uther's office next to the conference room, the king slapped the prince's face. "How dare you defy me in public. You are the worst son a man could have. Where is your loyalty? Where is your respect?"

Arturus held his stinging cheek, fighting back tears. Uther, a warrior who once beheaded five men in battle, had never touched him before in anger, and Arturus had no idea how to respond.

"For your insolence, you are banished from my sight. I expect you to support me, not stab me in the back. You are an ungrateful son who deserves nothing from me. Leave! Now! I will make your excuses to the Council."

Arturus shook from fear and hurt. He had only spoken his mind, and wasn't the Council a place for discussion? He thought of running to his mother, but he wasn't a child. Instead, fuming like the hobbyist's forge his father gave to him on his fifteenth birthday, he stormed to his palace apartment. He packed a change of clothes, borrowed a horse from the stable, and galloped out of the city to a small hotel in a border town, where he cried in his room for an hour. On the road, he texted Merlin, but no one else.

Merlin showed up the next day.

As it happened, the town had a blacksmith who had injured himself on the job. He allowed Arturus the use of his tools and his forge if he completed some of his backlog. A week after his arrival, Arturus leaned his elbow on the table beside Merlin's book and the rock. "Last month, you were into frogs. Are you into rocks now?"

"I found this on the riverbank. It isn't like the other river stones. Most of those are basalt and sandstone."

Arturus picked it up. "It's heavy, too." He set it down with a *thonk*. "Reminds me of a bloom from iron smelting."

Merlin looked up from his book, as if an idea had come to him.

"My father is losing it, Merlin. Don't get me wrong. He's better than other fathers I know." Arturus decided the slap was an aberration, though the memory still hurt. They hadn't spoken since the incident. His mother, however, told him he brooded over it.

"At least your father was around. Mine?" Merlin shrugged.

"Mine started bringing me to privy council meetings when I was five or six. I'd play in a corner with my Knights and Beasts game. The adults didn't think I was listening, but I was. Father asked me questions about the discussions later."

"A lot of kids would've been bored to death."

"Father and his ministers made me feel important. After a while, I started giving my opinion to Father in private. One thing he wouldn't let me do was speak up in the meetings. He said I was too young and inexperienced."

"So you finally opened your mouth in public and he banished you from Camelot."

"He was wrong. I kept telling him that he needed to get the Viridian kingdoms together. This was after a Lucian incursion that destroyed a border post and killed a dozen knights. Cameliard reached out to me, thinking I could persuade Father to be more aggressive."

"He thought you were challenging him. If you studied history, you'd know the stories about princes getting rid of their fathers."

"Why would I do that? I was just speaking my mind."

"He over-reacted. He might be a little afraid of you."

"That's crazy." Arturus considered the suggestion. "Do you think so?"

"Wouldn't be the first time it's happened. He looks at you sometimes like a shepherd looks at a wolf. Wary. Worried."

Arturus wasn't sure what to make of Merlin's observation. The thought of deposing his father had never occurred to him. Once a powerful chieftain, Uther had grown conservative, even timid. He preferred to hoard what he had, rather than nurture its growth. He distrusted his neighbors, especially Cameliard, who jostled with Uther for leadership of Greater Viridiae.

"I heard things on the net, the news chans, everywhere. A lot of people were agreeing with you. That would scare any political leader."

Arturus narrowed his eyes. "How do you know so much about politics? You collect frogs and rocks."

"Unlike you, I read."

"I'm not as illiterate as you think. I found one of Father's intelligence reports on his desk. It scared the shit out of me."

"So what do you think we should do?"

Arturus' frustration boiled over. "Maybe Father was right. I don't have the experience to speak up or lead anyone. Maybe I'm the idiot."

While Arturus was tall and large, Merlin was wiry and a lot shorter. His bookish ways earned him taunts from other children. In the palace school, Arturus intervened in Merlin's fights with bullies more than once. Merlin repaid his friend with tutoring sessions in math and science.

Merlin fingered the metallic rock on the table. "Remember that chemistry prep text, the one for the admissions test to The Keep?"

"It gave me a headache."

"It was about the chemistry of steel, the uniting of carbon and iron to make something stronger than either alone."

"Everyone knows that."

"People also want to be inspired. Facts rarely do the trick. Magic does."

"I thought you wanted to be a scientist, not a magician."

"I'm learning that one is related to the other, at least in ordinary people's minds." Merlin picked up the rock. "Take this ataxite, for example."

"Never heard of it."

"Science has known since before the Dissolution that it's made of iron and nickel. Thing is, it comes from space. It's a piece left over from a meteorite. To some people, maybe subconsciously, it's a gift from the gods, mysterious and impressive."

"And your point is?"

Merlin reached into a knapsack at his feet. He brought out another ataxite, a little smaller than the one on the table. He pulled out another handful of pitted rocks about the size of his fingernails. "I found all these along the shoreline. Gaia knows how long they've been there, but I think they're from the same meteorite."

"Still not following."

"Look at them, you lunkhead. The big piece is Viridiae. The next biggest is the duchy of Cameliard. The other ones are the independent cities and mini-states. You're a blacksmith. What do you do with chunks of iron?"

Arturus' face lit up. "Make something."

"Forge these pieces of a heavenly object into a tool and you've got a symbol. That's another thing I've learned with all my reading. People need symbols to understand big ideas."

"What about a sword?"

"Perfect. Can you do it?"

"I've never made a full-sized sword. I'll have to do some research. But I get what you're saying, Merlin. It's a great idea."

* * *

Arturus dived into the project. He watched netvids and read metalworking articles from his favorite online magazines. After discussing his planned design with Merlin, he heated all the pieces of ataxite until they glowed a fiery orange. Using a power hammer, he pummeled them together into a lump about twice the size of his fist. Over many weeks, often with Merlin holding tongs or fetching tools, Arturus divided the mass of iron and nickel into three pieces, eventually drawing them into squared rods about a meter long. After heating, hammering, reheating, and more hammering, he welded the three rods together until they formed a rough blade. More weeks of grinding, filing, and hammering followed, until finally, after three months, Arturus had a double-edged blade with its unmistakable blood groove down the center.

One step remained: polishing. Merlin wrote to a jeweler friend, who sent him a box of aluminum oxide sandpaper. Arturus rubbed the surface of his creation over many long hours, and when he finished the final buffing, Merlin marveled. Woven into the metal, like mirrored meanders of a stream, dark streaks of iron alternated with lighter streaks of nickel. In Arturus' hand, the blade seemed to float in the air like smoke, though Merlin could barely lift it.

"You are the magician, Arturus. I could never have created this."

"It was your idea. I couldn't have done it without you."

"I think it's time that you asked your father's permission to come home."

"I already have. We leave in the morning."

Arturus worked all night on fitting the hilt, pommel, and guard. A leather craftsman in the town made a simple scabbard tooled with the dragon sigil of the Arturii.

Over the months of work, Merlin uploaded dozens of videos of the process to the royal family's netsite, and by the time the sword was finished, tens of thousands of people had watched them. News chans picked up the videos, and a journalist traveled from Camelot to write an article with quotes from the prince and his friend.

Merlin had laid the groundwork for Arturus' triumphant return from exile.

When Arturus and Merlin arrived at the palace, Uther shook Merlin's hand and embraced Arturus. "I'm glad you're home, son. I regretted sending you away. Did you know that? But I couldn't back out. That's part of what makes leadership hard. I'm happy that you made something of your time away. May I see it?"

Arturus handed Uther the sword in its scabbard. Uther drew it, his arm still steady twenty years after the last time he had wielded a sword in battle or in the lists. "It's well-balanced, and I can feel the strength of it. I wish I was young again so I could test it in the field."

"With respect, Father, it's meant as a gift, but not to you."

Uther's eyes narrowed as he returned the blade to its home and owner. "I don't understand."

Arturus drew himself up. He'd talked over this moment with Merlin. He was determined to get his way. "I want to speak to the Council. Tomorrow, at the next meeting."

"After what happened last time? Impossible."

"I don't think you can stop me."

"Are you defying me again? You've been home five minutes, and already you're threatening me."

"Please, Father." Arturus did not want to reopen the rift between them. "I have something to say to the Council."

"And that is?"

Arturus straightened his back. "I'm sorry, but that's for their ears."

Uther walked to the window, which looked out to the public square surrounded by government buildings and the people's assembly. "I'll admit I underestimated you, Arturus, both before I exiled you and during your time away. I won't make that mistake again."

Merlin had predicted that Uther would resist allowing Arturus to speak. He'd researched the rules, and thought Arturus had a chance to go on his own.

"You appointed me to the Council. Everyone thought it was a gesture only, and meaningless. But your appointment gave me the right to speak. It's the Council rule."

Uther's face turned red. "Don't tell me the rules. I'm the president of the council. I'm the king of Viridiae. I interpret the rules. And I say you will not speak. If you do, consider yourself banished, permanently. Now get out."

Despite Merlin's prediction and its fulfillment, Uther's declaration nearly broke Arturus' heart. He loved his father, even though he disagreed profoundly with him about the Lucian threat and how to combat it. Arturus and Merlin departed Uther's presence, and they sat on a bench in the hall outside Uther's office.

"That didn't go well," Merlin said.

"You said it wouldn't."

"I hate it when I'm right sometimes." Merlin scratched the back of his left hand. "What are going to do?"

"Speak tomorrow, like I said. Otherwise, everything we've done this summer is pointless."

Once a year, in September, the Council gathered to begin a new session. The leaders met in a century-old hall below Camelot's stone citadel. Typically, the new president was chosen informally long before the ceremony in order to avoid a public debate over leadership, which Uther thought made the Council appear weak to friends and foes alike. However, at a certain point in the ceremony, the previous session's president called for nominations for the new session's president. Arturus planned to take advantage of this moment. And he had a secret ally.

"May it please the Council," Uther intoned before the dozens of viscounts, mayors, princes, ambassadors, dukes, and others with speaking and voting rights, "I call for nominations for president of new session."

The mayor of Perditon, the second largest city in the region after Camelot, rose as if his back was stiff from sleeping in an unfamiliar bed. "Your Majesty, the citizens of my city, whose ships trade from its seaport across the Peaceful Sea to nations as far away as Nippon, China, and Bharata, offering recycled metals and rare earths, bringing back food, clothing, and machines, are pleased with your leadership of the Council these many years. We are happy to propose and nominate King Uther Pendragon of Viridiae for another term."

Enthusiastic applause completed the ritual.

"I am honored again by your confidence and your nomination, Mr Mayor," Uther said. I'm happy to again accept the nomination." Uther glanced at his notes. "Are there further nominations? Hearing none—"

The Duke of Cameliard rose. "I have a nomination, Mr President."

Uther's mouth gaped. In the quarter century since Uther had ascended the throne and sat on the Council, no one had offered a competing nomination to the one prearranged at dinners, drinks in private quarters, and late-night netmails. Uther wasn't sure what to do.

"If I may remind the president, the ancient rules allow unvetted nominations from the floor."

Uther hadn't read that in the rule book. "This is out of order, my lord duke."

An elderly woman so bent that she barely changed her height as she rose from her chair said, "My grandfather told me stories of the days before everyone agreed to a new president before the ceremony. One president took his seat only after single combat with the other nominee. But the call for other nominations never went away. The Duke of Cameliard has a right to name his champion, so to speak."

Uther's face went white with anger, but he had no choice. "Very well. Proceed, my lord duke."

"I nominate Arturus Strong-Arm."

The gasp around the table echoed the shock from the public gallery, where a hundred prominent citizens watched the proceedings. Thousands more tuned into the news chan broadcasting the event. Arturus was ready. He stood, waiting for his father's customary recognition.

Uther glowered at his son as if he were an infected sore on one of his beloved war horses. Arturus took on a steady, almost proud mien, careful not to appear disrespectful to the king in front of the most important people in Viridiae. He wouldn't be cowed, though.

Uther spoke through gritted teeth. "The chair recognizes Arturus, Crown Prince of Viridiae. Do you wish to tell us why you are qualified to serve as president?"

"Your Majesty," Arturus began with a slight bow, "many on this Council have known me since the day you first brought me to learn at your side. I leave it for them to judge whether I am qualified. I rise to argue for something far more important."

"Pray, tell us what that might be." Uther barely held his sarcasm in check.

Arturus turned to Merlin, who handed him a long box, polished, but made simply, with brass hinges. On the top, two kanji characters— 兼併 —were written in gold. Arturus laid the box on the table with a reverence reserved for religious objects.

"With your permission, sire, I would like to give a gift to this Council, and all the people of Greater Viridiae."

Uther nodded, his curiosity competing with his fury. Arturus unlatched the box. Slowly, as if it were a fine piece of porcelain, Arturus removed the ataxite sword, sheathed in its leather scabbard.

A second gasp rippled through the crowd. A few called out in anger, "A weapon! It's forbidden. No weapons at the Council table!"

"Yes! It is a weapon, but not the kind of weapon you believe it to be." Arturus spoke from his diaphragm, as Uther once taught him. "I made this with my own hands. No doubt many of you saw me working the iron and nickel that fell from the heavens. I pounded this sword from the stones found by my friend Merlin, and it was a different feeling than other metal I've worked. I was making something more than a weapon. I'm not superstitious, but I know an energy was there. I can't describe it, but it was there as I hammered those fragments into an object, and an idea, of beauty and strength. This sword has power that will strike fear into anyone who challenges us." Arturus gulped. He thought his words tumbled out like fortune sticks, which made no sense until you studied them.

The crowd rose almost as one, arguing with one another, pointing fingers at the council members. Uther sat unperturbed, suspicion twisting his face.

Holding the sword at its balance point, Arturus lifted it over his head. "I do not offer a sword, my friends. I offer synthesis, singularity of purpose, and harmony. I have named this sword 'Kenpai,' a word from the people of Nippon across the Peaceful Sea. It means 'uniting.'"

Silence overcame the crowd. One or two people began to applaud, and the clapping spread through the room. A few held back, including Uther.

Arturus laid the sword on the table, in front of the open box. "The Lucian Empire is at our doorstep. It will not knock politely, and ask permission to enter. It will break down our doors, slaughter our people, and plunder our property. We must unite to face this threat. No amount of equivocation or appeasement will delay them. We need to show them that together, forged into one nation, they should fear us, not we them."

The applause was so loud, Arturus feared the citadel's walls would crack. He was joyous. His gamble had worked. Merlin had understood that the people wanted nothing more than a strong leader to help them face the threat. Arturus was the one man in Viridiae who could create *kenpai* among his countrymen and women.

"I have one more thing to add," Arturus said as the applause died down. "I thank my lord Duke of Cameliard for honoring me. Regretfully, I must decline his nomination."

Cameliard's eyes flashed, as if Arturus had betrayed a secret agreement. But a moment later, he relaxed, understanding what

Arturus had in mind.

"Instead, Your Majesty," Arturus said, "I would like to endorse your nomination for another term as president, on one condition."

Uther pursed his lips. "Which is?"

"You allow me to lead a joint expedition of knights and soldiers from across Greater Viridiae against the Lucians. I will carry Kenpai at the expedition's head. I pledge complete victory to you and to our people. We will not fail."

Cheers and screams of elation competed with pounding feet on the floor and fists on the council table. Arturus had never seen anything like it. He turned to Merlin, who was subdued, despite his smile. He had suggested the move, which gave Arturus what he wanted, but allowed Uther to save face, though he might accuse Arturus of blackmail.

Fortunately for Arturus, Uther didn't. Instead, the king raised his hand, and the noise subsided. "I thank the prince, my son, for his endorsement. Nominations are now closed. The clerk will call the roll."

The vote was nearly unanimous, with a few write-ins for Arturus. A member moved for approval of Uther as president by acclamation, and the motion passed unanimously by voice vote. Cameliard made another motion to appoint Arturus as commanding general of the Army of Greater Viridiae, which also passed without dissent.

Later, after the evening celebrations of Uther's election and Arturus' appointment, the prince found Merlin alone on a palace terrace. An orange harvest moon loomed above the peaks of the Range of Needles. Merlin set his cup of ale on the balustrade. "We've done the right thing, haven't we, Arturus?"

"I think so. People are excited about our chances to defeat the Lucians. Maybe the fight will lead to a stronger alliance, maybe a better country."

Merlin gazed at the garden spread before them. "I can't help but think of the thousands and thousands of people, soldiers and civilians, who won't see the better days. Will it be worth it?"

"We can't know, but we have to try, don't you think?"

Merlin looked at the glowing moon and grinned. "Here's to amateur blacksmiths."

Arturus touched his mug to Merlin's. "And to rocks from the sky."

CHAPTER 9: TRUTH AND LIES

Sir Percival blinked, having forgotten for a moment that the Lucians held him prisoner, and that hundreds of his comrades had died on their march to Transietum. Over the years, he had heard Arturus relate an anecdote about a general's bad luck in a battle, or describe a diplomat's distracting tic, or some other bit of bonhomie. Percival had never heard Arturus tell a real story, particularly about his own family, and about something as mythic as the Arturus Strong-Arm's Sword from the Stones.

Arturus Longshanks, Strong-Arm's grandson, had told the story wrong.

If they suspected the problem, Dardarius and Adrian didn't show it.

"Your grandfather was an amazing man, Majesty," Dardarius said. "To hear the tale from his descendant is a privilege. Thank you."

"I'm proud of my family history, General."

"We share that feeling, sir. I have a question or two, if you don't mind."

Percival tensed. Did Dardarius know?

"What happened to the sword?"

Arturus folded his arms. "No one knows. It was lost after the war that briefly united Greater Viridiae. After the Lucians were defeated—"

At this, Adrian raised his head, his hand inching toward the hilt of a dagger.

"Be easy, nephew." Dardarius put his hand between the king

and the Adrian, as if preventing a coming blow. "We are all soldiers here, and the events we're discussing took place nearly 80 years ago."

Adrian frowned, but relaxed. Percival eyed the tribune, certain he would have to kill him one day.

"After the Lucians were defeated," Arturus reiterated, "Uther died, and Arturus could not hold the Council together. The infighting devolved into a civil war, but the outcome was a single state, our present Viridiae. Historians regard Arturus Strong-Arm as the founder."

"That's too bad, that it was lost," Dardarius said. "Imagine if the sword was discovered. Imagine the price it would fetch!"

Percival frowned at the insult to his country's heritage. The sword would be a holy relic and priceless. "A few fakes have turned up over the years."

Adrian said, "The Duke of Cameliard. He's also a relative of yours, is he not, Majesty?"

"Of a sort. He is the great-grandfather of my wife, Guinevere. You see, the Cameliard family believes it has a claim on the Viridian throne. Lawyers and historians have argued about it for decades. I love my wife, and it suits the country for our families to be united in this way."

"A political marriage, if one ever existed," Dardarius observed. "And dangerous, I might add."

Arturus' face was blank, but Percival guessed that Dardarius knew of Guinevere's involvement in the attempted coup before the invasion.

"Let me ask about Merlin." Dardarius touched his chin. "I'm led to understand that he's an old man, but if he knew and helped your grandfather, that would make him—"

"More than 100 years old," Arturus said, completing Dardarius' thought. "As you may know, some of our citizens live well into their 120s. It's one of many legacies of the Old Civilization's tinkering with the human genome."

"Yes, some of our people live that long, but Viridiae seems to have more than its share."

"When they're not murdered by Lucian raiders," Percival said.

Arturus touched Percival's arm. "I beg pardon, General. We are both very tired, and it's been a long evening."

"I don't take offense, Majesty. Some of our people," Dardarius glanced at Cantwell, "have minimal self-control. One last point, if I may." He reached for a tablet on his desk, swiped through it, and showed Percival and Arturus a portrait of a middle-aged man in formal, if old-fashioned military dress. "My grandfather claimed he fought Arturus Strong-Arm. Arturus wounded him, right here." Dardarius pointed to his left arm, above the elbow. "He showed me the scar when I was very young. I don't suppose you know anything about this story?"

Arturus considered a moment. "I don't remember a mention of my grandfather wounding a member of the Dardarian clan. He killed so many Lucians, that I suppose he lost track of mere woundings."

Dardarius laughed. "Well said. It seems that nearly every Lucian soldier's family has a story of an ancestor fighting Arturus the Great in single combat, and losing. Mine included."

The general stood, a signal that the evening was over. He extended a hand to Arturus, who took it out of courtesy, managing a light smile. Percival gauged his king's visage, and imagined respect, even friendship, on the surface. Underneath, duplicity undercut the warmth.

* * *

Two of Dardarius' personal guard escorted Percival and Arturus to their tent, but along the way, the elected king of Viridiae greeted his fellow prisoners of war. Battery-powered floodlights shone on a huddled mass of prisoners divided into ragged, sickly groups of about two dozen and guarded by legionaries. They couldn't touch their monarch or hand him their gifts, but Percival watched their eyes brighten as he called encouragement to them across a three-meter gap.

Once inside their quarters, Percival poured a measure of water into two cups, giving one to Arturus. The king studied the liquid, but didn't drink.

"Percival, when I see our comrades treated like insects, I feel that I have failed."

The statement alarmed the young knight. If Arturus lost hope, Viridiae itself was lost. "Majesty, those men and women out there need you. You saw their smiles. They don't believe you've failed. We lost a battle, many battles. But the war isn't lost. Not yet. If that were true, Dardarius would've crowed it to the heavens."

Arturus hung his head.

"Don't you see, Majesty? As long as Merlin is alive, and not in Lucian hands, you will stay alive, and perhaps the rest of us. We might even see home again." Percival surprised himself with his words. In the days since his attempted escape and recapture, he'd come to understand some of Arturus' thinking. The king also needed a friend who would support him in the darkest times.

Arturus sipped his water.

"Majesty, let me say this. As long as you have your mind, you have a weapon. I think you knew that when you lied to Dardarius."

The king grinned. "I knew I picked an intelligent man as my aide."

"Explain to me, sire. That story you told, it's a lot like the story I heard from my mother when I was a boy, apart from a few details."

"What was wrong about it?"

"With all respect, I think you know." Percival lowered his voice, expecting that ears surrounded his tent. "Historians have researched this tale like almost no other. At university, I learned the most likely version."

"Which is?"

"Your grandfather didn't make the sword. The injured blacksmith made it, though with your ancestor's help. Merlin found fragments of pre-Dissolution steel by the river, not iron from heaven. There may have been a large bridge at the site a thousand years ago."

"The bridge's location was confirmed only last year."

"The most embarrassing fact of all: The sword broke on the first day Arturus Strong-Arm used it, and that was during training. The sword was far too brittle and poorly made. It was probably melted down to make other weapons." Percival switched to a whisper. "What if Dardarius finds out that you lied to him?"

"He's a cultured man, but I doubt he cares much about Viridian folklore. My telling gives the story extra credibility. Lying about an ancestor is an unseemly thing, beneath my station." Arturus chuckled. "Besides, the other parts of the story are true: Uther's dithering, Arturus' banishment and return, his speech, and his appointment as supreme commander. That's what matters."

"I don't understand."

"I know a lot about Dardarius, my friend. Our spies kept us apprised of Lucana's politics, public and private. Dardarius' clan has nursed a grudge against Empress Vetrania and her clan, the Cardeans, for generations. Dardarius' clan has a similar story of an ancestor who saved the nation, only that man was murdered by the Cardeans, who supplanted the Dardarians as Lucanus' leaders."

Percival thought a moment. "Were you trying to make some kind of personal connection to Dardarius?"

"Yes. It's a tiny chance, but maybe a friendship between myself and him could lead to better treatment of our comrades. He seems to respect me, wouldn't you agree? Once we get to Lucana, I might even be able to use his respect to get us released, perhaps traded for Lucian prisoners."

On this point, Arturus' thinking was wishful at best, but Percival kept silent.

"Most importantly, I want to stoke his ambition. I'm almost certain he wants to be emperor. Why not show him how it's possible? Maybe not exactly in the way Arturus Strong-Arm did it, but that he could achieve his goal, if he gambled."

"You're appealing to his vanity, but you did it without fawning over him." Percival grinned. "Majesty, you're a good storyteller. A hidden talent, perhaps?"

"Don't jump to conclusions, Percival. I've only planted a few seeds. I have no idea if they'll grow, or if they'll turn out to be poisonous. Like my grandfather said, we have to try."

Percival agreed. It was the only hope they had.

CHAPTER 10: THE ROAD TO ONTARI:IO

Saddle sore and weary, Dindrane struggled to keep up with Guinevere and Lancelot on the almost invisible track. Taking the role of guide for the trio, Lancelot avoided the main trails and remnants of pre-Dissolution roads. She stuck to smuggler's routes and game trails, especially after they crossed into disputed territory between Viridiae and Ontari:io now controlled by Lucanus. The rolling, windy flatlands had changed hands several times over the centuries as the power of surrounding nations waxed and waned.

Apart from old campsites, the occasional pre-Dissolution concrete ruin, and the discovery of rare unicorn spoor, the road was quiet. Dee was struck by the spare beauty of the mountains. Historical records claimed year-round glaciers once covered the peaks. She tried to imagine the scene lost to the planet's warming ten centuries ago.

Surveying the scene in her light armor, Lancelot pointed out one of the monuments left from the Old Civilization. Standing like sentinels, a handful of towers from an ancient wind farm reminded the travelers of the achievements of the Old Civilization, one that had failed.

Dee remembered a lecture by Merlin while she was at Camelot University. The Old Civilization's greatest achievement, the Great Machines, had kept the climate balanced for nearly a thousand years. With the loss of the Grail from Viridiae's Great Machine, the climate had grown unstable. "The Old Civilization thought wind power would stop the Warming by replacing carbon-based fuels," Dee said. "It was a good idea, but it came too late."

"Quiet," Lancelot ordered. "Listen."

The towers loomed tall as the trees in the rain forest on the shores of the Peaceful Sea west of Perditon, Viridiae's second city, which Dee visited once. It was dirty, noisy, and exciting. As she remembered the city's press of people and traffic, she heard a scream. "What was that?"

"A dying human," Lancelot said.

A low glottal growl rumbled over the hill, but Dee could not see its source.

"Is it possible, Lancelot?" Guinevere said.

Lancelot indicated a concrete pedestal stained brown with rust at the top of a low rise. Leaving the horses tied to a bush, all three crawled on their bellies until they viewed a shallow valley. A biped animal, at least three meters tall, pecked at a corpse. Another corpse lay a dozen meters away. Three horses ran over the next hill.

"I've heard of basilisks, but I've never seen one," Lancelot said.

"Are you serious?" Dee said.

"The Old Civilization engineers were pretty clever," Guinevere said. "They made questing beasts and unicorns. Why not basilisks?"

The creature resembled a rooster, but its feathers were stunted, and its head was closer to a snake's than a chicken's.

"They're incredibly dangerous. They say even horses can't outrun them."

"They didn't outrun those Lucian soldiers," Dee said. "Poor devils."

"Better them than us," Guinevere said.

"Hold on," Lancelot gulped. "We might be joining them."

Like a dog sniffing the air, the basilisk raised its head. Even at this distance, Dee saw its reptilian eye blink.

"Go, go, go!" Lancelot barked.

Forgetting caution, the three Viridians ran back to the horses. Dee heard a pounding, and it wasn't her heart, though it thumped against her chest. Behind them, the basilisk stopped at their previous hiding place, sniffing the ground. It spotted the travelers, and plodded down the hill.

"Run!" Lancelot took off like a shot.

Guinevere followed, with Dee centimeters behind, slowed by her lead of the mule with their supplies. The basilisk gained on them, its toothy beak snapping at the mule's hindquarters. Dee screamed in fright, but kept control of her mount and the mule with its precious food and water. After a few hundred meters, the basilisk slowed. Dee glanced behind her, and the creature stopped, visibly tired. Dee and her companions didn't slow or stop for another kilometer.

Breathing as if she'd run the distance on foot, Dee pulled up to Lancelot. "What happened?"

"Maybe it couldn't go further, like trying to run after a full meal."

Guinevere laughed. "Maybe those unlucky Lucians saved our lives."

* * *

Dee swayed with exhaustion. "Are we going to make camp soon?"

"We have another hour of light," Lancelot said. "We need to burn as many kilometers as we can."

"Can we at least get close to a hilltop? I want to see if we can pick up a net signal."

Just before Dee and Lancelot began their mission, the Viridian intelligence agency gave Dee a special tablet with extra sensitive antennae designed for weak signals. They instructed her to find the highest point in the area and aim the tablet toward Camelot.

Lancelot pointed at a low ridge. "How about there?"

Passing fallen and half-buried generator blades, preserved by their carbon fiber construction, the travelers reached the crest. Dee adjusted the app at the foot of a tower caked with rust. "Got a message. Shall I open it?"

"Can it wait until we eat something?" Guinevere said.

Lancelot, finally ready to quit for the day, led the group to a jumble of boulders that served as a windbreak. All three women had plenty of practice setting up camp by this time in their journey. Water was plentiful, as was forage for the three riding horses and single pack mule. Wearing woolen wraps against the cooling evening temperatures, they sipped tea made with water boiled on a battery-powered fire. They wouldn't risk a real fire, fearing the smoke might attract roaming Lucians or another basilisk.

"If it weren't for the war," Dee said, "I could almost imagine myself on vacation. Percival and I went on plenty of camping trips when we lived with our mother."

"Have you felt anything from him since he was captured?" Guinevere said.

Dee considered. "Maybe a feeling when we crossed into the occupied territory. I think he's alive, but I can't be sure. It's like seeing a ship through a fog. Maybe it's there. Maybe not."

"It must be frustrating," Lancelot said. "Sometimes I think I can feel Arturus' presence. He's almost certainly alive. He's of no value to Dardarius dead."

Dee applied her decryption key to the message on her secure tablet. The message transformed from a tangle of symbols to readable text.

Headquarters of the Armed Forces of Viridiae

Guinevere, Royal Consort of Viridiae; Dame Lancelot du Lac; Miss Dindrane Rathkeale

Greetings.

I write to you from a field in Lothia, my ancestral lands, where thousands of living heroes wait patiently for news of your success. Our spirits are high, our hope undiminished, and our faith in you boundless. I offer you news of victories and setbacks, which you may wish to relay to your hosts in Villefroide as evidence of Lucanus' threat to their security.

I do not believe in holding back bad news, for it can strengthen

resolve, even as the recipients grieve. The prisoners taken by the Lu-
cians at the battles of the River Colum and Camelot are marching
toward a transit point where they will be loaded onto freight cars
and shipped to Lucana far to the east. Our scouts trailing the column
have found hundreds of exposed corpses. We believe Arturus and
Percival to be alive as hostages, as promised by General Dardarius.
Despite his care for our king and his companion, the Lucian com-
mander is guilty of a war crime, in our view. We will exact revenge,
when the time is right.

Dee paused, digesting the news. The stricken faces of Guinevere and Lancelot revealed their feelings.

The Lucians are consolidating their victories in Viridiae. Any re-
sistance is put down with property confiscation and murder. In one
case, an entire town was burned to the ground and the city council
and mayor killed. I am heartbroken that I cannot offer any military
support for the ad hoc resistance at the risk of exposing our rebuild-
ing armed forces to further degradation.

Lancelot huffed. "I would've taken a squadron of knights and
slaughtered an equal number of Lucians. I sometimes wonder
about Mordred's aggressiveness."

We are striking blows in defense of our country. A squadron of
our best knights attacked a Lucian supply column, killed most of the
legionaries, and captured a dozen electric trucks full of weapons and
food. We feel that hit-and-run attacks are our best strategy until we
can build a new army to send against the occupying forces. As you
discuss these tactics with the Ontarii, seek their advice. They have
perfected the art of guerrilla warfare on their frontier with Lucanus.

Lastly, Galahad and Bors are making progress through the Hot
Lands, and they've already met with a number of tribal leaders, who
are noncommittal. I ask you to make the best possible speed to the
Ontari:io border and onward to Villefroide. Time is not on our side.
Mordred, Lord Lothia
Commander-in-Chief

Prime Minister of Viridiae

"I see that Mordred has appointed himself Viridiae's leader," Lancelot said. "Perhaps he's happy that we, Galahad, and Bors, not to mention Arturus, are out of his way. Perhaps he's accomplished his coup d'état after all."

"Hush, Lancelot," Guinevere said. "Who else has the political connections and military experience to lead Viridiae now? Mordred's letter is sincere and his advice sound. Let's take it at face value."

Lancelot swallowed the last of her coffee. "I don't doubt his patriotism. I just don't trust him, just as I don't trust the Lucians to leave us alone. Or bandits, for that matter."

"Why haven't they found us, Lucians or bandits?" Dee said.

Lancelot glanced upward at a tower, its top jagged, like a beast with its head torn off. "Maybe they're frightened by ghosts. I feel surrounded by them."

Lancelot volunteered to take the first watch and bid her companions good night. Dee turned down the electric fire and followed Guinevere to the three-person tent. As night insects sang a lullaby, Dee re-read the letter. "My lady, do you trust Lord Mordred?"

Guinevere unraveled her braids. "One can never trust a politician. The sincere ones never tell you their true motivations or intent. The insincere ones simply lie."

Dee offered to brush Guinevere's luxurious dark brown hair. "Which kind is Lord Mordred?"

"He leans toward sincere, even earnest, but he will lie if it suits his purpose. No leader is pure." Guinevere allowed Dee to redo her braids. "It's none of my business, Dee, but I've heard that you and Mordred were lovers."

Guinevere's frank statement took Dee aback, but she was happy to share her secret with another woman. "For a time, my lady. He's an attractive, powerful man. And he has good taste in art."

"But?"

"I'm not interested in a long-term relationship with any man, especially now. Before the war, my career was taking off. You helped me a great deal, my lady, for which I'm very grateful. I'm glad to be serving my country now, but I hope to return to my project for the Great Audience Hall when the war is over."

"That could be many years, Dee. How will you grow your skill? Light tapestries require time and expensive equipment."

"I have my tablet. I can sketch ideas and dream. When you are reunited with His Majesty, I'd like to paint a portrait of both of you."

A shadow passed over Guinevere's face. "I hope that's soon."

"May I ask how you and His Majesty met? I mean, I know the story of your marriage, but I'd like to know about the first time you saw him."

"I saw him several times over the years, ever since I was small. My father would bring me along on his trips to Camelot, and I would see Arturus at parties and such."

"You make it sound as if your father was showing you off."

"I wouldn't be surprised if that were true. He was always keen to keep the Duchy of Cameliard closely aligned with the old kingdom of Viridiae, even though it existed in name only after Arturus the Great united the country."

"Sounds almost barbaric."

"Arturus and I were lucky. Our marriage was political, to be sure, but we actually fell in love. He was handsome and broad-shouldered. He sent me beautiful gifts, but nothing gaudy or over-the-top. He was the crown prince, but he was as good a man as I'd ever known."

"You're lucky, my lady."

A sly look crossed Guinevere's face. "Most young couples today, if they like each other, will spend the night together after a short time getting to know each other. Arturus and I were forced by our positions to adopt some very ancient practices, such as having a chaperon when we took a walk or visited a museum. And according to an old Cameliard custom, I had to be certified as a virgin the day before our wedding."

Giving in to her curiosity, Dee wasn't quite sure how to ask her next question without being nosy. "And what was the result?"

Guinevere threw her shoulders back. "That my virtue was intact."

Dee could wait no longer. "Seriously?"

Guinevere laughed. "Of course I wasn't a virgin. Though I was young, I was an independent woman by that time. I'd graduated from the Cameliard Institute and I was working at the duchy's Environment Ministry. I had had several lovers over the years, male and female."

Dee scratched her head. "You mean the doctor lied?"

"At the request of my father, of course. I know it sounds crazy, but life is full of fictions that people cling to, as if letting go of them might result in the disintegration of society. As far as the public is concerned, I married Arturus as innocent as new fallen snow. Him, too, by the way, though society had to be satisfied with his sworn word on the marriage contract."

Both women giggled like teenagers who finally understood a piece of the adult world.

Dee whispered, "And how did the wedding night go?"

"Both of us were ravenous. We didn't leave the bedroom for three days. The servants slid food under the door as if we were prisoners in the dungeon."

"A prison of love?"

"You could say that." Guinevere yawned. "I'm sorry, Dee. I'm tired and tomorrow is another long day. Good night."

With that, the Viridian queen zipped herself into her sleeping bag and lay on her side, leaving Dee with her thoughts. Soon, Dee fell asleep as well.

Four hours later, Lancelot tapped Dee's shoulder. "Your watch, Dee."

By now, Dee was used to the routine. Each of the three women took part of the night for watch. Dee had the middle watch on this night. Without complaint, she pulled on a sweater and a second pair of long pants and joined Lancelot. A coffee pot steamed over the dim, artificial fire.

"I heard you laughing earlier," Lancelot said. "A good joke, I hope?"

How much of a semi-private conversation with Guinevere should she share with Lancelot? On the other hand, Dee considered Lancelot a friend. "We were talking about Guinevere's wedding to Arturus."

"I've heard that story, too. Did Guinevere tell you about the window scandal?"

"No." Dee sensed a juicy story.

"It happened while I was posted to the citadel. I saw the whole thing myself. The morning after the wedding, a news chan photographer caught the royal couple standing at the east-facing window watching the sun come up. They were naked as jaybirds. It caused a scandal." Lancelot stifled a laugh, as if afraid to attract unwanted attention.

Dee covered her mouth to quiet her guffaw.

"She was so beautiful." Lancelot uttered the words with a tinge of nostalgia, or regret. She sipped from a cup.

"You'll be up all night, Lancelot."

"It's decaf. Besides, I'm thinking I might sleep under the stars instead. It's not that cold."

On previous nights, Lancelot had taken her place in the tent after Dee had assumed the watch. Not tonight. Did the discussion of Guinevere and Arturus upset her? Dee wondered if a portrait of the king and queen might have to include an image of Lancelot in the background, perhaps peering from behind a column in the palace. Avoiding a reference to her might be less than truthful. Whitewashing reality, even for her friends went against her artist's aesthetic demand for truth.

* * *

Lancelot steered Dee and Guinevere toward a remote border village in the continent-dividing mountain range that, once crossed, descended into Lucanus proper. The village sat at a crossroads that abutted the southwest corner of Ontari:io. Just as the Lucians pushed against Viridiae's border with raids and incursions—and now a full-scale invasion—the Empire pressed north against Ontari:io's lands along a border stretching 4,500 kilometers from the village to the Eastern Ocean.

Coming down out of the mountains in a pouring rain, Dee spotted a compact community nestled among rolling foothills, not much different from the small town in Viridiae where her mother, Eleanor, owned property. But the bucolic scene was marred by thousands of refugees, stretched into a kilometer-long line on the main road leading into town.

"Remember our story," Lancelot said. "We're refugees from the fighting in Viridiae. We have relatives in Villefroide. Say as little as possible. Lie as little as possible. Are your documents at hand?"

"What if we're recognized by someone in the queue?"

"Keep your hoods on and pray that we blend in."

After weeks on the trail, obeying Lancelot was easy. Dee had fantasized about a bath and a real bed in the border town, but that prospect appeared as distant as the mountain peaks above them. After a full day in the line, Dee spotted the Lucian border post, about 200 meters from the border itself. A half-dozen legionnaires stood guard outside.

"There'll be more soldiers in the buildings," Guinevere said.

Dee touched the passport in her shirt pocket. The Viridian intelligence agency had also altered her ID chip in the skin between the thumb and forefinger of her right hand. Despite her companions' reassurances, her heart thumped. She wasn't used to traveling like a spy.

The town's main street was lined with small shops, horse troughs, and electric carts parked at an angle. Empty booths on an open lawn suggested a weekend produce market. A cart trundled by, and Dee exchanged three Lucian dinarii for three loaves of fresh bread and a measure of butter. The prices was outrageous, but she was tired of the freeze-dried rations, which were almost gone.

The border post waited at the far end of the main street. Two single-story buildings sat on either side of a gate across the road. Chain-link fencing topped with razor wire stretched into the hills to the right and left. The legionaries leaned against their pila, while an officer sat in a booth, swiping through a tablet. Ahead of Dee and the others, a group of refugees, perhaps a family, was allowed to pass.

"The Lucians don't look as if they're expecting anyone, other than refugees," Dee said.

"The soldiers aren't exactly the flower of Lucanus. They look half-asleep." Lancelot kept her hand near Arondight, hidden under a saddle blanket.

Guinevere volunteered to talk the trio through the gate. Dee was too young to be credible. Lancelot was too blunt. If the plan to reach Villefroide and convince the Ontarii to attack Lucanus was destined to fail, this was the most likely place, at least so far. Guinevere smiled at the centurion, but kept her eyes down in respect. He set down his tablet.

"Papers." The officer was a thin man in his early thirties. A scar cleft his cheek.

Guinevere handed over three Lucian passports. The centurion gestured Dee and Lancelot forward. If the forged papers failed, they might be killed on the spot. All three passed their hand under the ID chip reader.

"Your last place of residence is listed as Cameliard. All three of you. What are you doing here?"

"My great-grandfather was a Lucian trader who married a local girl," Guinevere said. "He came from the Sinarion clan. Perhaps you've heard of it?"

The officer shook his head.

"After your legions crossed the Viridian border, our neighbors drove us out. They never liked us, and frankly, we never liked them. My family has been thinking of moving to Villefroide, where we have relatives. My second cousin is a diplomat. She—"

"Enough." The centurion raised his hand and rose from his chair.

Dee's heart raced as he approached her horse. If he noticed

her anxiousness, she hoped he'd see it as intimidation. She kept her eyes down and rehearsed her story in her head. The best way to maintain a lie was to stay silent, unless questioned, then tell as much truth as possible. After a desultory inspection of her horse's panniers and her shoulder bag, the officer moved on without a word. He had missed the secret compartment in her saddle with her tablet and its encrypted documents.

The officer stopped at the pack horse, and then Guinevere's animal. He rifled through her belongings with more thoroughness than Dee's. The queen stepped forward, as if readying an objection, and the officer turned toward her. Instead of saying anything, she smiled, keeping her eyes on his. Dee had never seen her look as pretty. She guessed the officer and her were of similar age, and he lingered on her face. Guinevere's gaze appeared to enchant him and frighten him in the same moment.

The centurion moved on to Lancelot. She had the hardest time playing the poor evacuee, looking the officer directly in the eye. He grimaced, then peered at her, as if asking himself a question. He took a step backward, his hand moving toward the hilt of his gladius, without touching it. Dee thought about what she might do if he attacked. Run? Defend Lancelot with her power to kill at a distance? He patted the saddle blanket on Lancelot's horse and found the pommel of Arondight.

The centurion lifted the blanket and withdrew the sword from the scabbard. Arondight's blade was razor sharp, yet worn. The flaked gold paint on its hilt and the frayed leather of its grip showed the effects of years of maiming and killing. Back on the trail, Lancelot hoped it would pass with little notice. Most travelers carried weapons to protect themselves.

"Fine workmanship." The officer grinned. "Is it yours?"

"It was my grand-uncle's."

"Not a Lucian design. Did your grand-uncle fight in the Viridian civil wars?"

Dee tensed. The officer knew more of Viridian history than most. Lancelot would have to embellish his story. Could she convince him?

"Yes," Lancelot said. "On the losing side."

"Ah." The centurion approached Lancelot. Arondight's blade reflected sunlight into Lancelot's face. "Have you fought with it?"

"Only bandits." Lancelot squinted.

The centurion's deliberate rudeness angered Dee. He was provoking Lancelot to trip her up.

"You've had a relatively recent encounter." The centurion indicated a pink scar on Lancelot's forearm. She'd told Dee that the wound occurred at the River Colum battle.

"That bandit lost." Lancelot smirked.

The centurion grunted, apparently satisfied. He handed Arondight to Lancelot and returned to his booth, retrieving his tablet. "You may pass, lady."

"And my family?"

The centurion looked up. "Of course."

A guard lifted the gate, and the Viridians passed under its bar. After a few meters, Dee breathed a sigh of relief.

"Mount your horses," Lancelot ordered.

Dee thought they had made through the checkpoint into the no-man's land that made up the border, but when she glanced behind her, the guards were moving about, as if suddenly awake. The Ontarii checkpoint was visible in the distance, but Dee had the sensation of it falling further and further away. They were still in Lucanus, and wouldn't be safe until they passed the Ontarii gate.

"Stop!" A loudspeaker blared from the Lucian side. "Stop now and return to the gate!" The centurion's suspicions were confirmed.

"Now!" Lancelot shouted.

Dee and Guinevere spurred their horses. The pack mule startled but its herd instinct took over. Lancelot galloped fifty meters or so, then turned around, drawing Arondight.

"Lancelot!" Guinevere called. "Don't fight them! We need you with us."

"I'm coming, my lady. I just need a few minutes."

Two horses flew through the Lucian gate carrying the officer and a legionnaire. Lancelot parried the legionnaire's lance and sliced backward into his kidney, knocking the soldier off his horse.

The centurion took advantage of Lancelot's awkward position and sliced down to Lancelot's shoulder. The Viridian knight dodged the blow. The combatants shouted at one another, but Dee couldn't hear the words clearly. She did hear the clang of metal upon metal, but Guinevere urged her onward. After an excruciating minute, they reached the Ontarii gate.

"I am Guinevere, Royal Consort of Viridiae. I demand you let myself and my people enter Ontari:io."

To Dee, the Ontarii guards appeared more disciplined and alert, though the ongoing fight in the no-man's land piqued their interest. Lancelot and the centurion swung their swords like madmen. Three more mounted Lucians headed toward the fighters.

A woman in a plumed cap exited one of the Ontarii buildings. Guinevere shouted her demand again. The Ontarii officer studied the queen's face and Dee's.

Another dust cloud caught everyone's attention. Two more horses galloped onto the grassy field from the Lucian side. The legionaries surrounded Lancelot, who waved a captured pilum to keep them at bay.

When Lancelot tried to break away, legionaries cut her off. She ducked several blows before managing to land one, knocking the soldier off his mount. Lancelot was tiring, and his capture, or worse, was imminent.

Dee had to defend her friend. Guinevere needed the knight and her fame to boost Guinevere's chances of success with the Ontarii. Stepping away from the gawking Ontarii soldiers and a frightened Guinevere, Dee took a deep breath, recalling her training with Ganieda before Camelot was destroyed. She closed her eyes and opened the palms of her hands, which hung at her sides, and concentrated.

Guinevere's shout broke her concentration, but Dee had done

it. Three of the Lucians lay writhing on the ground, vertebrae in their backs crushed like eggshells. Lancelot broke off her fight and raced toward the Ontarii post. The centurion and his remaining soldiers galloped after Lancelot.

The Ontarii officer barked a command. Panting after her mental attack on the Lucians, Dee saw a squad of Ontarii leap through the gate and position long pikes five or six meters in front of their checkpoint. After another shout in Ontarii, the soldiers let Lancelot pass, then closed up ranks. The Lucian horsemen pulled back their reins. The centurion came up, his arm bleeding profusely. As they stared at each other, Dee sensed the Lucian centurion and Ontarii captain knew each other well.

"Is there a problem?" the Ontarii captain said in Lucian. He motioned Dee, Guinevere, and Lancelot through the gate.

"They're spies," the centurion said.

"They look like refugees to me." The Ontarii officer shrugged. "You're wounded, my friend. You should see to it."

Realizing an argument was pointless, the centurion snarled and wheeled around his horse. The other Lucians followed close behind back to their checkpoint.

An Ontarii sergeant ushered the Viridians into a park-like grove of trees behind the Ontarii gate. Thousands of other refugees milled about, some with tents, others huddled under carts as shelter. Despite the brush with failure, Dee hugged Guinevere, relieved they had made it safely through the border. A sweat-soaked Lancelot beamed.

Guinevere approached the Ontarii officer. "Thank you, captain. I send greetings from Lord Mordred of Viridiae."

The captain, whose name was Tintan, maintained a serious mien. Dee could not take her eyes off the woman's face. Diagonal bands of light and dark pigment covered it from hairline to chin.

"We've been expecting you, my lady." Tintan bowed slightly. "You and your party are under arrest."

CHAPTER 11: VILLEFROIDE

Tintan and two of her musketeers accompanied Dee, Guinevere, and Lancelot to a holding area with several hundred genuine refugees fleeing the war.

"We must confirm your identities before admitting you," Tintan said.

Dee's encrypted tablet contained electronic versions of the Viridian documents declaring their status as diplomats. Lancelot bristled at giving up Arondight while Ontarii functionaries filled out forms.

"How long are we expected to wait, captain?" Guinevere said.

"I cannot say, madam."

"My government notified Villefroide that we were coming. Weren't you given any instructions?"

"I was told that a senior Viridian might arrive at my border station, or she might not. The frontier with Lucanus is long and porous. I've reported your arrival, but my superiors have said nothing more."

Days passed with no word from the Ontarii government or the Viridian embassy in Villefroide. Dee felt forgotten by an inscrutable system. Even Guinevere's status as Arturus' wife carried little weight. Tintan kept Dee and the others away from the refugees. Guinevere wanted to visit them and encourage their spirits, but Lancelot agreed with Tintan that staying apart was best for security reasons. Lucian spies and assassins could easily hide in a crowd of people who knew little of each other.

Three days later, a well-dressed man of about thirty-five

turned up and asked to see the special detainees, as the Ontarii referred to the Viridian visitors. Like Tintan, the man's face was striped, though the alternating light and dark strips were thinner and subtler. Perhaps they signified social rank?

"I am Nock, a deputy assistant to the western regional manager of diplomatic investigations for the Foreign Ministry of Ontari:io. Whom, may I ask, is Lady Guinevere?"

Guinevere identified herself and introduced Lancelot and Dee.

Nock bowed to all three. "A pleasure, I'm sure. I apologize for the wait. I'm here to ascertain the purpose of your visit."

Guinevere invited Nock to sit at a table. "I'm sorry that I can't offer you more than water or apple juice as refreshment."

"Thank you, kindly, but I won't be staying long." Nock was business-like and efficient. Dee caught a whiff of high-quality cologne.

"I'm surprised, Mr Nock," Guinevere said. "I'm here on a diplomatic mission of the highest urgency and importance. My government indicated that I was traveling to Ontari:io to see President Jarnay. We wish to discuss matters of security related to the Lucian threat."

Nock folded his hands on the table. "Forgive me, my lady. I've been asked to relay our queen's regrets that she will not be able to discuss anything with you at this time."

"Why not?"

"Furthermore, we are unable to issue diplomatic visas for yourself and your party."

Lancelot spoke up. "You can't be seriously thinking of sending us back to Lucanus. They can easily identify us and kill us."

"You entered our country without permission, Dame Lancelot, notwithstanding Captain Tintan's gallant actions. You are in Ontari:io illegally."

Dee tuned out the polite, if tense, back-and-forth. She was enthralled by Nock's amazing facial bands, which she noticed on other Ontarii in the compound. She had never heard of the peculiar markings, and she couldn't resist the urge to record what she saw. She found her tablet, which had a drawing app, and she hurriedly sketched a head and shoulders portrait. After droning an explanation of Ontarii's immigration procedures, Nock stopped to see what Dee was drawing. His eyes flared in shock.

"Oh dear, I'm sorry, Mr Nock. Did I do something wrong? It's just that—"

"No, Ms Rathkeale." Nock smiled. "But I've never had my portrait done before, and it's a bit of a surprise."

"I sincerely apologize if I've offended you."

"Please, you've offended no one, least of all me. I'm quite flattered." Nock adjusted his cravat. "You see, most Ontarii can't afford portraits of this quality, though I aspire to have one done someday."

"This is just a sketch."

Guinevere jumped in. "Dee is an accomplished painter. Before the war, she was commissioned to create a monumental light tapestry honoring Viridian history. That was before the Lucians attacked Camelot. For all we know, they've destroyed her work."

Dee cringed at the half-truth. "That's not—"

Guinevere hushed Dee. "No need to be modest, my dear. We were all breathless with anticipation. You've pledged to complete the work once the war is over and Camelot restored to Viridian control."

"A light tapestry?" Nock's eyebrows lifted. One was dark. One was light. "I'm unfamiliar with this technique."

Dee cleared her throat. "It's a type of visual art using laser light. There are various forms, but most combine two-dimensional imagery with three-dimensional animation. For my commission, I took a lot of inspiration from the Revisionist style—"

"Mr Nock," Guinevere interrupted, "I was hoping to present Dee to President Jarnay, who is one of the most important patrons of the arts in Ontari:io, if not the continent. She'd appreciate the introduction, but if you insist that we have to leave Ontari:io..."

"I'd be glad to do a proper portrait of you, Mr Nock." Dee caught on to Guinevere's idea. "Your face is full of wonderful character. I might even work it into my commission in Viridiae's

Great Audience Hall."

Nock's eyes jumped from Dee to Guinevere and back to the sketch. Dee had stumbled onto the man's vanity, and she could offer a gift of real value. For her part, Guinevere hoped to leverage his desire for advancement. What career bureaucrat doesn't want to attract the eye of higher ups?

Nock tapped a finger on his dark chin. One of his white stripes bisected his left eye. "It's true that Ms Rathkeale's talent could add value to Ontari:io's visual arts scene. I'm sure many young artists would benefit from a lecture, perhaps?"

"Name the time and place." Dee didn't like public speaking, but Nock's resistance was crumbling.

"Let me make a call or two. Oh, this is exciting!" Nock clapped his hands in glee, bowed, and promised to return.

"Bit of a suck-up, wouldn't you say?" Lancelot said after Nock departed.

"Did you catch the look on his face when he saw Dee's sketch? He practically melted into our arms."

"It's just a sketch. I've done a million of them." Dee doubted the power of a simple, one-off image.

"It's not a sketch, Dee," Guinevere said. "It's our ticket to Villefroide."

* * *

Nock proved to be a master at manipulating Ontarii bureaucracy. He obtained an entry visa intended for medical emergencies on the pretext of a laceration inflicted on Lancelot by the Lucians during the dash for the border. Dee and Guinevere were listed as nurses to the injured knight. Satisfied that the letter of the law was met, the border agent stamped all three Viridian passports. The party, including Nock, headed northeast toward Villefroide.

As it happened, Captain Tintan departed with them on long-planned leave. A distant cousin to President Jarnay, she promised to do what she could to secure an audience, if Nock could not. The five travelers enjoyed a cordial relationship, despite the differences in rank and role. Dee almost believed she was on an adventure, until she received another communication from Mordred. The prime minister described the Viridian position as desperate, even as more recruits arrived daily for training.

Tintan sat for her own portrait at the hotel the day before the train departed for the capital. She donned the cap with the modest feathered plume she wore the day the Viridians arrived at the border post. "I've been meaning to ask you something, Ms Rathkeale, about your escape from the Lucians."

"How many times have I asked you to call me 'Dee', captain? I've never met a more formal people."

"I'll try harder, mmm, Dee." Tintan cleared her throat. "During the fight with Dame Lancelot, three of the Lucians seemed to spontaneously suffer injuries serious enough to take them out of the fight. I noticed an intense look of concentration on your face."

Dee avoided Tintan's gaze as the stylus in her right hand flew over the tablet's screen.

Tintan ignored Dee's discomfort. "At first, I thought it was simply a coincidence, but the more I think about it, the more doubts I have. Can you shed any light on this?"

Tintan had saved Dee's life, as well as Guinevere's and Lancelot's. She didn't think it wise to blurt out the truth of her genetic legacy. but she had to say something.

"I'm sure you know about the DNA manipulation by the Old Civilization?"

"Know of it? It is a constant topic of conversation among the Ontarii elite."

"How so?"

"I overheard your admiration of Nock's bandeau."

"Yours are amazing as well. Are they inherited?"

"Early in Ontarii history, just after the Dissolution, several dozen leading families wanted to set themselves apart from the population. They had their DNA altered to produce bandeau, with a particular pattern for each family. Over the centuries, the altered genes spread throughout the population. Each pattern also developed a meaning. Mine, for example, suggest a military family."

"That seems natural." Dee concentrated on getting the shades of pigment correct in Tintan's bandeau. They ranged from a deep, almost purplish black to pinkish white.

"The width of my bandeau also suggests that someone in my family background was a farmer."

"You mean they represented furrows in the earth?"

"Something like that."

Dee still hadn't answered Tintan's question about the injured Lucians. "Viridiae has a history of DNA manipulation as well, but it's not something we're proud off."

"It's difficult to talk about."

Maybe Tintan would let her off the hook if she claimed a taboo.

"Still, I'm curious."

No such luck. Dee sighed. "I have some psychokinetic abilities."

Tintan's concentration on Dee intensified. "Of what kind?"

"Please, captain, do we have to talk about this?"

Tintan let out a breath. "I'm sorry, Dee. I'm trained to identify, well, threats. Snapping a bone at a distance is a powerful weapon. But I've overstepped my bounds."

As if released from a pair of cuffs, Dee swiped a few strokes on her tablet. She wouldn't have to tell the full story of her abilities, at least not yet. "Would you like to see what I have so far, captain?"

Tintan grinned. "I'm flattered. I can't wait to see it completed. Another sitting tomorrow?"

Dee agreed.

* * *

After three days of rolling hills and farmland viewed from the steam-powered train, the slender, pointed towers of Villefroide rose on the horizon. When she wasn't working on Tintan's portrait, or sketches of the landscape, Dee read up on the city and its culture. She tried out her knowledge on Nock at breakfast a few hours before their arrival.

"Villefroide was founded soon after the Dissolution, correct, Mr Nock?"

"Indeed. A group of refugees from the ancient United States of America joined other refugees from parts of the old nation of Canada at a luckless seaport on the Bay of Hudson. Sea level rise had drowned the port."

"The refugees fled the southern latitudes. Farming was nearly impossible."

"The nation-states had gutted themselves fighting over the scraps."

"How did the immigrants survive?"

"The founders restored the docks, built sailing cargo vessels, and traded over the Freezing Sea in summer. By this time, the sea was nearly ice-free. Vessels from other ports called on Villefroide, and it grew into the richest trading zone on the continent, due to its central location."

"It's an amazing history, Mr Nock."

Nock tilted his head in thanks. "It's not without its troubles, Ms Rathkeale. As Ontari:io's strength grew, other powers grew jealous."

"The Lucians, no doubt."

"They managed to create an empire out of the ashes of the Old Civilization. They are forever looking to the north for new land and resources."

"And the west." Dee sighed, thinking of Camelot.

"Except that the Empress Vetrania had other motivations for her invasion, no?"

Dee wondered why the Ontarii always managed to ask uncomfortable questions? International relations and the mission to recruit the Ontarii was Guinevere's territory. Why did Mordred send Dee with Guinevere and Lancelot in the first place? She was an artist, not a diplomat, despite her passport. She often felt useless, like an extra wheel on a four-wheeled cart. That didn't stop her from forming opinions, however.

"I'm not an expert in politics, Mr Nock, but I think the empress is afraid."

"Please, I'd like to hear your thinking."

"Why else would she take such a risk to steal the Grail from us, if she feared that she could not make her own Great Machine work properly?"

"These kinds of fears can make individuals and nations do reckless things."

"That's why we're here, Mr Nock. Perhaps her fear will lead her to attack Ontari:io."

"We don't have a Great Machine in Ontari:io. What do we have to fear from Lucanus?"

"What if she succeeds? What if she manages to repair her Great Machine? Her power and prestige would grow. She might conquer all of Viridiae, and then turn her sights on Ontari:io."

"Seems unlikely, Ms Rathkeale." Nock contradicted his comment by furrowing his brow.

"It's possible, don't you think? Despots who succeed at expanding spread themselves like a cancer until they are stopped."

Nock leaned back in his chair as the train slowed in Villefroide's suburbs. "Ms Rathkeale, you should give yourself more credit. Perhaps you should be the one to make the case to President Jarnay."

Dee could not imagine substituting for Guinevere, but Nock's observation surprised her. The argument seemed obvious. Vetrania endangered everyone, and an alliance was the best way to stop her.

It was also the best way to bring Arturus and Percival home.

* * *

Villefroide mornings teemed with birdsong from the maple trees beyond Dee's window, but the day promised more of the waiting that had bedeviled the Viridians since their first steps off the train. The skeletal Viridian embassy staff, in the dark about Guinevere's arrival in the city to maintain security, scrambled to find accommodations, finally putting them up in the ambassador's residence. Lancelot bunked with the officer commanding a squad of knights that guarded the embassy, while Dee shared a room with Guinevere.

Dee hardly saw the queen, except in the early mornings or late at night. "Do you have any hope of seeing Jarnay today, my lady?"

"I have hope every day." Guinevere adjusted her blouse and jacket. She'd purchased Ontarii women's business wear to replace the road-worn traveling clothes. Jarnay's invitation might come at any time. Or it might not come at all.

"It's been almost three weeks. How long can we wait?"
"As long as necessary." Guinevere applied light makeup in the Viridian style. Tailored for the bandeau, Ontarii cosmetics didn't looked right on the Viridians' more even tones, which tended toward caramel. "How is your portrait of our host coming?"

To combat her boredom, Dee worked on a portrait of Jarnay. This time, however, she executed the image as a light tapestry, borrowing some equipment left over from a Viridian cultural exhibition before the war. Unlike her monumental work in the Great Audience Hall back home, Dee intended Jarnay's likeness to hang in the executive's private quarters. Working from photographs and videos, as well as her official biography, Dee focused almost exclusively on Jarnay's face, hoping to capture the subtle changes in each band. The transitions from one band to another proved tricky, and she sought help on artists' forums in the Ontarii social nets. Could she find a hint of the woman's essence, even though she'd never met her? Many artists sympathized with the Viridian cause against Lucanus, and Dee soon found a technique that worked.

At the beginning of their sixth week in Villefroide, Guinevere received the message she'd waited for: President Jarnay would give her 15 minutes that morning. After all her begging and preparation, Guinevere expressed a sudden bout of anxiety. "What if I'm unable to persuade her, Dee?"

"You shouldn't worry, my lady." Dee adjusted Guinevere's hair in a modest style currently popular among female leaders in Villefroide. "Our cause is moral and just. President Jarnay is an intelligent, compassionate woman. She gained the presidency on her reputation as a hawk on resisting Lucian aggression."

Guinevere studied Dee in the mirror. "Will you come with me to the presidential palace?"

"Is that permitted?"

"Lancelot will be there. I want you there too. I need all the support I can get."

"Of course, my lady. It's a great privilege."

Dee advised Guinevere on the color preferences of the fashionable Ontarii, though both women added a splash of green, Viridiae's national color. Guinevere, however, had trouble concentrating. "Your hand is shaking, my lady. Perhaps we should postpone."

"No, I'll feel better once we reach the palace. I haven't felt this nervous since I was appointed to the Round Table. I probably should've felt more nervous then, but I was younger and a little over-confident."

Dee could hardly imagine a more poised and careful leader.

"Have I ever told you the story of my time on the Siege Perilous?"

"No, my lady."

"I was only 19. It was one of the most important experiences of my life."

CHAPTER 12: GUINEVERE AND THE UNICORN

The annual Red and White gathering of 150 knights, elected and appointed, erupted. Gallery spectators shouted. The knight's retainers protested. On the real-time screen above the well of the Government House chamber, Viridiae's citizens poured out praise and scorn.

The ball of red glass shocked Guinevere. It lay in the palm of her hand, and it terrified her with its opportunity. Each of the other Knights of the Round Table held a white ball. They had nothing to fear, nor a path to glory. Gaia, or the gods, or random chance, had given Guinevere the Siege Perilous. If she could pass its test, maybe everyone would finally take notice of her.

Arturus II oversaw the ceremony. He could send her to her death, or worse.

Amid the tumult in the hall, a tall, white-mustachioed knight in formal tunic demanded recognition. "Majesty, I must object in the most strenuous terms."

On his dais, the elderly Arturus lifted a hand, which brought a measure of quiet. "On what grounds, Sir Caris?"

"The honorable Sir Caris has no grounds, sire." Guinevere defended her selection. Her reputation and ambition depended on it.

Caris made his case with a curl to his lip. "Dame Guinevere is barely more than a child. She is brave, I'm sure, but she has no military training. The Siege Perilous quest is arduous and demanding. She may have to spend weeks or months alone in a wilderness. I doubt even her charm and obvious allure would dissuade an attack by a questing beast or a troll."

Scattered snickers echoed in the chamber. Guinevere closed her fist around the Red Ball to control her disgust and frustration. Her beauty was always the ticket that got her in the door. Once inside, it proved a curse. No one looked past the bright eyes, perfect skin, classic features, or proportioned figure. The Gaia-given traits blocked interest in her keen and discerning mind, as lead blocks the invisible rays emanating from rare elements.

Nonetheless, she wouldn't be goaded by the Table's most vocal conservative, even if she had never accepted a quest of any kind before. "Sire, my personal qualities are not important. I am a Knight of the Round Table and I have won the Red Ball in a fair lottery."

"You have been a knight at this table for a single day, my lady." Arturus had just confirmed her appointment. "The Siege Perilous is not a trivial thing."

Guinevere's brand-new formal tunic pinched her. "I take the quest as seriously as Sir Caris, Your Majesty, perhaps more so." Men and women had always stood side-by-side at the Round Table, but Arturus had reformed the Round Table to attract more than military minds. Guinevere and her newly appointed and elected peers recognized the moment's importance when it came, and all worked hard to earn their seats. Here was her chance to prove their worthiness.

"I submit, with all due respect, that you do not have the strength for it," Caris said.

"I have earned many trophies in athletic contests."

Caris laughed. "I refer not to your physical strength, but your strength of will. I fear you will, as children say, 'wimp out.'"

The accusation mystified Guinevere, though she regretted her peevishness. What was he talking about?

Arturus intervened. "Enough, Caris."

Caris bowed. "My apologies, Majesty. I am merely concerned

about maintaining and increasing the honor of this Table." He puffed out his chest. "I expect the test Your Majesty chooses will be difficult and dangerous in the extreme, as tradition demands —"

"You are out of order, sir, and edging toward contempt for this body." Despite his age, Arturus commanded respect. His father, Arturus the Great, founded the Viridian nation. "The Red Ball is selected, and the quest is mine to charge."

Quests given to knights chosen for the Siege Perilous typically involved climbing mountains, sailing the oceans, or infiltrating the Lucian Empire. If Arturus gave Guinevere a difficult test, and she failed it, no one would ever take her seriously now, or in the future.

Caris ignored Arturus' threat of contempt. He spoke for a large faction of the country. "I do not believe My Lord Duke of Cameliard, if he were here, would countenance subjecting his beautiful daughter to an ordeal that might kill her."

Guinevere bristled. "It's not up to you to decide what I may do or not do, Caris."

"I would be happy to oversee an intensive course of physical and mental training that would prepare you."

"Sire, this is outrageous." Guinevere nearly crushed the Red Ball in her fist. "I'm not a child. I have shown in many ways that I'm more than capable. If Sir Caris were in charge, the Round Table would be populated with men who know nothing but swords, pistols, and riding."

Arturus narrowed his eyes. "Surely, Caris, you're not implying that our reforms opening the Round Table to a broader set of our citizenry have been misguided?"

"Of course not, sire." Caris did not meet Arturus gaze. "But high school trophies and good grades at Camelot University are not qualifications for a quest worthy of the Siege Perilous. Let me remind Your Majesty that Dame Guinevere acquired her seat at the Round Table when her father resigned due to ill health. Your sire, Arturus I, reserved the seat for the Cameliard family as a reward for its support during the Civil Wars. Dame Guinevere is not of that class of people who've risen through the ranks, so to speak."

The truth of Caris' words hurt Guinevere. By inherited right, she belonged at the Round Table. Along with her beauty, her privilege masked her abilities. Only the best minds got into the honors program at Camelot University, but no one at the Round Table seemed to care.

Arturus lowered his chin in thought. "Caris, I believe you are speaking with the best interests of Viridiae at heart. I have taken your words into consideration. Before going further, I'd like to satisfy Guinevere's curiosity about the test I have chosen for this year's candidate to the Siege Perilous."

Guinevere's heart quickened. She hoped it would not involve killing someone or wanton destruction of property.

"Dame Guinevere, my test for you is this: Capture the Unicorn of the North, and bring it to Camelot within a month's time. Should you accomplish this goal, we will be honored to seat you in the Siege Perilous. Fame and respect will be yours forever."

The murmurs in the crowd began before Arturus finished. They rose to a crescendo, led by Caris. "This is unprecedented, Your Majesty. A girl of 10 could accomplish this quest. It's unworthy of the Siege Perilous. Good warriors, men and women, have died for this honor."

Inwardly, Guinevere breathed a sigh of relief. On its face, the test was easy, compared to tests for other knights. But was it too easy? What was Arturus playing at?

"I have one thing more. For both of you, Caris and Guinevere."

Guinevere's eyes met Caris', and she saw unease. Arturus was about to change the rules.

"Caris, I respect tradition as much as you, but things must change, especially as we face rising threats from the Lucians. On the other hand, I would never forgive myself if I sent Guinevere on a quest for which she was unprepared, physically or mentally."

Guinevere wanted to argue, but she held her breath.

"Therefore, I appoint Sir Caris as Dame Guinevere's second, to assist her in the test in every way he sees fit, save for accomplishing the test itself. That is for her only."

Guinevere and Caris' jaws dropped in unison. Tradition demanded that knights questing for the Siege Perilous achieve it alone. No one had assisted the chosen knight, not even at the command of the king.

"Sire, I'm grateful for Sir Caris' help, but I'm capable of passing the test on my own. I don't need any help."

Arturus voice rose above the pandemonium. "You will work with Sir Caris and you will leave as soon as possible." The king stood from his throne and departed.

Guinevere despaired. The Red Ball had signaled a chance to be seen and heard on her own terms. If she passed the test, she'd be more than a privileged child with good looks and good grades. She'd be a fully fledged Knight of the Round Table, a member of the meritorious elite of Camelot and Viridiae.

Instead, she had a babysitter.

* * *

Guinevere winced as she eased her herself off her horse. The raw spots on her buttocks complained about another day in the saddle. The skin would callus in time, but the indignity inflicted by Arturus still hurt. Caris' presence was a constant reminder. From the moment they left Camelot by its north gate, Guinevere kept her distance from the knight, despite his questions to her about "orders" and "plans." She suspected he was mocking her. The fact was, Guinevere had no time to develop a plan or orders. Tradition demanded that Siege Perilous knights leave the city within an hour of their charge with only a horse, weapons, and supplies for a week.

Instead, she researched, downloading everything she could find on unicorns onto her tablet. One of the first links was a revelation.

"You've captured the Unicorn of the North, Sir Caris?"

"And brought it back to Camelot, yes, my lady."

"But it escaped?"

Caris turned his head without answering, as if embarrassed, though it was hard to tell. He was of the same generation as her father, Leodegrance, men and women for whom pain, especially emotional pain, was endured without complaint or comment. Her father, for example, never talked about the death of Guinevere's mother from cancer. However, when the subject came up, his eyes would brim with tears.

"You are one of the few people who's seen a unicorn alive in the wild, Sir Caris." Maybe the elder knight would be useful. "Where do you think it might be?"

"I haven't the faintest idea, but I found my unicorn as far from people as you can imagine, and still be in Viridiae."

"According to my research, the creature was last seen in the remote northwestern corner of Viridiae, near the Lucian border. That would seem to be the logical place to start a search."

Caris nodded. "As you say, my lady."

"Some sage-biologists believe a population lives in the far north, perhaps along the shores of the Freezing Sea."

"That's a long way to go for an old man like myself."

Guinevere didn't want to go that far either, so she had to hope that the last sighting was not a mirage, and that the creature had stayed in the area.

"Tell me what you know about the beast if you please, Sir Caris. Are the descriptions and images accurate?"

"They are ferocious horse-like creatures. The needle-sharp horn can tear you to pieces, so it's said."

"Did it harm you?"

"I managed to capture it without hurting it or myself."

Guinevere smiled at that. She disliked seeing animals in pain. She scrolled through her notes. "Viridian sage-scientists aren't sure of their origins. One hypothesis goes like this: Prior to the Dissolution, when the world fell apart, people began experimenting with genetic editing. A few tried to create mythical creatures imagined since the beginning of human history. They combined the genes from a horse, a goat, and a sea creature called a narwhal to build a unicorn."

"It is truly ironic that human beings a thousand years ago had the arrogance to play Gaia and construct a chimera that symbolized purity in ancient times."

Caris knew more of the subject than he let on. The man was opinionated, but not prideful.

Over the following days, they'd developed a kind of truce, neither hostile nor friendly. He was an experienced outdoor traveler, and she paid attention to his habits, learning how to start a fire in his preferred way, or finding fodder for the horses. She had never attempted a journey like her quest before, and he spent years on military campaigns in the Hot Lands or against Lucana.

On this day, however, he changed his routine. After she helped him set up the pair of one-person tents, he asked to be excused. Taking his horse, while leaving his camping gear, he said he would be gone for a few hours, returning by sundown.

Guinevere waited, nervous that he might abandon her to the cold.

He appeared with furred bundles hanging from his saddle. He'd set snares and caught two rabbits. He gutted and skinned the carcasses.

"Did you have to do that right in front of me?" Guinevere turned away. Unable to watch Caris spit the carcasses for roasting, she dug into a pannier for the package of dried fruit and found two moldy bits of apple. Disgusted, she gave them to her horse.

The meat dripped juices over a fire. "You'd better eat something." Caris held out half a rabbit.

Guinevere retched. "I don't eat flesh." She wouldn't meet Caris' gaze. "You probably think it's stupid."

"On the contrary, I admire it. The methane produced by livestock contributed to the climate change that led to the Dissolution. I wonder if the Old Civilization would've survived if it had brought its meat habit under control."

Looking at the rabbit, all Guinevere could think about was its last moments as it choked to death. "Then why are you eating it,

Sir Caris?"

"I'm hungry, and meat is high in protein and energy. We'll need both to fight off the wet and the cold." Caris glanced at the sky, which had clouded over.

Guinevere imagined the silenced screams of the rabbit.

"Do not pity the rabbit, Dame Guinevere. It is fated to be prey, just as some people are."

"I hope you're not referring to me." Guinevere regarded the haunch, undecided whether she could swallow the cooked muscle.

"Prey can learn to be predator, when it comes to human affairs."

"You're mistaken about me, if you think I will be like the sheep, rather than the wolf."

Caris sucked his fingers. "I know what you want, Guinevere of Cameliard, but you haven't got what it takes to get it."

"How do you know so much about me?"

"Everyone knows the Cameliards have a grudge. Your family's been hanging on to it for nearly a century."

"That is none of your business."

"On the contrary, my lady, it is the nation's business."

When her father's illness left him bedridden, she'd suggested taking his place at the Round Table. She was his oldest child, and she could think of no better way to honor his service to the nation than to keep the seat in the family.

"You must be referring to the Civil Wars, Sir Caris. If it weren't for the Duchy of Cameliard changing sides to support Arturus the Great, Viridiae would still be a gaggle of squabbling states, instead of the power that it is."

"Arturus was smarter than you gave him credit for. He promised your great-grandfather lands to expand the Duchy, but he never followed through. Arturus knew how to keep his rivals in check. You're bent on revenge."

"If you're questioning my loyalty—"

"As I see it, the only way to resolve your family's grudge is to have a Cameliard on Viridiae's throne."

"I have no such ambitions, Sir Caris." Guinevere had to dissemble, or risk an accusation of sedition.

"You're a bad liar, my lady, and you have a worse fault."

"Really?"

"You pity the prey." Caris chewed more of the rabbit. "You won't eat what Gaia has offered in this rabbit. You lack ruthlessness, my lady. No king, or queen, can survive without it."

Caris' assertion stung. That was the thing she had to show, that she could trample on something or someone, or no one would respect her, or fear her. So far, she hadn't impressed Caris. But was compassion a weakness? "What makes you an expert on ruthlessness, Sir Caris?"

Caris did not answer. Instead, he tore off another chunk of meat. Life fed on life to survive, and while the Old Civilization had abused this fact to fatten itself, eating a rabbit to stay strong was hardly a sin against the earth. In a manner of speaking, monarchs, in order to survive, fed on their adversaries, enemies, and friends.

Guinevere took a small bite, chewed once, and swallowed, hoping she could keep it down. A sip of water helped.

Caris watched her, enjoying his portion. He moved his mouth into a half-smile, begrudging Guinevere's attempt to learn a lesson. She noticed his approval.

"You once picked the Red Ball, Sir Caris."

"That has been one of my misfortunes."

"I think of it as a great honor."

"Of course, it is, my lady. But that does not mean the result is what you hope for."

"How did you feel when Arturus gave you the task of finding the Unicorn of the North?"

Caris shrugged. "I succeeded. I brought it to his menagerie, where it stayed for three years. Then it escaped."

"Forgive me, but you're not making sense. You succeeded in capturing the unicorn, but it escaped. That sounds like failure to me." Guinevere enjoyed a chance to gain advantage.

Caris was thoughtful. "All I know is that Arturus said a week after I brought in the beast that I hadn't achieved the quest. I've never understood what he meant. The unicorn's escape was an entirely different mystery. No one knows how it managed to get out of its pen. I have a feeling the king knows, but he hasn't said a word to anyone."

With no experience at court, and only her father's warnings and admonitions about court life, Guinevere didn't know how to interpret Caris' story. Was Arturus setting her up for another humiliation?

Caris grew taciturn as the days passed. He scanned the dim horizon, as if expecting to see something he didn't like. His quietude got under Guinevere's skin. Perhaps it was the rain. Maybe she'd hurt him by pointing out his failures. He was courteous, however, when they set up camp or prepared meals.

The travelers sat on a jumble of rocks eating a cold lunch of salmon berries, jerky begged off a passing hunter, and rainwater. "Are you troubled about something, Sir Caris?"

"We're too close to the Lucian border."

The Unicorn of the North was last seen in Nighthawk Valley, according to the hunter. A ridge that flanked the valley's eastern rise served as the legal border between Viridiae and Lucana.

"At this pace, we'll cross into the valley in a few hours."

"What are the chances of actually encountering a Lucian?" Guinevere said. "We're still on the Viridian side of the border."

"Borders mean nothing to the Lucians. Conquest is all they understand."

Caris had fought in the last war with Lucana.

"Do you think the Lucians would have gone after the Unicorn on their own?"

"They would see it as a propaganda coup. 'See how Lucana takes from Arturus at will.' They'd wave it in front of our noses to disparage us."

If the Lucians had captured the Unicorn, or it had simply wandered off further north into the Frozen Lands, Guinevere's misery of a sore butt and the mountain cold would count for nothing. She would've wasted an opportunity of a lifetime to make a name for herself.

"We should go, my lady. Too long in one spot is dangerous."

The rain eased, and as the sun approached the western peaks of the Range of Needles, they reached a pass into Nighthawk Valley. For the first time in the journey, Caris strapped his fighting sword and single-shot pistol to his hip. Guinevere had a sword and pistol as well, but she had no practice with either. They descended toward a shallow river through broken sage and basalt outcrops. Clumps of cottonwood crowded both banks of the river.

"Perfect cover for an ambush," Caris observed.

Other than footprints, hoof prints, and a long-cold camp fire, the searchers found no signs of a Lucian patrol, or a Viridian patrol, for that matter. The nearest Viridian strong point was fifty kilometers south. Stretched thin, the Viridian military thought these lands too remote to defend effectively.

"A weak point ripe for exploitation, if you ask me," Caris said.

Twilight ended their search for the day, and stars peeked around the broken clouds of evening. Caris killed two more rabbits, and Guinevere had an easier time with her meal. They sipped fresh-ground coffee made with filtered river water. She volunteered for the first watch. They had only a few days left to find the unicorn before Arturus' deadline.

Caris set his cup on a flat stone. The metal reflected the campfire's flames. "Dame Guinevere, may I tell you something?"

"It's about time we dropped the formalities, don't you think? Call me Guinevere. I doubt anyone at court will hear."

"I knew your father."

"How so?"

"We were both posted to security duty at the Viridian consulate in Aurelia, down south in the Hot Lands. I was there only three months."

Leodegrance had listed the great city-state on the Peaceful Sea as one of his favorite posts as a young man. The city was famed for its technological prowess and carefree culture.

"I never saw him fight an enemy, but he was formidable in the lists. I remember thinking that I would not want to meet him in battle."

"I'm sure he would remember you," Guinevere said, "if you were to visit us in Cameliard."

"Maybe, but I'm only a knight with a little bit of land and a bagful of strong opinions."

Guinevere thought back to the Siege Perilous ceremony. "You've opposed the changes Arturus has brought to the Round Table."

"Some of them."

"Including the one dropping military service as a prerequisite for appointed positions?"

"I confess to it. I have no problem with people without military backgrounds getting one of the elected chairs. But I see the appointed chairs as a kind of meritorious elite. Without people who know the capabilities of the Lucians, how will we defend ourselves successfully?"

Guinevere stayed mute. It was not a moment to start an argument, despite her view that an elite could easily turn in a cabal, even an oligarchy.

"There," Caris said, "I've opened my mouth again. Arturus has made his decision, and it's my duty to abide by it."

"Sir Caris, let me be frank. I have a feeling that you and I would disagree on many things, even fundamental things. But I hope I am not patronizing you by saying that we both believe in our country and its values."

Caris nodded.

"I'd also add, hoping that it does not embarrass you, that while I was not happy about your appointment as my, well, guardian, I am glad you've come. I don't think I would've made it this far without your help."

"I don't think you would've made it, either."

The comment took Guinevere aback.

"Having said that, I've been impressed with your persistence and your willingness to set aside your discomfort in the quest for something larger. I'm considering whether to revise my opinion of you."

Guinevere felt as if she'd been shot with an arrow. What did he mean, exactly? She didn't get a chance to request a clarification.

* * *

Guinevere and Caris reached the place where the Unicorn of the North was last seen, but the valley was uninhabited and rarely visited. Local knowledge was scarce.

If Guinevere could not go to the unicorn, perhaps it would come to her. The ancient sources on the creature claimed it could be trapped by a maiden. The DNA engineers would've loaded all the expected characteristics and behaviors, at least for the casual observer. Would the unicorn sense her presence, and at least investigate?

Caris hated the idea. "You'd be exposing yourself. Gaia knows what other monsters might be looking for a meal."

The engineers had also created questing beasts, griffins, even a horse with wings.

"I don't see any alternative, other than wandering around, hoping for a sign. We've only got a few days left. Do you have any better ideas?"

They followed the river north until they found a broad, treed plain with a thin undergrowth. Large, four-footed animals might move easily under the cover, attracted by the vegetation. Caris identified elk tracks and spoor, but no other signs.

Guinevere found a dry place in the grass and laid out a horse blanket. Donning a brightly colored jacket and brushing her long, black hair, she caught Caris staring at her. "I might as well make myself presentable."

"An easy task, my lady."

In the late afternoon, after hours of boredom, the sun came out, bathing Guinevere in golden light. She tipped her head back to soak in its rays. A rustling, louder than the mice she'd heard in the grass on the edge of her blanket, made her open her eyes. She sat still, fearful of frightening the visitor or triggering a predator's instinct to attack. The rustle turned into a struggle and she heard a loud grunt which sounded an awful lot like Caris. He had taken a position underneath a bush decorated with blood red berries.

"Like I said, the woods are full of predators." Caris emerged from the forest, his pistol drawn, pushing a man ahead of him. He wore the uniform of a Lucian legionnaire.

Guinevere jumped up. The soldier gazed at her in a familiar way. She'd seen that look at thousand times from young men when she walked into a room of strangers. It was disbelief.

"Speak up, man," Caris said. "Tell my lady your name."

"I am Hubertus." Cowed, he dropped his pock-marked gaze to the ground.

One legionnaire meant more, maybe hundreds, nearby. Guinevere's palms sweat.

Caris said, "What are you doing out here?"

"I was just out for a walk. My family owns land like this. I was homesick."

Guinevere felt pity for the young man, probably a conscript.

"I saw you," Hubertus said to Guinevere, his voice thick with hard vowels, "and I thought you were a goddess, come to comfort me. You see, it's lonely out here and—"

"Enough blubbering," Caris said. "Where's the rest of your unit?"

Hubertus shook his head. He may be a conscript, but he wouldn't betray his friends.

"Sir, I am Guinevere Cameliard, and this is Sir Caris. We are both Knights of the Round Table, and we are searching for the Unicorn of the North. Have you seen it?"

Hubertus licked his lips.

Guinevere took a step toward the legionnaire. Despite her desire that men see her as an intellectual equal, she was ready to use her beauty to advantage, remembering her father's admonition never to waste her gifts. She took Hubertus' hand. His jaw dropped. He was intimidated. "Help us in our quest, dear Hubertus. Have you seen the creature?"

"I have seen it, my lady." Hubertus' eyes flicked back and forth between Guinevere and Caris, who forced back a grin.

"When?" Guinevere struggled to contain her excitement.

"Today, my lady."

Guinevere remained impassive, though her heart leaped with joy. She kissed Hubertus on the cheek, and he nearly melted into the grass.

"Steady, lad." Caris pressed his gun into the Lucian's spine. "What would your mother think of your consorting with one of Arturus' favorites?"

Hubertus swallowed hard.

"Take us to a place where we can see your camp without being seen ourselves," Guinevere said. "I will reward you for cooperating."

With Caris alert to deception, the trio walked up a hillock covered with dense bushes. Shouts and an unearthly braying, like an angry mule, rose in volume. His gloved hand covering Hubertus' mouth, Caris encouraged the prisoner to edge closer to the commotion.

Through a break in the trees, Guinevere spied the cause of the ruckus. Three Lucian soldiers strained to control a snow-white beast with ropes. Guinevere caught herself before she cried out with delight. The creature appeared just as the books and images described: cloven hooves, a goat-like beard under its chin, and a twisted horn on its forehead. Fighting to break free, the unicorn's flowing mane and long tail awed Guinevere, and she understood why Arturus wanted it back in his collection. Its wild ferocity symbolized the power and threat that a nation could bring to bear on its enemies. Caging one suggested it could be unleashed.

Also mesmerized by the unicorn, Caris had loosened his grip. Hubertus slipped out, screamed and bolted down the hillock toward his compatriots.

"I guess your spell is broken, my lady." Caris handed Guinevere his fighting knife and drew his sword. "You get the unicorn. I'll take care of the Lucians."

Caris ran after Hubertus into the camp, yelling his war cry, and slashing with his sword. Guinevere sped toward the unicorn. When it saw her, it stopped struggling against its bonds. The books were right again: When it encountered a maiden, it turned docile as a kitten. Guinevere cut the ropes, fashioning one into a makeshift halter and lead. She didn't have to coax the unicorn into following. All it took was a mild tug.

Glancing over her shoulder, she steered the unicorn away from the fight. Caris challenged three of the four soldiers. What happened to Hubertus? Guinevere imagined him running off in fright or embarrassment. Instead, he emerged from behind an oak tree, brandishing a sword.

"I don't know who you are, but that's our unicorn. Give it to me." He held out his left hand for the lead, keeping the sword in his right hand.

Guinevere pointed Caris' fighting knife, still in her hand, at Hubertus.

She had no idea what to do. The *clank* of sword against sword behind her meant Caris wouldn't rescue her. She wasn't about to give up her prize. Technically, the unicorn belonged to Arturus. Maybe she should argue the case to Hubertus. He seemed intelligent, if immature. She could demonstrate her intellectual gifts, as well as her ambition. She sometimes fantasized about making a grand argument at the Round Table for her family's right to gain election to the Viridian throne, and having the country beg her to declare her candidacy for the seat when Arturus died. On the other hand, back in the meadow, she saw how she could manipulate a man with her demeanor, and she resented his shallowness. An advantage was an advantage, especially if it worked against a man ready to slice you in two.

Guinevere gambled on a fantasy. "Is this any way to treat a princess?"

"What?"

"Knights are supposed to protect princesses, especially damsels in distress. But you're threatening to kill me. You have no honor."

"I only want the unicorn."

Guinevere's struggled to buy time. She thought delaying Hubertus with nonsense might give Caris a chance to help. But the fight two dozen paces away showed no sign of ending. Guinevere was on her own. Hubertus and she were a year or two apart in age, but he was nothing more than a cog in the great Lucian military machine. She was a noblewoman, if not actually a princess, with ambitions far higher than Hubertus could ever reach.

A piece of her realized what she was doing. She shaved off bits of Hubertus' humanity, turning him into a creature she could look down on. She pitied poor Hubertus, and that allowed her to let go of pity, and see him as nothing more than a barrier to push aside for a greater good—her greater good. Even though the attitude didn't come easy, it came easier than she expected. Ruthlessness was not an inborn talent. You could learn it, like how to start a fire.

"You dishonor me, sir, but I will give you your unicorn to save my reputation. Take it from me." Guinevere offered the unicorn's lead, but in a way that encouraged Hubertus to step forward.

The young man took the bait. His eyes on the rope, he didn't see Guinevere's right hand drive the point of the knife into his neck below the jaw. Before his fingers touched the lead, he dropped like a stone. Blood surged around the blade with the last beats of his heart.

Guinevere vomited.

Caris' fight ended, and he arrived with two of the Lucian horses. He took in the scene of Hubertus' death. "Hot work for both of us, eh, my lady?" His eyes glinted with the thrill of battle. One of his three opponents sprawled by the camp fire, also dead. "The other two have run off, but they'll regain their courage soon."

"Did you hurt either of them?" She thought of Hubertus and his innocent enthrallment. Nothing would ever thrill him again.

"Not in any way that won't heal in a week or two." Caris studied the unicorn. "Congratulations, Guinevere. I only half-believed we'd find it."

115

She wanted to get back to Camelot as soon as possible. Her stomach churned.

"Don't be sorry about what you did, my lady. He was a soldier, trained to kill or die. You did what you had to do."

Did she really defend myself? Or did she kill poor Hubertus because he was inconvenient? The unicorn didn't seem to care. It kept its placid gaze on the maiden who had lost her moral virtue.

"Let's go, my lady. We're just inside the Lucian border, if I'm not mistaken. The patrol is likely to come back with friends."

Returning to their camp, the two knights packed as quickly as they could and released the Lucian horses. The riders and their prize galloped toward Camelot, aiming to beat Arturus' declared deadline three days hence. Guinevere forgot her saddle sores, her hunger, and the rain. But guilt colored her anticipation of the reception back home. As she watched the unicorn through the trees surrounding the Lucian camp, it appeared confused, apprehensive, even depressed. It had enjoyed freedom for years before its capture by a few boys, and now Guinevere held it in bondage. What made her different from the Lucians?

* * *

Thousands greeted Guinevere and Caris at Camelot's north gate. As long as she held the unicorn's lead and kept it close, the creature remained calm, as if it saw only Guinevere, and didn't see the waving banners and screaming children. She resented the unicorn's tranquility as she walked it into a special enclosure in Government Square. She wanted it to fight, to bray, to bellow in protest, yanking at its halter hard enough to break her arm. She wanted to dominate it, win, and feel triumphant, even victorious, with her ego stroked by praise from the poorest tramp to the richest nobleman. Instead, she felt as if she had condemned a child to prison and a life sentence. She was committing a sin, not earning glory.

After nearly a month in the wilderness, she longed for a rest. The Court had other plans. A dame knight in charge of protocol whisked her to a palace apartment and told her to dress in a formal gown of green satin brocade. King Arturus II would fête Guinevere that night at a gathering of the Round Table. She had no choice but to acquiesce. At least she got a shower and a snack.

The dinner and ceremony resembled a coronation in its opulence and cheerfulness. The previous two quests for the Siege Perilous had failed, and the seat had remained empty all that time. The capital starved for a party. At the climax of the celebration, Arturus invited everyone to toast Guinevere in celebration of her accomplishment. Then he asked her to tell the story of the quest.

Caught unawares, Guinevere had no idea what to say. The adrenaline of the unicorn's capture had worn off, leaving her spent. As she tried to think of a way to beg off, Caris stood at his place next to hers on the dais.

"Your Majesty, I realize I may be breaking protocol, but I beg leave from Dame Guinevere and yourself to speak."

Caris' request put another, unwelcome layer of intrigue on the quest. Would Caris criticize her again for her lack of experience or qualifications, as he had done during the Red Ball ritual? Would he chastise her impractical concern for rabbits, her murder of a Lucian soldier, her imprisonment of an innocent mutant creature? Guinevere braced herself for ridicule.

Caris told the story from the beginning, delivering a report as factual as it was bewitching. He left nothing out, not even the death of Hubertus. Guinevere listened carefully, tears rising in gratitude, because Caris avoided the chance to demonstrate her unworthiness or incompetence.

"My lords and ladies," Caris said, "when His Majesty appointed me to accompany Dame Guinevere, I was angry. How could he humiliate me by making me a nursemaid? However, I'm here to tell you that Dame Guinevere is worthy of the Siege Perilous and your respect. She is very young, but she will do great things for our country and our people."

After the applause died down, Guinevere blurted out a few words of thanks, even though Caris had stolen a bit of her thunder. She was too tired to complain, and she was distracted by the king, who appeared disappointed. What was wrong now? Before she could ask if it had anything to do with her, he bowed and left the table to mingle with other guests.

Guinevere had achieved her goal. She'd won glory and a place as a woman of power. Nonetheless, she couldn't shake a feeling of incipient loss, that she'd missed a crucial detail, that something was unfinished. Sick with fatigue, she said good night to Caris and the guests. Instead of returning to her palace rooms, she headed for the unicorn's enclosure.

No one guarded the unicorn, and in the small hours, no one but Guinevere visited the beast. The creature lay down on its belly, legs bent under its body, head bent as if depressed. Guinevere called out. The animal perked up and rose, trotting over to its captor. Stifling a sob, Guinevere stroked the creature's forehead as it snuffled a greeting. What had she done? Was it right that a beautiful living thing, man-made or Gaia-made, rot in captivity to satisfy a human ego? Was her lust for approval a justification for ruthlessness? The victory was hollow.

On impulse, remembering the rabbit in the snare, choking to death, Guinevere lifted the catch of the unlocked gate and beckoned the unicorn to follow. The act thrilled her, as if she was disobeying an edict from her father, but it felt right. Wary that she might be spotted, she led the unicorn through the empty streets of Camelot to the north gate and past the somnolent guards.

The unicorn took its cue and galloped off into the night. Freedom overcame the maiden's spell.

Guinevere's heart soared. Tears of relief flowed like rain.

"Congratulations, Dame Guinevere. You've achieved the heart of the quest." The voice belonged to Arturus, who stepped out of the shadows.

"Your Majesty!" Guinevere wiped her eyes and smoothed down her gown. "I'm so sorry, but I … I mean, you saw?"

"I did, my friend."

"But it belongs to you, and I've released it."

"That was the point."

Guinevere shook her head in confusion.

"I told you to capture it and bring it to Camelot. I had no intention of keeping it."

"My lord?"

"Did Caris tell you the story of his quest for the unicorn? How he had captured it, brought it here, and that it had escaped? I was the one who released it, when he did not. That was why he failed the quest."

Guinevere though it over. "Are you saying the capture and return of the unicorn was not the quest you gave me?"

"That was the assignment, but not the quest. The Siege Perilous is about testing yourself, to see what you might learn, and to see if your core goodness remains. The true danger is losing yourself in a quest for something as diaphanous as glory or fame."

"Caris said I had to learn ruthlessness to survive."

"There's truth in that, especially for kings. Before his quest, Caris was a rising star at the Round Table. But Caris lost something during his quest. I'm not sure what it was, but afterward, he faded from view. I missed him."

"Why did you ask him to go along with me?"

"You had no experience. He did. Maybe I wanted to give him a second chance."

"He failed again, but I didn't. I still don't understand, Majesty."

"I knew you had a core of compassion. I wanted to see if it would survive the strain of a quest. It did. You've learned how to suspend your pity when necessary. That's a skill all leaders must learn. But in your heart of hearts, ruthlessness pains you. That means you're still human, still empathetic. It makes me happy to see it. You know, I've been watching you, just as I watch everyone who might be a rival."

"Majesty! I would never—"

"I'm old. I know what's coming. That's the curse of age. We know the future, because we've seen the past. You are going to be Queen of Viridiae someday, just as I am king today."

"I would never presume—"

"And you will need to suspend your pity in a time of crisis. Releasing the unicorn tonight may well be your last act of compassion."

Arturus' explanation put Guinevere's quest in perspective. She'd remember the lesson. What's more, his prediction rekindled her ambition. She wanted to be the chosen leader of Viridiae, and she would have to climb to the throne on the backs of friends and foes alike. That was the nature of achieving power. When the time came, she would reign in her competing urge to empathize, though she vowed to keep a place for it in her heart. More unicorns, beasts of light and magic, might come her way.

Guinvere finished her story as Dee put the last touches on a braid in Guinevere's hair. After a moment, Dee said, "Did you ever see the unicorn again?"

"No, I didn't, but I heard that it had returned north, perhaps to be with other creatures of the Freezing Sea. I'm happy for it. I hope it stays free."

CHAPTER 13: THE PORTRAIT OF QUEEN JARNAY

As Dee changed into her own newly acquired Ontarii business wear, she thought about Guinevere's courage and independence in agreeing to go on the quest for the Unicorn of the North when she was only nineteen, six years younger than Dee was now. She felt a new bond with the queen, though it was not something to brag about. Both had blood on her hands: Dee to defend her brother from trolls, Guinevere to protect her future. Both women might be called to kill again, though Dee hoped she was wrong. She'd rather create than destroy.

On a whim, Dee packed her light tapestry equipment. She'd gone to scheduled meetings before with powerful people, only to be told the meeting was delayed or canceled altogether. She could work on the portrait during the down time.

The official car from the presidential palace delivered the Viridians a quarter hour before the scheduled meeting. The trio waited in a vestibule. Guinevere was as nervous as Dee had ever seen her, though she did her best to hide it. The survival of Viridiae was riding on her success.

At three-quarters past the hour, Nock entered the vestibule from a hidden door. He greeted the Viridians warmly, but Dee sensed trouble.

"The President will see you now, my lady, but I'd ask you to be patient. Don't get your hopes up."

"Has she already decided against helping us?"

"Diplomacy is founded on the arts of patience and persistence. I think you may consider a 'No' a 'Maybe,' but don't push too hard."

Guinevere's face took on a new measure of anxiety, but she was determined. Lancelot, dressed in a borrowed formal knight's uniform, had little to add, apart from military matters.

A double-door opened, and an usher invited the Viridians into a large office with a sitting area. At one end of the office, Jarnay sat at a polished desk with a pair of aides, one of them Tintan.

Jarnay stood and reached out to Guinevere. Nock took care of introductions.

"I apologize for the delay in meeting with you, madame," Jarnay said. "I'm sure you understand the delicacy of your situation."

Dee found Jarnay far more striking in person than her images suggested. Her height, three centimeters taller than Guinevere, gave her a presence that reminded everyone in the room who was in charge. Her fit figure balanced the worry lines around her eyes, which settled on Guinevere in an inquisitive, but not condescending gaze. Jarnay took charge of every encounter with friend or foe.

Standing with her shoulders back, Guinevere presented herself as the representative of a powerful nation, even if it was back on its heels. Like the athlete who forgets nervousness before a major competition, she'd lost all hint of anxiety. "I understand Ontari:io's relationship with the Lucians completely. Like you, Viridiae shares a long border with the empire. In our case, Empress Vetrania decided to violate that border."

"I am genuinely sorry to hear about the troubles your country is facing, madame." Jarnay invited Guinevere to take a place next to her on a settee. "Have you met Vetrania?"

"I've not had the pleasure."

"It is not a pleasure, I can assure you," Jarnay said. "She is an implacable ruler. She gets what she wants by any means necessary."

"That should not include unprovoked invasions."

When would Guinevere get to the point? Dee fidgeted. Half of the Viridians' allotted time with Jarnay had passed.

Jarnay glanced at Tintan and the other aide, introduced as Jarnay's defense minister. Apparently, Tintan was more than an officer at a remote border post. "Vetrania tests our borders on a daily basis. It's all my military can cope with, though an invasion appears unlikely."

"Let me come to the point, madame president." Guinevere looked Jarnay in the eye. "We're asking for Ontari:io's help to regain our country. Lucanus is stretched thin, despite its prowess on the field. If Ontari:io were to, well, distract it, it might react by countering your move, giving us a chance to regain our territory and put Vetrania in her place."

Jarnay rose to study the garden outside her window. "What does Ontari:io have to gain by this unprovoked encroachment on Lucanus?"

In its weakened state, Viridiae had little to offer Jarnay except friendship.

"We believe Lucanus does not expect a two-front war. Vetrania will rethink her strategy. If Ontari:io inflicts enough damage, she may sue for peace immediately to prevent a catastrophe."

"Your analysis assumes this is an ordinary expansionist adventure by Lucanus. There's more at stake, madame."

"Our analysis assumes nothing, madame president. Vetrania has the Grail that belongs to my country's Great Machine. The Great Machine on Lucian territory is failing." Guinevere's voice rose. "Our greatest mind, perhaps the greatest mind on the planet, knows more about the Great Machines and the Grail than any other person. We might have even helped Vetrania, if she had asked. All of us have a mutual interest in maintaining the earth's climate. Instead, she stole our Grail and kidnapped my husband Arturus to exchange for Merlin. I can't be sure she might renege on the exchange and even kill my husband, once she has Merlin. I'm asking that you help us restore the balance, and I promise you that Viridiae will be a friend to Ontari:io forever, and that Merlin will work to repair both Great Machines so that humanity will survive the crisis."

Dee wanted to cheer Guinevere's performance, but Jarnay appeared unmoved.

"Vetrania rarely backs down from a challenge," Jarnay said. "She may decide the risk of retreat is greater than the risk of attack. You may be correct that her military is stretched to the limit, but I wouldn't be surprised if she counter-attacked with everything she has. If Ontari:io was unable to resist, both our countries might be lost."

Dee swallowed hard. The Viridian mission was on the verge of failure.

Jarnay turned to Lancelot. "What do you think, Dame Lancelot? Can the Lucians win a two-front war?"

Lancelot glanced at Guinevere, who nodded slightly, giving her permission to speak. "The Lucians have one of the best armies in the world. Their navy is also powerful. But their invasion of Viridiae was unprovoked and criminal. We have right on our side."

Jarnay looked at the dame knight as if she were disappointed in the answer. Dee thought perhaps she was seeking a justification for helping Viridiae to counter the objections of her advisers, and neither Guinevere nor Lancelot had provided one.

"What about you, Ms Rathkeale?"

"Madame president, forgive me, but I have no expertise in military matters."

Jarnay eyed Dee, as if recognizing her. "I understand you are a great artist, Ms Rathkeale."

Dee face flushed. "I worked on some sketches for Mr Nock and a portrait of Captain Tintan to pass the time on the train."

"They showed me the results. My compliments."

Dee glanced at Guinevere, who grinned in encouragement. "If you don't mind, madame president, I've been working on a portrait of yourself."

Jarnay was intrigued. Everyone likes to know how other

people view them. A portrait was a rare opportunity. "I'd like to see it."

Quickly, Dee set up her light tapestry projectors and hooked up her tablet. Her heart beat faster. She'd never shown a piece to a foreign chief of state. In a moment, Jarnay's face floated in front of a wall, flanked by ordinary two-dimensional scenes of Ontari:io life already on the wall.

Jarnay's mouth opened slightly, as if shocked. A surge of panic ran up Dee's esophagus. Had she offended the president somehow? Had she just destroyed Guinevere's chances of gaining a critical ally in the war against Lucanus?

"Extraordinary. Nock, do you see this?"

"Yes, madame president. It's as I explained, is it not?"

"Where did you learn to create pieces like this, Ms Rathkeale?" Jarnay could not pull her eyes off the play of color and the subtle animations. "I feel like I'm looking into a magical mirror."

"Thank you, madame president. I studied at Camelot University. My teacher and mentor, Ganieda, also helped me." Dee cleared her throat. She needed to keep her emotions under control. "Part of the arts school was burned by the Lucians. And I've heard nothing from my mentor since leaving Viridiae."

Jarnay turned to Guinevere. "I neglected to visit last year's cultural exhibition, madame. That was clearly a mistake, if your country produces talent such as this. I must apologize."

"No apology necessary, madame president. But, if I may, what you see here may be all that's left of Viridian culture, if Vetrania is not stopped. If she conquers all of Viridiae, the three of us may be forced to live in exile. What's to stop the same thing happening to Ontari:io and its cultural talent?"

An usher tapped on the door and announced the next appointment. For a second, he was distracted by Jarnay's portrait.

"Give us a moment. I'm not quite finished with our distinguished Viridian guests." Jarnay turned to Guinevere, Lancelot, and Dee. "I do not have the power to simply order my people to help Viridiae. But that does not mean I have no sympathy for your cause. I'm no fan of Vetrania or her adventures. She is a threat to both of us, and it would be tragic to lose a talent such as Ms Rathkeale's to barbarity. I'll see what I can do."

Dee breathed a sigh of relief. It wasn't an outright 'No.'

"And Ms Rathkeale, I would be pleased if you would complete your portrait. I think I might find a place for it here at the presidential palace."

Dee's heart swelled with pride. Jarnay had breathed new life into Viridiae's cause.

CHAPTER 14: RITUAL SACRIFICE

Victor's Avenue cut through the heart of Lucana, with one end at the soaring sandstone Victory Gate and the other end at the Regia, the complex that included the imperial palace. Flanked by his senior officers and trailed by his general staff on the broad, tree-lined boulevard, Robert Dardarius rode in his open-air limousine at a walking pace past bleachers crammed with ordinary citizens screaming his name and waving Lucian flags. At a predetermined spot, the motorcade stopped, and he stepped out to greet the crowd. A girl child in a blue and white pinafore dress ran out and handed him a bouquet of blue irises, playing perfectly the part of spontaneous, patriotic acclamation. A half-dozen state media cameras, on drones and on shoulders, broadcast the moment to tens of millions.

The horses of royal guards clopped around him at a slow trot. He waved every few moments, almost automatically, because he couldn't stop contrasting the joy in the faces of his fellow citizens with the memories of the journey from Viridiae to the capital's outer precincts. In a black moment, one of his officers had calculated that if you had laid the graves of the prisoners who had died end-to-end, each corpse's foot would touch the next one's head from Lucana to Camelot. They laughed over the math in the officers' mess, but the images of a putrefying trail of death haunted Robert's dreams.

Within the hour, the entire nation would witness one more death.

The two-kilometer journey ended at the main grandstand.

Robert saluted the Lucian flag and passed a temporary platform about the height of a standing man. Two banks of steps, one in front and one behind, let to the platform's deck. On the deck, a little to the side, a black cloth covered objects on a table. In the middle of the platform was a pole about a half-meter thick and two meters tall. The carpenter had set a horizontal slab of wood into a notch on one side of the pole, making the assembly look like an uncomfortable chair with no arms.

Ignoring the device, Robert climbed a third set of stairs toward the imperial box, which was festooned with banners and canopied against the burning sun, which was rapidly heating the paved public square. Robert greeted applauding senators, ministers, and other grandees. When he reached the box, he saluted the empress, fist over his heart. A trickle of sweat made its way beneath his formal tunic to the small of his back.

Vetrania Katrina Cardea, Commander-in-Chief of the Army, First Admiral of the Navy, President of the Senate, Governor of Lucana, Supreme Priestess to the Gods, Empress of Lucanus, acknowledged Robert's salute with a nod. She turned up the corners of her full mouth, which added a razor-sharp edge to her stern eyes and pointed nose, the mirror image of her father's, who styled himself "Lance-Thrower." Robert imagined how many enemies she had impaled by that look.

"Welcome home, General Dardarius. Congratulations on your victory." Vetrania's voice had the moist thickness of Lucana's summer humidity.

A camera drone hovered a meter away.

"I'm grateful for your welcome," Robert said with slight bow of his head. Rumors persisted that Vetrania took power by killing her father with a stiletto. Robert knew better than to believe rumors, but he guessed the truth was far more frightening.

"Your victory is a gift to the state. Do you bring an offering of thanks to the gods?"

"I do, madam. I ask permission to present it."

Vetrania assented, as the ritual demanded of the Supreme Priestess. Robert took his seat on Vetrania's right. Her consort,

Marron, a man who spent half of his life drunk and the other half in brothels, lounged on her left. Vetrania openly despised Marron, whom she had married for his family's connections and money. Robert pitied Marron for having to tolerate a marriage with a woman as cruel as Vetrania. The thought brought forth a memory of his own wife, Cecily, who had died giving birth to his son. She would've taken the seat just behind Robert, and he would've kissed her in greeting. As it was, an old courtier occupied the chair.

The crowd settled down from its cheers, anticipating the next act in the triumphal parade. Over loudspeakers and through the ear buds of those tied into the net, a drummer pounded a slow beat on timpani. All faces turned toward the Victory Gate in the distance, visible as a black dot through the shimmering heat. Robert thought of the battle on the River Colum, of how his phalanxes of legionaries marched into the mix of disciplined knights and rabble of Viridian volunteers. On a monitor mounted on one of the imperial box's posts, he watched the same phalanxes march through the gate, helmets, armor, belts, and sword hilts polished to perfection. A rolling cheer reached him at the box, and his pride swelled. An ancient poet had written about "we happy few" on the eve of a battle, and Robert understood the reference to brotherhood.

The first Lucian units arrived, led by their officers on horseback. They entered Regia Square and took places, rank upon rank, to the left and right of the main grandstand. The crowd noise subsided to a murmur as the steady timpani took a mournful turn. The spectators' hushed conversation gave way to jeers. The prisoners had appeared.

Arturus, accompanied by his aide Percival, rode in a single-axle wooden cart drawn by an ancient swayback horse. No one worried about an attempt at escape; the populace would've torn them apart. Instead, the crowd hurled insults, booing and laughing at the monarch. Robert had brought down his enemy from kingship to poverty, and the crowd ridiculed Arturus for his weakness. However, the victorious general found he could not inflict the same humiliations on the Viridian king as he had other barbarian chieftains. This time, he allowed Arturus and Percival to bathe and don clean clothes for the ceremony and ride unfettered. Arturus held himself as regally as he could in the rickety cart. Percival's hatred of the crowd was palpable, even in his stony visage.

Behind Arturus walked the surviving prisoners, three thousand in all, hobbled by shackles, bound neck-to-neck with meter-long wooden staffs. Even at the height of the grandstand from the pavement, Robert heard the clink of chains and grunts of men and women at the limits of endurance. A full twenty minutes passed before all the prisoners shuffled by the imperial box. Another ten minutes passed as trucks piled high with booty from Camelot trundled by, everything from furniture to paintings to lawn ornaments to an orange cat in a cage.

Once again, the crowd quieted, but their shoes scuffed the paving stones, as if caught between a decision to leave or watch the approaching climax of the triumph. Escorts shunted the Viridian prisoners to a corner of the square, packing them tightly for easier control. All had full view of the platform and its strange chair. Arturus and Percival climbed down from the cart and sat on a bench in front of the platform.

As if heralding the third act of the triumphal ceremony, the crowd's voice changed again. A donkey pulled another cart with a wooden cage. A single, naked, terrified Viridian prisoner, chosen at random, cowered inside, unable to stand or even kneel. The populace of Lucana shouted at him, demanding his life for relatives and friends lost on the campaign. Hawkers sold rotten fruit, small stones, and paper bags of feces to the crowd, which threw the trash and sewage at the victim. Some tried to approach the cart to punch him or stab him with knives, but legionaries held them back with their pila.

By the time the prisoner reached the platform, he leaned against the cage's slat, knocked insensible by a rock to his temple. Two legionaries opened the cage and dragged him out. They mounted the steps, their straining arms lifting him along. The soldiers placed him on the grotesque seat, tying his arms behind the pole. His head lolled, and the legionaries dropped a leather strap over his forehead, tying lengths of hide together at the back of the pole to keep the prisoner's head in place. The victim opened his eyes and screamed before the legionaries gagged him.

Hovering cameras captured every moment. Robert kept his eyes on Arturus. One moment the king watched the prisoner, helplessness tearing at him. The next moment, his face slackened, as if he understood that could do nothing to stop the ceremony's climax. Despite the accolades of the people and the empress, the pain in Arturus eyes stole some of Robert's pride. All the victorious general could think of was escaping the spectacle for a goblet of Napene wine at home.

A glance from the empress brought Robert back to the moment. She stood, the sash of office limp over her business-like outfit. All the guests in the grandstand rose with her. Guards prodded Arturus and Percival to their feet. A huge broad-shouldered man, robed entirely in black except for his thick arms, mounted the steps behind the groaning prisoner. The robed man wore a full-head metal mask with holes for eyes and mouth and a long crow's beak for a nose. The man represented Corvus, the Lucanan god of trickery and death.

The crowd, which had moved toward the platform and large monitors placed along Victor's Avenue, silenced itself, though the air sparked with tension. The prisoner's eyes darted about as his breathing grew heavy. He knew something was about to happen to him, but he had no idea what. The robed man turned toward the imperial box. He looked at Vetrania, but Robert thought the man searched his face for a command as well. Vetrania did nothing for long seconds. Would she surprise everyone with the unexpected? Not this time. She stretched out her hand, her long fingers and thumb splayed, the only decoration a ring on her second finger with the double-eagle seal of her office. A moment passed, and she clenched her fist.

The robed man lifted the cloth from the table. He raised a

loop of hemp rope, dropped it over the top of the pole and the prisoner's head, and drew it tight around the throat. The groaning stopped, but the gag popped out of the prisoner's mouth. His eyes bulged as the executioner twisted the rope tighter and tighter using a thick piece of wood. Though Robert was too distant from the prisoner to hear it, he imagined the sound of straining hemp. The prisoner's face purpled as his body convulsed. Eventually, he stopped moving, save for a twitch in one leg.

The executioner held the garrote tight a full three minutes, his sweating arms bulging with the strain. When he relaxed, the crowd went into a paroxysm of dancing, hugging, and back-slapping. They had celebrated their victory and their revenge with a blood sacrifice. They were sated, until the next time. Robert blinked, sending his own prayer to Corvus, asking that he never witness such a spectacle again.

CHAPTER 15: A SURPRISE FROM VIRIDIAE

Robert Dardarius showered and relaxed with a massage in the bedroom suite of his suburban Lucana home. As his trainer broke down the knots in his shoulders and back, he let his eye fall on the image of his wife, Cecily, and his son, Damien. He could never look at either without feeling a lump in his throat, but he kept photos of them always in view, as a reminder of his love for them.

Damien died first, of leukemia. Robert recalled the last time he saw his son alive, in a hospital room, tubes running into his neck and hand, dripping Gaia-knew-what poison into his six-year-old body. The doctors said he was getting stronger. They promised Damien would run into his arms when he returned from the emergency deployment to Lucanus' northeastern frontier with Ontari:io. Cecily urged him to go; all would be well. Ten days later, Damien was dead, his mother at his side, and Robert raced home to bury him. The couple locked themselves in this room, and they cried together for three days. Guilt over abandoning Damien when the boy needed his father most never left Robert.

Cecily died a year later at Vetrania's hands after renegade Dardarians tried to assassinate the empress. Robert squeezed his eyes shut, pretending to the masseuse that he had found particularly tough knot. In reality, Robert was forcing away the memories and the rage. He needed to keep his wits about him, or he might suffer Cecily's fate. Nine years had passed since Cecily's death. The pain had dulled, though the seductive laughter of his wife haunted Robert in his dreams. The opportunity for justice would come in good time.

The masseuse paid and dismissed, Robert donned loose casual wear appropriate for welcoming guests. He'd invited Adrian and his wife Marcella to his home for a glass of Napene wine. A servant announced Adrian as Robert lounged at his natatorium. The two men embraced.

"Where is your lovely wife?" Robert said.

"Working late at the palace, as usual, sir. Vetrania wouldn't let her go early, even though we haven't seen each other for months."

Robert frowned. Vetrania would find any way to get in a dig against him, even if it was through his nephew's wife.

A servant set down a cheese dish and water glasses, the condensation dripping down the sides in the air-conditioned room.

"How did you leave our prizes, Adrian?"

"All the prisoners are settled in. We lost two more today to malnutrition, but the death rate is nearing zero."

"And what about the financial arrangements?"

"Your share of the proceeds from the sale of these prisoners' contracts is going into the veterans retirement fund."

Robert didn't need the money. That's why he gave it charity. But Adrian needed his share, if he was to buy a house with Marcella and start a family.

"And what of our special prisoners?"

"They are in separate quarters in the Regis fortress, as you instructed, sir. Arturus was quite upset. He asked me to request quarters nearer his ranks."

"Admirable, but impossible. I can't risk his person. We need a healthy bargaining chip."

"I'll relay the message. You probably heard, sir, that Vetrania wants to see him tomorrow."

"Yes, that's on the agenda of my debrief with her. Find a way to give Arturus and Percival a little dignity. I really prefer they be treated as guests rather than chattel."

"Of course, sir."

The servant announced Marcella's arrival. She walked in, petite but full of drive. Pundits claimed she had enough energy to power a small city. Robert leaned down to accept her friendly kiss. "You are more radiant than the last time I saw you."

"Adrian hasn't told you?"

Robert straightened. "Are you keeping secrets from me, nephew?"

Before Adrian could find his words, Marcella said, "He's a modest man, uncle. We're pregnant."

Robert laughed. "Congratulations to both of you. But how —" Robert found himself flushing. "Adrian's been with me for months. He didn't take any leave."

"We've kept it to ourselves. Vetrania is jealous of anything that takes the spotlight away from her. But I'm starting to show, so we can't keep it a secret any longer."

Marcella had the instincts of her father, Verus, head of the Verusian clan, and Robert's political ally.

"How is your father taking the news?"

"He's over the moon. You'll see him tomorrow at the debriefing."

The thought warmed Robert's heart. He sensed that a crisis was coming, more than the problems with the Great Machine. He'd need Verus' help.

"We've all missed you, uncle," Marcella took a chair next to the pool. "Lucana feels, well, less stable, when you are away."

Robert put his finger to his lips to silence Marcella. The general swiped on a tablet and touched an icon. "I had the estate technician install some extra protection before I left. I want to make sure we have no eavesdroppers. "

"You don't trust Vetrania?"

Without commenting on his purpose, Robert touched another icon. It started a separate app that recorded every word poolside, including Adrian's and Marcella's. Robert regretted the violation of his family's trust, but he'd learned long ago to hedge his bets.

"I trust you to tell me more in person than what I read in your emails, Marcella."

"I always assume they are intercepted by Vetrania's spies."

The servant poured three glasses of Napene wine.

"How is our 'Mother of the Land'?" Robert sipped the smooth vintage.

"As vicious and grasping as ever." Marcella grunted in disgust. "It's a wonder any of us don't have a knife in our backs at her whim."

"Sounds like things have hardly changed since my departure."

"They've gotten worse." Marcella accepted a deep red glass of wine. "She's threatening to fire the entire science advisory committee if they can't come up with a fix to the Grail device within 10 days. She's already forced the head of the Science Institute into retirement."

"Things could be worse for him."

Marcella laughed. "He died last week in a gardening accident."

"A what?"

"The news chans said he tripped on a stone and fell onto his clipping shears." Marcella pointed to her chest. "Right into his heart."

"Tragic." Robert couldn't help his sarcasm. Ministers and minions out of favor with Vetrania often suffered unexpected illnesses or freak accidents.

"When you see her tomorrow," Marcella said, "make sure there aren't any pointy tools in the room."

Robert sighed. He could play the court intrigue game as well as anyone, but it was tiresome and wasteful. Campaigning was difficult and dangerous, but at least you got away from the jungle of the palace.

"Tell me more, Marcella. You are the best-connected woman in Lucana."

"Vetrania is beside herself with anxiety." Marcella tapped her painted fingernail on the chair's arm.

Adrian cleared his throat. "Sir, they're only rumors, but..."

"Don't worry, Adrian. I trust you. And Marcella."

Adrian breathed in, and glanced at his wife. "You might be next, sir."

Robert forced a grin. "In what respect?"

"She's very unhappy with the results of the Viridian campaign." Even as the youngest staff member for the National Security Committee, Marcella was in almost daily contact with the empress. Marcella knew her mind as well as anyone.

Robert said, "I don't see why. I brought her a king."

"But you didn't bring her Merlin," Adrian said. "That's what she wanted."

"I already know that. It will take a little longer, that's all."

"That's not how she sees it," Marcella said. "She thinks you're playing games. She thinks you're trying to undermine her."

From the beginning of the trek east from Camelot, Robert understood his precarious position. He'd failed at his mission, to bring the foremost scholar and scientist in Viridiae to Lucana to fix Lucanus' Great Machine. A successful repair would solidify Vetrania's authority. Robert threatened that success.

"I don't know what she's so afraid of," Robert said.

"What's happening in the palace isn't as important as what's happening out in the country," Adrian said. "Harvest yields are down, livestock are losing weight, and doctors are seeing the first signs of widespread disease among Lucanus' poorer people. The sage-scientists believe a good portion has to do with the unstable climate."

"I will get Merlin, eventually. The Viridians will do anything to retrieve Arturus, even if it means trading their most important scholar."

"If you don't get him soon, you might wind up with a pair of garden shears in your belly," Marcella said.

Marcella was right. A misstep, and Robert could suffer the scientist's fate.

"Well then," Robert said, "I'll make sure I'm wearing extra strong armor."

* * *

After the horrifying execution at the end of the triumph, Percival had brooded in a corner of the cell he shared with Arturus for hours. He couldn't shake the memory of the man's silent scream, and the cheer of the populace as his eyes nearly popped out of his head.

Equally dazed by the experience, Arturus felt the need to process its monstrousness, despite Percival's wish to forget it. "The Lucians," Arturus explained, "believe they must gift a prisoner to their death god, Corvus, as compensation for their victories. Ordinarily, the prisoner is the highest ranking person in the group. In some other war, that person would've been me. But I'm more valuable alive than dead."

"Why didn't they take the second-highest ranking person?" Percival said.

"I don't know. None of my generals survived the battle. Or they escaped. You're the only knight among the prisoners, and Dardarius promised you to me. Ironic that the king of Viridiae survived to be captured, don't you think?" Arturus shook his head. "Maybe picking a victim at random is the Lucians' idea of fairness."

"They're nothing but bloodthirsty savages dressed in tailored suits." Percival spat on the concrete floor of their cell.

Arturus stared at the narrow window where the wall met the ceiling. Percival had wasted energy trying to reach it in a vain hope of another escape attempt. When a guard spotted him, he called for backup, entered the cell, and landed a fist on Percival's temple. Percival fell unconscious for a moment or two. When he awoke, Arturus was arguing with the guard, who dared strike Dardarius' special prisoner. Percival could barely understand the conversation, but a few minutes later, a new guard brought bread and water. Percival managed to swallow some of both.

Percival awoke the next morning to a blinding headache and more shouts from guards. Arturus nudged him on his palatte, urging him to get up and dress. Arturus held clean tunics, underwear, and sandals. A large bowl of water and two towels sat on a small table. After so much slow death, poor meals, and humiliation, Percival imagined himself in a luxury hotel. He splashed the water on his face and dressed, leaving the old clothes, teeming with vermin, for the guards to destroy.

Cleaner than he'd been since the battle on the River Colum, Percival blinked when the guards led him and his king into a small courtyard surrounded by similar cells. Percival couldn't see into the dark interiors, and no sounds came from them. It was impossible to tell if they were occupied or not. The guards paused to place him and Arturus in shackles, and as they worked, Percival heard murmurings from beyond the 10-meter, crenelated wall. The indistinct voices had a familiar quality.

"Your Majesty, do you hear them?"

"Shut your fucking mouth," a guard ordered.

Arturus listened. "They're our comrades."

The guard tightened a binding on Arturus' wrist. He winced, then recovered. "What's going to happen to the other prisoners, guard?"

"None of your business, Your Majesty." The guard stretched out the last words in a mocking tone.

"You can at least tell us if they're alright," Percival said.

"Another word out of you and I'll send you to the hospital."

"We're both soldiers," Arturus said. "One soldier to another, what's going to happen to them."

Arturus' plea appeared to reach the sweaty guard. "They're government chattels now. They'll be rented out to farmers and rich households as labor. My brother is a contractor. He has two chattel laborers." The guard grinned.

Arturus nodded. "I thought as much."

"Quiet, now, the both of you. You'll have plenty of opportunity for chatting about chattel—" The guard laughed at his joke "—when you meet the VIP."

"Who is?"

Without answering, the guard pushed his charges into the

back of an electric cart with smoked windows. Percival could see out, but no one on the street could see in. He had no idea where they were going, but the trip took him and Arturus through a cityscape not that much different than Camelot's. Steel and glass towers loomed over them and streets teemed with pedestrians. Shoppers ducked in and out of stores. Children played in a park. Unlike Camelot, which was built on hilly ground, with the citadel overlooking the rest of the city, Lucana spread out from the Regia on a nearly flat plain, giving it the impression of stretching out forever.

The trip lasted only a few minutes. The cart arrived in the same courtyard as the previous day's triumph, but by a different, modest entrance. Whomever invited Arturus wanted to keep it a secret, or at least keep others from noticing. Ordering the Viridian pair out, the guard removed the leg shackles, but not the wrist bindings. He handed them off to another guard with a far grander uniform. Percival recognized him as a Saepian, one of the Lucian imperial guard. He beckoned Percival and Arturus to follow. Two other Saepians of lower rank followed the Viridians.

"Whatever happens, Percival," Arturus whispered, "stay calm. Don't let your emotions cloud your judgment."

They came to a small foyer with a cast bronze double-door at one end. The reliefs depicted legionnaires slaughtering people Percival didn't recognize. An odd fragrance wormed its way into Percival's awareness, a mixture of blood and decaying wood. Percival tried to speak to Arturus, but he was hushed by the Saepian officer. Arturus offered a wink, and Percival got the impression he knew exactly what was about to happen. A tiny yellow light blinked near the bronze door.

"You will follow my lead." The Saepian officer warned Percival and Arturus with a stare. "If you so much as move a centimeter from my side, my soldiers will kill you instantly."

Percival turned to look at the two lesser ranking Saepians, who gripped the hilts of their short swords without drawing them.

The light blinked green, and the double-door opened with a

ponderous creak.

"His Royal Highness, Arturus, King of Viridiae." The bellowing voice belonged to a bulky man in a ceremonial robe. "Sir Percival Rathkeale."

The officer stepped into the cavernous hall. Percival and Arturus stayed close, mimicking the officer's pace. The flat soles of their prison sandals beat a light tattoo on the marble floor. A group of men and women gathered around a desk, obscuring its occupant. As the prisoners approached, the group turned its attention to the new arrivals. Percival recognized Dardarius and Cantwell. Both were in crisp uniforms, dark with the red ochre favored by the Lucian military. Percival didn't know any of the other Lucians, such as an attractive, petite woman who stood near Cantwell. Never far from his mind, hatred of his captors threatened to overwhelm Arturus' command to stay calm and mask his feelings.

As the subordinates stood aside, Percival recognized the woman at the desk. He had never seen her in person, but her angular features and sharp eyes were as familiar as his dearest friends'. Like all young Viridians, he'd grown up knowing Empress Vetrania as his country's vilest enemy. Percival perceived nothing in her face but contempt, hidden behind practiced cordiality. Percival instantly distrusted her. Every movement suggested an ulterior motive, every inflection of her voice a lie, or at least a calculation with intent to dissemble. She could have occupied her place in Lucian society only through deceit and fraud, the opposite of his king, Arturus.

"At last we meet, Your Majesty." Vetrania's voice was as smooth as polished obsidian. "I have read so much about you and your interesting family."

"And I, yours." Arturus said evenly. He stood straight, shoulders back.

Vetrania stepped out from behind her desk. She sized up Arturus as if judging a race horse. "I would shake your hand in polite greeting, but my security staff deems you a psychopathic killer." She grinned, as if passing a secret message. "You might have a poison embedded in your hands."

Arturus glanced at this bindings. "It's more likely I'd be carrying a disease caught by my comrades on the road to Lucana."

"Really? What sort of exotic pathogen?"

Arturus shrugged. "Dysentery, cholera, any of a number of illnesses abused prisoners suffer. Not to mention malnutrition."

"Abused?" Vetrania raised an eyebrow. Ignoring Percival, she stepped around Arturus, who faced forward, while keeping his eyes on her as long as he could. "I understand our tribune, Adrian Cantwell, has done an outstanding job of keeping our Viridian chattels alive for their new lives in Lucanus. Attrition is to be expected. I'm disappointed in you, Arturus. You should be grateful to him."

Percival glanced at Cantwell. Back in the prisoners' camp by the River Colum, he had said much the same thing.

"I suppose I shouldn't be surprised at your attitude." Vetrania folded her arms. "Frankly, I don't understand what Dardarius sees in you."

A puzzled look crossed Arturus' face.

"He admires you. Did you know that? He told us a story of how you denied opportunities for better treatment when you saw your soldiers suffering."

Dardarius' cheeks flushed.

"The story of your grandfather's sword is entertaining, if fanciful. Dardarius suggested we publish it, maybe in a volume of myths from cultures Lucana has rescued from barbarity."

Dardarius looked away as Arturus reddened.

"I suggest it go into a children's book." Vetrania waved her hand. "You know, the kind with simple illustrations and one-syllable words."

Arturus fought to keep his temper in check. "Did you call me here to humiliate me, Empress?"

"No. Well, yes, a little bit. I need to show my people that you are far smaller than some of my aides think you are." She stole a look at Dardarius. "There are people within my circle who get a little too big for their britches, as I think the Viridian saying goes. It's apt, because Lucanus is teeming with people who don't know their place. A few hurrahs from the mob, and their heads expand two hat sizes." Vetrania gestured with her hands around her head to illustrate her point.

"What else do you want with me?" Arturus said.

"Not much, really. I wanted to meet you, to be sure. I'm not impressed, but you have served your purpose."

Arturus gritted his teeth. "Stop playing games with me, Vetrania. I am my people's elected monarch. They and I deserve—"

Vetrania slapped Arturus across his face. A ring on her finger cut Arturus' cheek. Percival stepped toward her, but the Saepians grabbed his arms before he could move any further. Dardarius stared at Vetrania, as if he was ready defend Arturus' himself.

"You are nothing," Vetrania hissed. "An elected monarch. What a stupid way to choose a leader. Ignorant people duped into picking a honey-tongued liar who can't even protect the country's borders. You are weak as a kitten." She stepped back, regaining her self-control.

"Now, Lord Mordred. There's a leader I can deal with. He's good. He's done far more damage to my army in Viridiae than you did. He's the one who deserves to be king, not you."

Despite Vetrania's motive for heaping praise on Mordred, who had tried to depose Arturus before the war, Percival took heart. Assuming what Vetrania said was true, Mordred was causing enough trouble for the Lucians in their newly conquered territory to get the empress's attention.

"Dardarius thinks we should release you, which might encourage Mordred to negotiate a settlement. Mordred wants you back, of course, but I'm thinking that's not a good idea."

Dardarius' face fell. "Madam, I thought we agreed. Arturus for Merlin so that the Great Machine could be repaired."

"We have Merlin in hand. Why should we give away our most valuable bargaining chip?"

Percival did a double take. "What? Merlin is here?"

Vetrania looked at Percival as if he were a pile of dung. "Yes, he is." She glanced at Arturus and feigned an apology. "Oh, I didn't tell you? He arrived at the palace only a few hours ago. And he's bearing a gift."

Arturus swallowed as he fought to regain his bearings. "I, I demand to see him. He is one of my closest aides. And my friend."

Vetrania shrugged. "Why not?" She snapped her fingers.

The bronze doors which welcomed Percival and Arturus opened. Two Saepian guards behind him, an elderly man with a close-cropped white beard stood holding a large box covered with a cloth.

Arturus' jaw dropped. "Merlin."

Prodded by the guard, Arturus' chief science adviser stepped forward, his pace tentative. He looked as if he'd walked a hundred kilometers. Had he walked alone all the way from Camelot? Percival's curiosity competed with his amazement. Merlin, here in the flesh!

Merlin stopped at spot next to Arturus. The elder nodded slightly to his king in greeting. Percival fought back tears.

"Place your gift in front of your king, Mr Ambrosius. Why everyone calls you by your first name is another one of those Viridian quirks that mystifies me. Anyway, Arturus can present it, instead of you."

Arturus was unsure what to do.

"Oh, damn you, stupid man," Vetrania said. "I already know what it is. Remove the cloth."

Arturus bent down, taking the corner of the plain, but high-quality cloth. The wrist bindings made the gesture awkward, but Arturus removed the fabric as if it were covering the face of a dead man. Percival half-expected to see the head of someone he knew, perhaps Guinevere, or Gaia protect her, Lancelot.

Instead, the box held the Grail.

Vetrania laughed. "You people amaze me. Dardarius arranged for a prisoner swap: Arturus for Merlin. Instead, Merlin brings me the Grail. Trouble is, I've already got the Viridian device. Now I have two!"

CHAPTER 16: MERLIN ASSESSES THE GRAIL

Within an hour of Merlin's arrival, Percival transformed from a prisoner-of-war to an assistant to the greatest mind of the age. Vetrania ordered Merlin to start work immediately, placing him in the hands of Verus, the head of the Science Academy of Lucanus. The large man, who happened to be the father of the young woman Percival noticed near Tribune Cantwell, took the assignment with equanimity, as if it were expected. Merlin, however, complained he had no assistant he could trust. He could not be expected to repair the Great Machine surrounded by Viridiae's sworn enemies, no matter their scientific credentials. Vetrania appointed Percival as Merlin's assistant. Before the knight opened his mouth to object, Arturus nodded in agreement.

Another Saepian military detail led Merlin and Percival away, escorted by Verus. Glancing back at Arturus, and reassured by Arturus' good wishes, Percival ached to question Merlin on everything from how he'd come to Lucana to how the war went back home. He had an inkling of the origin of the Grail in Merlin's box, but he feared a conversation might reveal too much. He bit his tongue as they sat in the back of another electric car, this time headed for the Science Academy.

Percival's mind jumped from Merlin to the Grail to Arturus. His king, still a hostage, was now alone. Percival guessed the Lucians would take him back to the cell they had shared, but Percival had no idea what might happen to him next. Would he rot for weeks or months while Vetrania decided what to do with him?

Now that Merlin was in Lucana, would she execute him and send his head to Mordred? What of Dardarius? Percival couldn't shake the impression that Vetrania's treatment of Arturus had dishonored the general somehow. If true, he wouldn't take the slight lying down, but the consequences were impossible to gauge.

Merlin said little during the drive to the Academy. Percival had never met the man, though he had seen him lecture at Camelot University. For a centenarian, Merlin looked forty years younger, another legacy of the DNA-engineering practiced by the Old Civilization. Lines creased his face, but they weren't so deep as to indicate pain or even excessive worry. On the other hand, the elder slumped in his seat, clearly exhausted from his journey. He smelled vaguely of horse sweat, and he didn't mention any companions. Apart from a bulging rucksack, all he carried was the pine box with the Grail. Percival prayed they could find a way to talk without fear of being overheard. The Lucians would record every word and movement of both men.

The 10-story buildings of the Science Academy encircled a large lawn dotted with dogwood trees. A cyclone fence surrounded the property, and the occasional surveillance drone mimicked the buzzing of bees. The car's passengers, including Percival and Merlin, were ordered out at a checkpoint for a security inspection. Presenting a tablet, Verus explained Vetrania's orders to the officer. The unsmiling woman insisted on searching Percival and Merlin, including the box and rucksack. She dumped the contents of Merlin's rucksack onto a table.

"Careful, please," Merlin objected. "Those are highly specialized tools. If they lose their calibrations because of your rough handling…"

"Is this necessary?" Verus said to the guard.

"I'm required to search for weapons and explosives. Unauthorized com devices are also prohibited. You know the procedure, sir."

Grunting her satisfaction, the legionnaire left the rucksack's repacking to Merlin, who wouldn't allow Percival to help.

Then the guard tried to touch Merlin's Grail. The scientist

snatched the box away. "I didn't come thousands of kilometers to have the most precious technology ever invented pawed like a knickknack at a flea market."

"I'm required to examine everything. How do I know you haven't hidden a bomb in there?" The guard flushed. "If you don't at least let me x-ray it, I can't let it in."

Merlin scoffed. "I know nothing about your infernal gadget. The Grail's circuits are delicate and sensitive. Do you want to be the one blamed for the failure of this experiment before it even starts?"

The guard looked to Verus for support.

Verus shook his head. "I'll personally vouch for the Grail's safety. My guest knows what will happen to King Arturus if it's a trick."

The guard relented. Merlin grabbed the box and held it close.

Once on the grounds, Merlin asked to see the laboratory with the Lucian Grail, which the traitorous knight Gawain had stolen from Viridiae, and handed over to Lucian spies days before their country's invasion. The faulty Grail object at the Lucian Great Machine in the northeast corner of Lucanus hundreds of kilometers away remained in place.

In the lab, bright light bathed the Lucian Grail in a clear plastic case. Hundreds of sensors, wires, and blinking computers surrounded the case like a halo. After so many months of focusing on day-to-day survival, Percival felt the magic of the Grail pulling at him again. A thousand years in the past, humanity had staked its future on a dozen machines to block the worst effects of the changing climate. At their nucleii were the Grail devices, and now they were failing. He was in the presence of two of the precious creations—one in the plastic case, and one in Merlin's pine box—created by a civilization ten centuries dead.

Merlin's affect altered. Until this point, he was a cranky, tired old man with no patience for fools. Like Percival, however, he gazed upon the Lucian Grail with a reverence once reserved for holy relics or the gods themselves. Merlin soaked energy from the inert device, which was round, like the earth itself, and covered with intricate circuitry burned into octagonal plates on its surface.

A cadre of lab-coated technicians and scientists hovered beyond the Grail's incandescence. Verus invited his colleagues forward.

"As I explained in the car," Verus said to Merlin, "I'm head of this institution. I'd like to introduce the team that's been examining the device."

One of the lab coats, a middle-aged man with dyed hair, presented himself with a short bow. Merlin waved him off.

"I don't have time for obsequiousness."

"But Professor Ambrosius," Verus said, "don't you want to hear what they've accomplished so far?"

"Obviously nothing, or I wouldn't be here." Merlin sighed. "I would like to see their notes. I assume you have notes prepared for me?"

The middle-aged scientist nodded.

"You'll have them immediately," Verus said.

"Excellent. Now, I want all of you out of the room, except for my assistant."

Verus coughed. "Professor, I really must object—"

"And turn off the lights out when you leave."

"What?"

"I prefer working in low light. These lights," he squinted, "give me a headache."

"Will there be anything else?" Verus' tone verged on sarcasm.

"Yes. Turn off any recording equipment you have, video, sound, all of it."

"You're not making any sense, professor. How are we supposed to learn from you if we can't watch you work, even after the fact?"

"Fine." Merlin started packing his equipment. "I'm going home. I can't work under these conditions."

Percival opened his mouth. Were they going back to Camelot without Arturus?

"Not a word, Sir Percival. I don't appreciate being treated by these Lucian imposters like some first-year dunce."

Verus stepped closer, lowering his voice. "I didn't want to say this, professor, but your king's life depends on your success. You have to stay."

Merlin narrowed his eyes at Verus, as if he were looking at a specimen of some disgusting slug. "I'm a scientist, Mr Verus. I don't care about politics. I came here because I wanted to learn more about the Grail and the Great Machine. When I heard you had a malfunctioning Grail, I undertook a perilous journey—with no help from your witless military—to examine it and perhaps repair it. I'm here to study the Grail and save the planet for future generations. Your empress and my king can hang, for all I care."

Percival gulped, along with most of Merlin's audience.

"Well, what is it, Professor Verus?" Merlin continued. "Do you give me a fighting chance to fix our respective Great Machines, or are you going to issue more threats?"

Verus looked as if he had inhaled a poisonous gas. Percival feared he might faint, but the bulky man stayed conscious.

"Very well, professor. Have it your way, but I demand a report within one hour."

Merlin breathed in and then out. Percival inhaled, but held it.

"A reasonable request, Mr Verus. Perhaps there's hope for you after all. You'll have my report in exactly one hour."

Verus nodded, his jowls wiggling. He waved off the lab coats and within a moment, the room was empty. The lights dimmed and to Verus' credit, the HVAC system grew quiet. Verus was taking no chances at upsetting the prickly, world-famous professor.

"Percival," Merlin said in a low voice. "I'm going to move around the device, as if examining it. Watch the cameras, but not too closely."

Confused, but with no choice to play along, Percival glanced at the three cameras pointed at the Lucian device. "I don't see anything, Merlin."

"Good," Merlin whispered. "When we came in, I saw that they all had the little red lights that usually mean they are active.

The lights are off now, and they didn't come on when I moved. They're not motion-activated."

"We should still assume we're being watched."

"Excellent point, young man. Surveillance is the norm. But we'll have to take the chance that whatever recording device they have running at the moment is not as good as the full suite."

"I'm sorry, sir, but I don't understand."

"I'll explain later. For now, stay very close, and follow my instructions to the letter. I won't repeat them."

"Yes, sir."

The instructions were short, and to the point. Percival's heart raced as Merlin delivered them. Merlin planned to gamble with all three of the Viridians' lives and perhaps with Viridiae itself, but Percival thought the plan had a chance. The only other choice was trusting Vetrania to live up to her word, and she had already proven herself a liar when she broke her promise to Dardarius.

An hour later, Verus knocked at the lab door, and Percival braced for Merlin's report.

CHAPTER 17:
ARTURUS COURTS
DARDARIUS

Robert Dardarius unclenched his fist and examined the palms of his hands. The indentations of his fingernails challenged him like a teacher's grades on a paper, and none of the marks were good. Vetrania's insults of Arturus, praising the king's internal enemies, and laying a hand on the man, were all meant as put-downs of himself. Marcella was right. Vetrania was afraid of failing to repair the Grail, but she was also afraid of him and his success. She could not take out her fear on him directly. People on the street would wonder why, further weakening her. Instead, she took it out on Arturus,

   who couldn't fight back.

Vetrania's treatment of Arturus had shamed Robert. He could do little to stop Vetrania. Her authority within the empire was absolute, and her power, though tenuous, was overwhelming. However, Robert could make Arturus' imprisonment more tolerable. With Percival now attached to Merlin, Arturus was alone in the cold interrogation cells of the intelligence service headquarters in the Regia.

Robert pulled a few strings. The head of the intelligence service once served with him on a minor campaign, and because Arturus was technically a prisoner-of-war, as well as a chattel prize, Robert had a say in his accommodations. After the call, Robert sent Adrian to the cells. An hour later, Adrian returned with a bedraggled, yet unbowed king of Viridiae. Arturus stood before his captor, who was equally uncertain about the next moves.

"Welcome to my home, Your Majesty."

Arturus took in the luxurious surroundings. "A home fit for an emperor."

Robert smiled. "My great-grandfather built it. He was the last of the Dardarians to sit on the Lucian throne."

Arturus said, "What do you want from me, General?"

Robert had no clear answer. He was ashamed of Arturus' treatment by Vetrania, but that was not something he was willing to admit up front. "Your accommodations don't fit your status, Your Majesty. I would like to offer you a place in my home."

"A gilded cage."

"House arrest, rather than imprisonment."

Arturus thought a moment. "What can you tell me of Percival and Merlin? I've heard nothing."

"They've been taken to the Academy of Science to examine the Grail. I know nothing more."

Arturus eyed the fresh grapes on the table next to Robert.

"Please, help yourself."

Arturus moved the bowl closer to himself, taking one, delicately, as if he were at a formal dinner. Robert noticed the tremble in the king's hands, and it pained him. Robert had never felt this way about a captured enemy before. He'd lost count of the bandit leaders, chieftains, and petty kings he'd defeated and captured over the years. None affected him like this monarch from the country they called the "Green Land." Arturus was strong, yet vulnerable. He endured his captivity with dignity, but he wasn't afraid to show his humanity. By Lucian law and tradition, Robert held Arturus' life in the balance, but he couldn't imagine harming him, at least not deliberately.

"I have news of your wife, Guinevere."

Arturus stopped chewing and swallowed.

"She is in Ontari:io. In Villefroide, as a matter of fact. She crossed the border with Dame Lancelot and a woman named

Dindrane Rathkeale. Do you know anything about this?"

"How could I? I've been your prisoners for months."

"I had to ask. Do you have any guesses?"

"Road trip?"

Robert laughed. "I'm amazed at you, Your Majesty. Your wife travels with her lover to the capital of Lucanus' strongest enemy on the continent. I'd be worried."

"About what?"

"Perhaps she was exiled by Mordred. Perhaps she's run off with her lover to raise an army to take what's left of Viridiae for herself."

"Or she may have gone in search of allies to turn back an invasion."

"All are possibilities. None have a chance at success, least of all the third possibility. Ontari:io is weak and decadent. All its people care about is money."

"But it vexes you."

"It's a formidable enemy. Our last war over Villefroide's aggression failed with thousands of Lucian casualties. My brother, Adrian's father, died in that disaster."

"My sympathies."

"Two of your other favorites, Sir Bors and Sir Galahad, have been seen by Lucian agents in the Hot Lands to the south. What might your knights be up to?"

"You know far more than I do, General."

Robert shifted in his seat. "Tell me about Mordred. What kind of man is he?"

"Ambitious. A good soldier. A brilliant politician. A loyal Viridian."

"But he tried to depose you."

"What are you getting at?"

"I'm just trying to understand my enemies. You're a fascinating people."

"I'll bet you say that to all the people you conquer."

"You don't believe me."

Arturus grinned. "Look, General Dardarius, I saw your reaction in the palace as Vetrania tried to humiliate me. I'm listening to you now, doing what interrogators do, trying to weave facts into a truth. But I don't think your heart's in it."

Robert's chest tightened. "I'm a soldier. I follow orders."

"Let me ask you a few questions. How did Viridiae threaten Lucanus?"

"All foreigners threaten Lucanus. We are surrounded by enemies."

"That's not what I asked. What did my country do to provoke an invasion?"

Arturus had laid a trap and Robert had stepped into it. He could lie, which Arturus would immediately spot, or he could be honest with a man he respected, despite his status as an enemy.

"I don't see any harm in telling the truth," Robert said. "Viridiae was a good neighbor."

"So the real reason was internal. Something was driving Vetrania to act."

"We needed Merlin. He is the only one who can fix the Grail."

"That's one excuse. What's the other?"

"I don't understand." In fact, Robert did understand, but he wasn't willing to admit it openly.

"Vetrania needed you out of the capital. Her hold on power is weakening, and there's only one man or woman in Lucana who can take advantage of that weakness: you."

Arturus was either well-informed or unusually perceptive. Probably both, Robert thought, as he locked eyes with the monarch. Of all Lucanus' powerful families, only the Cardeans and the Dardarians had the strength and resources to rule, and the Cardeans had ruled for three generations. The breakdown of the Lucian Great Machine had undermined Vetrania's hold on the Lucian throne, which created an opportunity for Robert to take what rightly belonged to his clan. But he could not share such sentiments with an enemy of the Lucian state.

"If you were a Lucian, I'd say you were encouraging sedition, Your Majesty."

"I'm merely offering the analysis you seek."

The statement shocked the general. Was that why he had brought Arturus to his home? To confirm the instincts that troubled him like a bug bite? In Lucana, where virtually everyone was a potential enemy, Arturus was an outsider with an insider's understanding. As a king, he knew the power game better than anyone, because he had to play it every day. He'd seen how friends would stab you in the back if it served their purpose, and he wasn't afraid to do the same thing, if it preserved the nation and himself. Robert might have allies in Lucana, even friends, but he had no one he could trust, except perhaps Adrian. He had to turn to an enemy to reveal the truth about himself and his destiny. He was meant to sit on the Lucian throne. And Arturus would show him the way.

"Your Majesty, you must be tired. I've prepared my late wife's painting studio as lodging for you while you are in my care."

"Thank you, General. But I'd be grateful if you returned me to my cell."

Why would anyone want to stay in that hellhole, Robert thought. "I don't understand."

"Percival will worry if I'm not near. He's young, and he needs a guiding hand."

"I'll bring him here."

"With all due respect, he's in more danger here than in a prison."

"My home is guarded by the best-trained soldiers in Lucanus."

"When Vetrania comes for you, I'd rather be as far away as possible."

Robert gave in. Arturus had seen through his offer. He'd invited the king to stay at his home to soothe his conscience. Arturus wouldn't suffer another humiliation.

After Arturus departed for his prison cell, Adrian picked at the grapes last sampled by the Viridian king. "His analysis of your situation vis-à-vis Her Highness was interesting. It's almost as if Arturus was trying to manipulate you."

"Of course he was, but that doesn't mean what he said about Vetrania wasn't true."

"You're walking dangerous ground, uncle."

Robert waved the servants and guards out of the room. He double-checked his equipment for interfering with listening devices. He hoped it worked as well as advertised.

"Adrian, how loyal would you say the Sixth, Seventh, and Eleventh legions are to me."

"They are as strong a force as Lucanus has."

"No, I mean, if I asked them to do something out of the ordinary, would they follow me?"

Adrian slowed his chewing and spat out a pit. "I suppose that would depend on the request."

"Answer my question, nephew."

Adrian viewed his uncle with a wary eye. "I'll say 'yes,' for now."

"And what about you, Adrian. Would you follow me?"

"You know I would. After what happened to Cecily, whom I loved like a sister, I would do anything to find justice for her."

"Justice." Robert mused over the word. "What a lofty concept. Everyone understands its meaning, but no one ever seems to get it, when push comes to shove."

"Are you saying, uncle, that it's time to balance the scales?"

"Nearly, but not just yet." Robert stood from his chair and gazed out the window, which looked toward downtown Lucana and the imperial apartments. Cecily had used that phrase, "balance the scales," not long before he lost her, before a clan war between the Dardarians and Cardeans nearly descended into chaos.

CHAPTER 18:
THE CARDEAN/
DARDARIAN WAR

The last war between the Cardeans and the Dardarians started during a chicken dinner. At that moment, nine years before, a few kilometers distant, a pounding at the front door couldn't break Robert Dardarius' concentration on the wall-mounted com screen and its crawl announcing "News Just In..." He and his wife Cecily watched the reports of the shots fired at the annual fundraising dinner for a homeless children's service. Empress Vetrania had hosted the dinner, but an hour had passed after the incident with no word from her. Robert swallowed, fearing the worst. He ignored the pounding.

"What's that noise? Aren't you going to answer the door?" Cecily squeezed Robert's hand, communicating her own anxiety.

"Let the servants answer it. I can't afford to miss anything."

The racket intensified, accompanied by shouts.

"The servants are too frightened to come out," Cecily said. "Gaia knows what's going to happen now. You'll have to answer the door yourself."

Robert growled, but assented. He sped to the door in his robe and slippers. He was supposed to attend the dinner with Cecily, but both had begged off after a bout with spoiled yogurt. Secretly, he was glad to stay away. Sparks always flew between him and Vetrania whenever they were in the same room.

He scanned the men via the security monitor. One of them

was Zeno, the head of his security detail, and the other was Matthew Dardarius Septimus, a distant cousin in the Dardarian clan.

"Matthew? What's this about?"

"You have to let me in. Please!" Sweat plastered a lock of black hair on his forehead. He gasped for breath.

Robert glanced at Zeno.

"I'm sorry, sir. I recognized him, but you gave orders not to be disturbed. He rushed past me—"

After both men slipped in, Robert closed the door. "Matthew, what is it?"

"It's the empress."

Robert noticed that Matthew wore a formal suit. "Were you at the dinner tonight?"

Matthew pursed his lips. "I was there."

Cecily came in to the foyer, her dressing gown swishing the parquet floor. "You disobeyed Robert, didn't you?"

Matthew ignored Cecily's question. "Listen to me, sir. I'm begging you as our clan chief." Matthew's eyes shifted from husband to wife and back. "Protect me."

"I shouldn't. I should hand you over." Robert's face flushed with heat. For months, he had argued with Matthew and his reckless friends about their disgust with Vetrania and her government. They'd seen their professors at university harassed after exposing the Cardean clan's illegitimate claim to power, kickbacks by contractors to Vetrania's clan members, and police violence against peaceful demonstrations. "I warned you and your so-called 'Agents of Change' against doing something stupid. Now you've done it, and look what's happening."

Robert pointed to the com screen. Hundreds of police fired tear gas into a spontaneous riot outside the pavilion where the fundraiser had taken place. "You're going to bring violence to my house."

Matthew gulped, but he knew his rights as a clan member. "Sir, I'm inside your walls. I demand protection."

Robert hissed. He turned to Cecily, who shook her head. Robert had no choice, however, not if he expected to remain clan leader when the family met at the next assembly. He touched Zeno on his muscled shoulder. "You know what to do."

The bodyguard half-led, half-pushed the young activist—now a terrorist—toward a door. The pair disappeared down a flight of stairs.

"You realize what you've done, Robert?" Cecily said.

"I'm bound by clan law and tradition to give sanctuary to any member who requests it. What kind of leader would I be if I ignored my own blood?"

"If Matthew was part of this plot, you're now complicit, Robert. Do you know what that means?"

Robert didn't want to think about the consequences of his obligation just then. Instead, he poured himself a whiskey, and gulped it down in two swallows. His burning throat cloaked the alarm that weighed on him like an approaching flood. On the com screen, cameras showed tables askew, chairs pushed away, food still on plates and wine in glasses. If the crawl hadn't said, "Government calls incident 'assassination attempt,'" it would have seemed like the ordinary aftermath of a pleasant, rather dull event. "If Vetrania is dead ..."

Zeno reappeared, without Matthew.

"It's too late now. What's done is done." Cecily took her husband's hand. "We have to think of our next move. Vetrania is a demon. We should hope she's dead."

"Madam." Zeno raised a paw-like hand in nervous caution. "The walls may be listening."

Cecily was always right. Robert married her because he fell in love with her. She was the most beautiful woman in Lucana, part of a family that had been allied with the Dardarian clan for generations. Elders scoffed at love-at-first-sight stories, but the poets knew its rare truth, as did Robert and Cecily. They loved each other from the moment they met at a May Day Festival. Fifteen years later, their love burned as brightly as it did then, but in a different way.

After Robert began a quiet, if dangerous career as a soldier, the true nature of their partnership emerged. When Robert's father died, the son became head of the Dardarian clan, the only family that had the power and wealth to challenge the Cardeans, Vetrania's clan, for supremacy in Lucanus. But his mind and heart was too steeped in family expectations, especially when it came to the Cardeans. Armed with her own perspective, Cecily knew better than he did when to act, and when to hold back.

"What should we do, Cecily?"

"We knew something like this might happen. We can follow the old traditions, or we can try another way. We—"

Before Cecily could finish, the news chan anchor came on, heralding a statement from the government. The video cut to a podium with the empress's seal of office hanging in front of a curtain. Robert anticipated an announcement he guessed would change his life forever.

The seconds ticked by. Robert thought of his great-grandfather, the last Dardarian emperor, murdered, his family was certain, after winning a key battle against the Missibams of the south. The official histories said he died in a riding accident, despite his acknowledged skill as a horseman. No true-blooded Dardarian believed the tale. The mystery languished for three generations before a researcher at Matthew's university turned up a letter that implicated the Cardeans, who were jealous of the Dardarians' popularity. A fearless independent journalist, who happened to be married to a Dardarian, published the letter, enraging Vetrania and encouraging her critics.

Robert gasped. Cecily stood beside him, eyes glued to the com screen. Vetrania walked up to the podium, tall and strong, her face stern, as if nothing had happened at the dinner, except under-cooked chicken.

"Ladies and gentlemen, I apologize for the delay."

Vetrania cleared her throat, her only sign of agitation.

"About two hours ago, a gang of terrorists attacked a group of peaceful Lucian citizens gathered to raise funds for charity. It appears I was one of their targets. Clearly, they missed."

Hesitant laughter rose from the out-of-sight audience, relieving some of the tension.

"I'm happy to report that all but one of the terrorists have been liquidated." An instant later, her visage transformed from confidence to menace. "Let me show you how my government deals with terrorists."

Vetrania signaled someone offstage, and the screen changed to a poorly lit alley. Hand-held floodlights played on three figures lined up against a wall. The camera zoomed in on each of the bloody and bruised faces, which contrasted with their dinner jackets and blood-stained white shirts.

The camera zoomed out and Robert heard an order. A volley of bullets slammed into the three figures, and they slumped to the ground.

Robert knew all three: two men and a woman. All were of the Dardarian clan. Cecily buried her face in Robert's chest. They had just witnessed the summary execution of three of his family.

The screen returned to Vetrania. "Security forces are searching for a fourth terrorist." The news chan cut to a video of a young man running toward a surveillance camera. Without a doubt, it was Matthew. "Anyone with information about this man should contact authorities immediately." Matthew's name, address, and clan affiliation appeared.

The whole country knew whom to blame.

"Attacks against the state will never be tolerated," Vetrania continued. "The conspiracy goes much farther and deeper than these criminals. Rest assured, people of Lucanus, that I will find the conspiracy and destroy it, root and branch."

With that, Vetrania left the podium, and the screen cut to the shocked and confused anchor.

"She's declared war on us," Cecily said.

"We started it. That's what people will think, anyway."

"She'll be merciless."

Vetrania's first move came within minutes. Zeno called Robert on the secure line, saying that plain-clothes state police were at the gate, asking if Matthew had shown up. A moment later, a knock on the front door ended the conversation. Robert opened the door and a broad-shouldered, gaunt man in a calf-length black cloak pushed his way in, followed by two others in black uniforms.

"I'm sorry to disturb your evening, General Dardarius."

Robert considered how to buy time. "This better be important."

"I am Major Kerillian, state security." He noticed the news chan on the screen. "I'm sure you know what happened this evening."

"I'll cooperate with your investigation, of course." Except if it means betraying Matthew.

Kerillian eyed Robert. "I'm sure you will. Your cousin, Matthew Dardarius, is a suspect in the conspiracy."

"He's not here." Robert guessed the officer would know he was lying, but he could not give up his cousin, at least not yet.

"I'm sure that's the case, but I'd like to conduct a search, nonetheless." Kerillian was willing to play games for now.

"I'd like to see your warrant," Robert said.

"You may not have heard the latest news, General Dardarius. The empress has declared a state of emergency. Civil liberties are suspended. I don't need a warrant." He flicked his hand at the uniformed officer, who stepped up.

Four of Robert's personal guard appeared and took places behind Zeno. Each put his hand on the hilt of his sword.

"We'll offer assistance as well," Zeno said, his tone unsociable.

Kerillian and Robert were at a standoff.

"Everything's fine, Zeno. This nice policeman was just about to leave to retrieve the search warrant he forgot in his office. Isn't that right, Major?"

Kerillian wouldn't be goaded into a mistake. He was outnumbered, and his pursuit had only started.

"There's another bit of news, General. Empress Vetrania has set up a tribunal, according to the Seditious Utterances and Actions Act, to investigate and try suspected terrorists and sympathizers. Your cousin will be one of the first cases, once we find him."

Robert reeled. Vetrania had suspended the constitution under the pretext of the assassination attempt. Now, his cousin Matthew was accused of treason, in so many words, as well as the Dardarian clan. The life of anyone with Dardarian blood or ties was at risk.

Kerillian and his men withdrew. The foyer of Robert's house emptied, except for Cecily.

"Vetrania can't do this."

"Yes, she can." Robert rubbed his arms, as if the heat of the evening had turned to bitter cold. "Vetrania won't stop until she's destroyed our family. It's about survival now, my love, nothing less."

* * *

Sleep was impossible for Robert, but not for lack of his need for it. Within minutes of Vetrania's announcement and the video of the summary executions, messages poured into his com account, and voice calls queued up like petitioners at the annual gathering. Some reported visits by state security looking for Matthew. Others demanded protection, which Robert ignored. One woman was arrested, and she asked Robert to post bail. It turned out she was already wanted on a theft charge and was merely caught up in the dragnet. His clan wasn't known for its purity of heart.

A large portion of the callers and message writers wanted revenge. They cared little for the crimes committed by the Agents of Change, only that the three executed criminals were family members. Robert had to stifle a laugh after hearing this from one caller, who was so distantly related to the clan as to be nearly a perfect stranger. Association with the most powerful family in Lucanus carried with it powerful emotions, including loyalty. It was a double-edged sword Robert found of little use in his life so far.

"What happened, Matthew?" Robert's cousin hid from state security in a room outfitted with enough supplies and weapons to outlast a siege. "Why did you try to kill Vetrania now?"

"Because she is destroying us." Matthew scowled. "And because you wouldn't act."

"You're blaming me?"

"We came to you, sir, months ago, asking for your help. You brushed us off as if we were children."

"You wanted me to depose Vetrania. You wanted me to engineer a *coup d'etat*, put Vetrania on trial, and execute her. How does violently overthrowing a government make things better for us? It just invites more violence, which hurts every Dardarian."

"What choice do we have? A thousand years ago, when Lucana was a village in a sea of corn, maybe we could've removed her from office legally, or voted her out. But now our country is run by a raging tyrant. The only way to get rid of her is to kill her."

Robert did not agree. Though Lucanus lost its obsolete democracy after the Dissolution, when the world fell apart, some of its emperors over the following centuries had ruled with an enlightened hand. The nation absorbed weaker states on its border, incorporated their peoples and economies, and defended itself against aggression. Decades passed in some eras without a major internal or external conflict. Lucanus was now the most powerful nation on the continent.

On the other hand, Vetrania met every definition of the tyrant Matthew despised. Robert, however, didn't believe removing her by force would improve his clan's lives. That was the argument he'd made before tonight.

"Sir, don't let my three friends, your family, die in vain."

"He's right, husband." Cecily stood at the door, her face heavy with exhaustion. In contrast, she spoke with conviction. "Vetrania has made a huge mistake."

"She seems to have the upper hand, as I see it."

"Tallies matter to some people," Cecily said. "Vetrania has killed three Dardarians. The scales of justice are out of balance. You have every right to retaliate in a way the Lucian people will accept. But you don't have to, if you make another choice."

"What do you want me to do?"

"This might be our opportunity to change things. Maybe we

can end this the endless cycle of family against family. It's such a waste."

Robert tensed his jaw. Now was not the time to challenge ancient traditions and expectations. It was fine to discuss turning people's lust for revenge and retaliation into something more constructive. It might be true that the clans needed to find a way past retribution for every slight. Now was not the time for change.

Cecily's plea, however, reminded Robert why he loved her. In a way Robert couldn't always fathom, she could stand apart from the moment and see a different path, even if it was impractical. Perhaps it was her artistic training, and maybe it was a deep family history of tragedy. In the long story of Lucanus' internal strife, her provincial clan always came up short. It was natural for her to seek a path to a permanent peace, free of the cycle of revenge.

"If I can find a way to prevent more killings, I'll do it, my love. But I'll make no promises."

* * *

How easy it would be to simply order Zeno to find three Cardeans and kill them? His people might expect him to do such a thing as a way to restore the clan's dignity, as would Vetrania, but Robert found the idea predictable and pointless. His reasoning had little to do with Cecily's odd, if interesting notions. Even if the scales of justice came back into balance, he couldn't imagine Vetrania would be satisfied. She wanted something more.

After a few hours of fitful sleep, Robert contacted Verus, a professor at the Lucian Academy of Science. Their personal history went back to college, but their families were allies going back generations, farther than either family could remember. Though the records were sketchy, Verus was probably related to the first Lucian emperor, Verusalian, who ended a long period of internal conflict in Lucanus' early history. Though his clan played only minor roles in modern Lucian politics, even a tenuous connection to the empire's founder gave Verus clout, and families often called on him to mediate inter-clan disputes.

"Verus, how are your connections in Vetrania's court?"

"At least as good as yours." Verus sat at Robert's kitchen table, braving the checkpoints Vetrania had set up all over Lucana.

"I don't have much contact with Vetrania's people. They regard the Dardarians with contempt."

"Then my contacts are probably better. The Verusians are not a threat to her."

"I need a go-between. This isn't an ordinary dispute. Vetrania is frightened, but she's clever. She'll try to turn this to her advantage. She'll want something to keep this situation from spiraling out of her control."

Verus sipped his coffee. "If it did, the blood would clog the gutters on every street."

"Can you arrange a meeting? Me and her?"

"I'll see what I can do."

True to his word, Verus made contact with Vetrania's staff, and a meeting was set for the following day.

Or so Robert thought. An hour before the scheduled meeting at Verus' house, Vetrania canceled. Robert guessed why. Early in the morning, Zeno came to him with credible rumors of another assassination attempt in the offing, but he couldn't track down the source or its veracity. Taking no chances, Vetrania canceled the meeting, but within hours, the rumors proved to be true.

Robert switched on the com screen at Zeno's request. The news chan anchor introduced a video posted by an unknown group calling itself Vengeance. One of the group had mounted a camera on his or her chest and recorded the attack. Despite a heavy police presence, the attacker managed to get close to a minister and his wife. The attacker killed the minister with a single-shot pistol and slashed the throat of his wife. She died in a hospital emergency room.

Robert confronted Matthew in the basement shelter. "What do you know about this?"

"Nothing."

"Zeno can learn otherwise."

Matthew regarded Robert. "You'd set one of your dogs on your own family? You're as bad as Vetrania."

Robert grabbed a handful of Matthew's thick, black hair and yanked the young man's head back. "You've demanded protection from our family's enemies. That doesn't entitle you to protection from me. Tell me now. What do you know of this new attack?"

"I swear to Gaia, I know nothing. I've never heard of 'Vengeance.' With all the new security, how could anyone get so close to one of Vetrania's cronies?"

Robert let go of his cousin's locks. He'd asked himself the same question.

Back upstairs, Cecily said, "What's the score now?"

"What are you talking about?" Robert paced the room.

"I'll tell you. Vetrania will learn, or she'll claim, that this new group is Dardarian. That means the Dardarians have killed three Cardeans to the Cardean's two victims. We're up by one. Who will be the third?"

Cecily's macabre reckoning repelled Robert, but her point was obvious. The incipient Dardarian-Cardean war had escalated, but Lucian justice demanded parity.

Robert's com filled with messages appealing for another killing.

Cecily went to Robert and took his hand. "You can stop this before it gets worse."

"I tried to meet with Vetrania, but she refused."

"Try again. Make an offer. Put a stop to this."

Robert agreed, but the inertia of tradition was almost unstoppable. As clan leader, his position was more symbolic than real. He had a few traditional powers, such as adjudicating intra-clan disagreements, blessing requests for adoptions of children from other clans, and officiating funerals of leading clan members. He couldn't, however, order his people to do or not do anything. Unlike Vetrania, his power was limited.

Nonetheless, he arranged a group-wide com message to his

family members to seek his approval before enacting a reprisal. He hoped respect for his position would slow the escalation and give him time to negotiate a settlement with Vetrania.

Either the tactic worked, or the clan's security forces had discouraged further rash behavior. Zeno had sent out his own messages. For three days, no one died on either side, even as Verus passed notes back and forth between Vetrania and Robert. The tension weighed on the city. The streets were empty; no one wanted to be caught in the crossfire.

Another meeting was arranged. Five days had passed since the assassination attempt by the Agents of Change. Robert arrived at Verus' house with Zeno and three other heavily armed guards. Vetrania arrived with her usual entourage of palace guard and courtiers, but left them outside the modest, if tasteful parlor. Robert and Zeno sat across from her and her only retainer, Kerillian, the security officer who had come for Matthew after the attempted killing.

"Major Kerillian is in charge of all security matters related to the events of five days ago." Vetrania sat straight, almost primly, on the sofa. She was dressed in a smart business suit with a pin representing the Lucian eagle on her lapel. Despite the attempt to hide them with cosmetics, Robert noticed the darkness of exhaustion under her hawk-like eyes. "Who is this man?"

Robert said, "Zeno Dardarius runs my personal security detail, Your Majesty."

Of all Vetrania's staff, Kerillian seemed an odd choice as her second. The empress was known to favor, then discard, lovers, as if they were last year's fashions. Kerillian might be one of them, though Robert had no way of knowing for sure.

Verus set down his tea on the low table that separated the parties. "We're here to discuss an end to the hostilities between the clans Cardea and Dardarius. I am merely the host, and my house is neutral ground. Nothing said here can be construed as actionable insult or law-breaking. Agreed?"

Robert eyed Vetrania. They nodded simultaneously.

"Clan Leader Dardarius has graciously requested that Empress Vetrania speak first to begin the dialog."

Robert listened as Vetrania recounted the events at the fund-raiser and subsequent days. He respected her calm, business-like approach to the matter, but he also detected a strain in her voice that was more than simple fatigue. At one point, she leaned slightly toward Kerillian, as if she needed physical support. The circles under her eyes grew pronounced.

"General Dardarius, do you have a response?" Verus said.

"I thank Your Majesty for her mostly factual rendition of these unauthorized attacks on her person. I'm personally glad to see that she is unharmed."

"You're a bad liar, Robert," the empress said. "You want me dead."

"That's not true, madam. I see no gain for my clan by your death."

"Another lie. You could've stopped these so-called 'Agents' months ago. They came to you for help."

Vetrania's knowledge of private conversations within the Dardarian clan didn't surprise Robert. She had all the powers of the state at her disposal, including electronic and human sur-veillance.

"Then you know I did all I could to discourage them."

"The point is, you failed. I blame you as much as them."

"As head of the Dardarian clan, I take responsibility for clan members' behavior."

Vetrania's shoulders relaxed. "That says well of you, General. To show your good faith, you must put this value into action."

"How so?"

"Immediately hand over Matthew Dardarius to Major Keril-lian."

Robert expected this. "Unfortunately, he has asked for protec-tion under our clan tradition and Lucian custom. He is a guest in my house."

Vetrania's voice rose. "Trying to kill the Lucian sovereign supersedes individual clan law. You know this, General. Hand him over."

"And what of the three deaths of my family? Their relatives have demanded vengeance."

"Two of my clan have paid the vengeance price." Vetrania looked away from Robert when she said this, as if she were in pain.

"And Matthew will balance the scales?" It was a foregone conclusion that Matthew would be tried, convicted, and executed.

"In part. I want something else." At this, Vetrania lost her fatigued manner. A new energy infused her. Robert braced himself.

"I want the Dardarian clan to renounce all claims to the Lucian throne now and forever. I also want you to pledge personal and clan allegiance to the Cardeans in all matters present and future."

Robert struggled to maintain his composure. He felt Zeno's eyes on him. If he'd been angrier, the room would've burst into flame. Even Verus, who practiced dispassion as an art form, rocked in shock.

"Your Majesty," Robert began, "my clan family would kill me before they ever accepted either declaration."

"Then the war will go on. And you will lose."

Robert breathed in. He let his breath out slowly. The Cardean claim on Lucian sovereignty never held much water because of the mysterious circumstances of William Dardarius' death. The Cardeans held onto power by mere fact of numbers, resources, and ruthlessness. After William died, his son tried to take his place, but he was unprepared, and Vetrania's great-grandfather pushed him off the royal dais. A purge followed, and the new emperor dispossessed the Dardarians of nearly everything, save the estate where Robert Dardarius made his home.

Today's clan was a shadow of a century previous, but Robert's military victories brought wealth and prestige back into the family. In hushed tones, a few elder Dardarians urged Robert to avenge his great-grandfather's usurpation. However, he saw little point in it.

No one, however, not even among the Cardeans, had asked for

what Vetrania wanted, until now.

"Well, General," Vetrania sneered, "shall there be peace?"

Robert needed time. "I must consult with my family. I'm sure you understand."

"Indeed. You have two days." With that, Vetrania rose, followed by Kerillian. "A warning: If any of my clan should die unexpectedly in the next forty-eight hours, I will hold you personally responsible."

Zeno sniffed, a sign of contempt. But Robert knew she was as good as her word. For a Cardean.

* * *

The attack on Robert's three-car motorcade started when an ordinary electric bus barreled between the first Dadarian car, with Zeno, and Robert's car, the second in line. Another bus slipped between Robert's car and the third Dadarian vehicle. Men and women in black uniforms with faces covered swarmed all three cars. Robert and his driver were cut off from support, but he'd been in ambushes before, and he kept a calm head. In the melee that followed, two of his bodyguards died, and Zeno was wounded, though not seriously. Two of the attackers died. Zeno identified them as Cardean clan soldiers.

The score, as Cecily might put it, was now five dead to four dead, with the Dadarians one short of the all-important balance.

At home, Robert excused himself to clean off the sweat and blood. In his bedroom, alone with his wife, his body shuddered like leaves in a high wind. He'd come within millimeters of death, and though bullets and arrows had come near him on the battlefield, he'd never been attacked by other Lucians. It felt completely different, as if someone you had trusted all your life turned on you in the blink of an eye. It was all so stupid and futile.

As Cecily held him on the bed, Robert's terror gave way to anger. He went to his armoire and removed body armor.

The act alarmed Cecily. "What are you doing?"

"Vetrania wants a war. I'll give her one."

"Robert, you can't."

"Stop!" Robert took a breath. He would not lose control, even in private with Cecily. "I know you believe what I'm about to do is wrong, but I disagree. Force only understands force."

Cecily took his hand, which eased Robert's fury. He relented to her gentle tug, and sat down on the bed beside her, his armor half-donned.

"My husband, you took the first steps toward peace. You've been attacked and nearly killed, but you survived. Don't let her provoke you. At least talk to her first."

Robert drank in Cecily's gray-brown eyes, and unbidden, a memory of their wedding night came back. He finally had her alone after three days of partying and feasting. Ever since that life-changing night, he could deny her nothing.

He touched his com. "Verus, can you get a call to Vetrania? I want to speak to her."

Verus promised his best, and ten minutes later, the palace called, saying Vetrania was on the line.

"Your Majesty, I'm sure you've heard."

"I have." Vetrania's face was ashen. "General, you must believe me when I say the attempt on your life was not ordered by me or the palace."

"Forgive me if I'm skeptical."

"Understandable, but like your clan, the Cardeans have, shall we say, undisciplined elements."

"I'm sympathetic to your dilemma. Perhaps you understand mine better."

Vetrania nodded, as if grasping an idea. "The perpetrators will be discovered and punished according to clan law and Lucian law. You have my solemn word."

"Very well."

"As for our previous discussion, nothing has changed. Agreed?"

"Agreed."

"Then I shall wait for your decision." Vetrania rang off.

Cecily, who was out of sight during the conversation, kissed her husband. "I'm proud of you. Another man would've sent a legion to the Regia."

"The slaughter would've been one for the ages."

"And you prevented it."

Hours later, a bulletin appeared on the news chan. A lieutenant in the Cardean clan guard had been arrested and charged with conspiracy, murder, and attempted murder. Vetrania had shown good faith.

* * *

As Vetrania's deadline approached, Robert made his decision. In some ways, it was difficult. In others, it wasn't. As clan leader, he had to weigh the rights and dignity of an individual against the benefit for the group. Under clan law, he was judge and jury, at least in the matter of Matthew's fate.

As he brought out his com to contact Zeno to make the arrangements, the captain knocked on the door to Robert's study. Cecily let him in.

"I have news, sir, that may change your mind."

"Go on."

"I have..." Zeno's voiced trailed off.

"Zeno, my friend, what's wrong?"

"I have contacts in state security and the Cardean clan security forces."

"I would expect no less. You've learned something important?"

"Yes, sir. The so-called 'Vengeance' group is a sham."

"I don't understand."

"Two people have told me this, General. The people who died, the minister and his wife, were on the wrong side of a feud with Empress Vetrania. They weren't even Cardean, despite the news reports. They were killed by mercenaries hired by Kerillian to eliminate Vetrania's problem. Blaming the murders on our clan was a convenience. I have more details, if you want them."

"So the score is really two Cardean dead—the convoy attackers —and five Dadarians," Cecily said.

Robert said, "I wish you wouldn't announce it as if we were at a soccer match."

Cecily pursed her lips. "Zeno, who knows about this?"

"Apart from the people I've mentioned, no one. I only got this information 20 minutes ago."

"You're sure of this?" Robert said.

"As much as I can be. At least Matthews' denial of any knowledge fits these facts."

Robert studied the objects on his desk. He alone would decide Matthew's fate. He reached for the dagger that his father said William Dardarius carried when he died. What were his thoughts a moment ago about the good of one versus the good of the many? For a brief moment, he wanted to resign as head of his clan, something no Lucian clan leader had done in living memory. He would be seen as a failure. People would say he had run from his duty, and honor mattered more to him than almost anything. Robert returned the dagger to its stand on his desk.

"Zeno, make the arrangements for Matthews' transfer to the government."

Zeno glanced at Cecily. "Sir. Madam. I, I…"

"Speak your mind, my friend," Robert said softly.

"Sir, I've served the clan all my life. You and I fought together in the north and the south. I've loved my job. I'm… I don't…"

"I'm grateful for all your service, Zeno. To the clan, and to me. I'd suggest asking for volunteers. Don't force anyone to do this."

Zeno stood, and brought himself to attention. "As you wish, sir." He took one step back, about-faced with as much dignity as Robert had ever seen, and left the room.

"That was hard for him," Cecily said.

"It's hard for all of us, but it's better to keep the butcher's bill as low as possible."

Cecily folded her hands. "What of Vetrania's other demands?"

"I've sent a message to Verus. He—" A text came through on Robert's com. "The meeting is set with Vetrania. You've been invited, my love."

"Why?" Cecily's eyes went wide.

"What's wrong? Are you worried?"

Cecily shook her head, but her denial was unconvincing. "I'm surprised, that's all. I've only met her once, and that was at a state occasion."

"I'd say this is as important as a dinner with strange food."

* * *

Scheduled for the next day, the meeting with Vetrania took place at a pavilion in Lucana's Crown Park, a thousand hectares of lawns, gardens, a lake, and paths enjoyed by every citizen. On this occasion, however, state security cleared the acreage for a hundred meters around the pavilion, throwing up barriers on the paved paths and stationing a hundred agents within sight of each other. Robert was grateful for Vetrania's caution. They both understood the dangers to their lives and their staffs' lives.

On the drive to the pavilion, escorted by a mix of palace guard and his own personal guard, Robert and Cecily watched the news reports of Matthews' transfer to authorities. They walked him twenty meters from the door of a police station to a horse-drawn cage. The episode was a propaganda show intended to humiliate Matthew and the Dardarian clan. Robert braced himself for invective sure to come from his own people. He touched Cecily's hand, and he felt as if he could survive anything, even the anger Vetrania was likely to loose on him shortly.

As before, Verus acted as referee, with Vetrania and Kerillian on one side of a table and Robert on the other, this time with Cecily, rather than Zeno, who asked to be excused from this particular duty. He waited with Robert's entourage.

Verus spoke first. "I propose—"

"Enough with your airy formality, Verus," Vetrania said. "It's no wonder your ancestors faded from glory to obscurity. You can't talk like a normal person."

Robert felt for his friend, but it was time the issue came to a head. He'd send him a bottle of Napene wine to smooth his feathers.

"General Dardarius," Vetrania continued, "I thank you for your decision to deliver your cousin to us. It is a great relief to me that the last of these would-be assassins is in custody. I can assure you his trial will be fair and the punishment just."

Robert maintained a deadpan expression. Matthew would be dead within days, a week at most.

"Now I must ask you about my other requests. Will you renounce your claim to the throne? And will you swear loyalty to me on behalf of yourself and your clan?"

Robert's heart beat faster. What he said next might change the course of Lucian history. It might mean the destruction of his family and perhaps his clan. He might even die at Lucian hands, but at least he could live with himself until that moment.

"Your Majesty, I must respectfully decline both requests."

A silence filled the room. Verus' eyes shifted between the parties.

"That's it?" Vetrania glanced at her lover. "You've nothing more to say, General?"

"No, ma'am, I don't. I put these questions to my clan, and few took them seriously. The feedback was universally negative." Robert shrugged, a gesture Vetrania would interpret as mocking her.

"I see. Well, it seems your entire clan is verging on sedition."

"With respect, ma'am, you can't arrest and try hundreds of thousands of clan members, not to mention their wives, husbands, children, and so on.

Vetrania shrugged herself, adding, "I have nothing more to add. I'd say the meeting was done. Do you agree?"

Robert opened his mouth, but said nothing. Verus's face paled. Something was terribly wrong, but Robert couldn't put his finger on it.

"I'm sorry," Vetrania said. "I'd forgot something. I'm placing your lovely wife Cecily under arrest."

Before Robert could react, Zeno burst into the pavilion and

moved toward Cecily, arms outstretched, face full of warning. He yelled, but a volley of bullets slammed into his back, and he pitched face down onto the polished floor. A dozen armored security men in government uniforms and balaclavas poured in, some stepping on Zeno's lifeless body. They surrounded Robert and Cecily, guns drawn. Shots and screams from outside filtered into the room. Kerillian grinned.

"General, you seemed to have forgotten that I have invoked the Seditious Utterances and Actions Act in my effort to maintain public peace. Your wife has violated that law."

A wave of terror flowed across Cecily's face. "I've never said or done anything against Your Majesty."

"Don't take me for a fool, Cecily. I have the evidence in hand. Major?"

Kerillian produced a small com device and pushed a button, playing a recording. "*Vetrania is a demon. We should hope she's dead.*" He clicked the button again. "*Vetrania is a demon. We should hope she's dead.*"

Vetrania sneered. "Is that enough evidence for you?"

"Robert, help me!"

Robert's horror nearly consumed him. He had the power of a king, at least of his clan, but in this moment, he was as helpless as a baby. "Let my wife go."

"Did you really think I would be satisfied with your cousin? Losing Matthew is nothing to you. I want you to pay a real price for your clan's arrogant behavior. Fortunately, your wife handed me a bargain. You and your pretentious family will suffer. Especially you."

Robert exploded in anger, leaning forward toward Vetrania. She flinched, but Kerillian's agents grabbed his arms before he attacked her. "You are a tyrant. You're a murderous bitch without an ounce of decency. Let my wife go. Take me instead."

"If it weren't for your position as clan leader, I'd arrest you too." Vetrania waved her hand. "But it wouldn't do. It'd cross a line. It might even make me vulnerable. Cecily is enough for now."

The security guards dragged Cecily away screaming. She begged Robert to stop her arrest, but he could do nothing. Five uniformed, faceless men held swords at his body. Life drained from him. He kicked himself. He should've foreseen the trap Vetrania had laid for him. She had no intention of stopping the war after taking Matthew into custody. The demands for loyalty and subservience were only meant to humiliate him and his clan. Soon all the world would know that he had misplayed a weak hand.

"If you harm Cecily, madam, there will be no peace between us."

"Oh come off it, General. Our clans haven't had peace for a hundred years, at least not since your great-grandfather squandered the throne, leaving us to clean up his messes. Your clan is nothing but a club of disloyal layabouts, thieves, and incompetent criminals. Cecily is just the latest example."

Vetrania turned on her heel and departed, leaving Robert alone with Verus and a squad of policemen and women who would love to cut him to pieces.

The last time Robert saw Cecily alive was ten days after Matthew was executed. He was allowed to visit her in the Regia prison for political detainees. They spent a long hour in a constant embrace. Cecily forgave him over and over again, blaming herself for failing to see the danger, and giving him hope that the long cycle of violence could be ended. He felt as if half of his soul was tearing away to vanish into some limbo from which it could not escape. Vetrania had commuted Cecily's death sentence to a terms of years at a prison camp at the edge of Lucanus near the border with the Hot Lands to the south.

No one ever returned from the camp. Vetrania's commutation was intended to torture Robert.

Months later, after no contact with Cecily, an envelope came with her wedding ring and a terse letter from the prison commandant informing Robert of her death. Though he had cried for days after he was dragged away from the Regia prison, he cried many more days by himself in their bedroom. He ordered the doors and windows covered in black, and they remained that way for a year.

Every day for that year, he kept a diary. Before he slept, he made an entry. Each entry was one sentence.

Empress Katrina Cardea Vetrania must die.

CHAPTER 19: MERLIN MAKES A TRADE

Sir Percival willed his leg to be still, but his nervousness had no other outlet. Behind him and two other men at the table, Merlin and Verus, the stolen Viridian Grail sat dormant on its mount. The lamps illuminating the dull gray metal device, encouraging it to awaken and take up its work, that is, to power the Lucian Great Machine. That assumed it was a power source. Maybe it was a control mechanism, or an interface with another device. Maybe it was just a complicated decoration, like a sculpture in front of a public building. The last speculation was the least likely, though no one knew for sure.

Not even Merlin.

Certainly not Verus and the army of scientists and engineers at the Lucian Academy of Science, which treated Merlin as a living legend. Never mind that their country's military had captured Merlin's king and regarded Merlin as his ransom price. Science was above all that, they asserted, especially when the planet's life was at stake. Merlin nodded appreciatively at their praise, and Percival mirrored the elder man's reactions. Gaining the trust of the Lucian academics was critical to Merlin's plan to rescue Arturus and return to Viridiae in one piece. With the true Grail, of course.

"Before I give you my report, Dr Verus, let me recapitulate my understanding to ensure we are all on the same page."

Verus and the scientist's hovering behind him listened gravely.

"Several years ago, the Grail device in the Lucian Great Machine—one of the twelve known devices on earth—completely failed."

"Correct. One morning, when our caretaker staff checked on it per normal procedure, it was inoperable. Scorch marks suggested an overload or a short circuit."

"You attempted a repair."

"It was futile. We couldn't even open it to see if the circuits could be rebuilt."

"In the meantime, you noted changes in the local climate."

"The changes happened quickly. Rainfall patterns, rising heat, drought. All affecting the region influenced by our Great Machine, roughly corresponding to the known geographic areas influenced by the other Great Machines in Europe, Africa, East Asia, and so on."

"Where is that failed device?"

"In a safe place."

Merlin rubbed his chin. "I take you don't want to tell me."

"It's not functional anyway."

Merlin shrugged. "If it's any consolation, Dr Verus, I've had my own problems getting my Grail to yield its secrets." He patted the pine box containing his device as if it were a resting dog.

"Your Grail?"

"Oh yes. This one belongs to me."

"How did you come by it?"

"That's not relevant. What's relevant, and outrageous, is your government's decision to steal a Grail device that doesn't belong to you." He pointed at the lifeless Viridian Grail on its mount. "And now you can't get your stolen property to work."

Verus presented a perfect mask of indifference. He wouldn't be provoked.

"On the other hand, I appreciate your desperation. Our Great Machine is also broken, and our fields are growing barren. It's only a matter of time before food grows scarce. Your great military machine has conquered a dying land. I hope you're proud of yourselves."

A lump formed in Percival's throat. He'd heard almost no unfiltered news about Viridiae since arriving in Lucana. He didn't trust the dire reports in the Lucian media, though they may have been more accurate than he allowed. He hoped he wouldn't return to a dead country.

"I don't understand something, Dr Ambrosius," Verus said.

"Just Merlin. I don't stand on ceremony."

"Why didn't you use your personal Grail to fix the Viridian Great Machine?"

Merlin waved his hands in exasperation. "Well, that was the plan until you people barged in the door. You know, invaded? I had finally teased out the secret to installing it when I got word from my government that you wanted me to fix your problem. I brought my Grail along, hoping it might offer a clue on what to do."

"Did it work?"

"What?"

"Bringing along your Grail to help you fix ours."

"Well, then, that's the heart of it, isn't it?" Merlin shrugged again. "The answer's no."

"Did you learn anything at all?"

"Nothing."

Verus face flushed. "But you only spent an hour examining our Grail. How can you expect to understand something so complicated so quickly?"

"You forget that I've been studying the Great Machine and its workings for half my lifetime. I know more about these gadgets than you know about pretty much anything. Those pre-Dissolution engineers were clever. They hid the Grail's workings pretty well. Or else, ten centuries later, human intelligence has devolved into something closer to a cockroach. I'm inclined to believe the latter scenario."

The scientists behind Verus murmured to each other. Panic rose in Verus' face. Percival wondered if he was frightened of failing to fix the Lucian Great Machine, or frightened of what Empress Vetrania might do or say when she found out.

Verus stood up from the table. "So this has been a complete

waste of time. You are nothing but a sham."

Percival perceived Verus' fallback strategy: blame Merlin.

Merlin raised his hands, hoping to halt the Lucian's tirade. "I'm not going away empty-handed. I'm expected to bring Arturus home. I intend to succeed. I have a suggestion. There's no guarantee it will work, but it's our best chance."

"I'm listening," Verus said.

"It's important to everyone, Lucian and Viridian, that at least one of our Great Machines is working. I propose to lend you my Grail, and take mine home to see if I can repair it. A simple trade among scientists. I have far more tools and more powerful computers for analysis in my lab in Camelot. Thankfully, it was spared your vandalism of the city."

"Why would we hand over our device to you?"

"Viridiae's device."

"Whatever."

"What choice to you have?"

Verus sat down again, but folded his arms. "How do you know your Grail will work?"

"I don't, but it's the only option I can think of. I have one condition."

"Yes?"

"Once my Grail device is up and running—" Merlin tapped the pine box— "you have to let myself, Arturus, and Percival leave immediately."

"I'm not sure Vetrania will agree to that. Arturus is valuable."

Merlin starting wrapping the box containing his Grail with cloth, preparing to pack it away.

"Wait a minute."

"I told you I'm not leaving empty-handed. I came up with a way both of us get what we want and you're stalling. Forget it!"

Verus turned to his colleagues, who stared at him, fearing Vetrania and the consequences of defeat. "I agree, contingent to the empress's approval. I can't offer more."

Percival let his face plead the case for accepting the offer to Merlin, but when the corner of the scientist's mouth twitched,

Percival was instantly reassured. This was all part of his plan.

"Very well, Dr Verus. I think you're negotiating in good faith. Bosses can be incredibly stupid. I'll give you that." Merlin unpacked his Grail for the second time. "I'll need some tools."

Within a few minutes, the stolen Viridian Grail was out of its mount. Merlin refused any help from the Lucian scientists and engineers. He handed the disconnected device to Percival, and it surprised him with its heaviness. If it wasn't a sold ball of metal, it was close to it.

Merlin instructed Percival to place the Grail next to his version, and hand him the latter. "Be quick about it, son."

Percival lifted Merlin's Grail, and it was lighter by far than the Lucian version. His mind filled with questions, but he remembered Merlin's admonition to pay attention to his cues and play along. Percival tried to pretend Merlin's Grail was just as heavy, but he feared his acting abilities were hopeless. As far as he could tell, however, no one in the Lucian group noticed the difference between the devices.

Merlin hooked up the power cables, poked at his device with a screwdriver, and ran a light cloth over the shiny metal sphere. He ordered the Lucians to throw the power switch. Within a second or two, red, blue and green lights glowed on the Grail, along with patches of white that reminded Percival of backlit, translucent glass. He also perceived a low hum. The object glowed and pulsed as if it had a beating heart.

The Lucian scientists cheered.

Merlin stood back, hands on hips, pleased with himself. Then he waved a finger. "Ladies and gentlemen, let's not celebrate too early. You will need to conduct a battery of tests, especially with some real world data, to see if the output will have meaning to your Great Machine. That said, I think we can call the first test a success."

Verus shook Merlin's hand vigorously. "I knew you could help us. Thank you so much."

"You're welcome. Now I'd ask that you take us immediately to Arturus."

Two Saepian guard members lounging near the lab door approached. With Merlin and Percival between them, they marched down the hall and out the Academy gate to the waiting van.

* * *

Percival sent a silent prayer of gratitude to Gaia when he saw Arturus in his cell at the Regia prison. Though they'd only be separated for a day, Percival had left his king fearing he might not see him again. At times, the despair of the march and the long train ride to Lucana had nearly broken Percival, and he leaned on Arturus for strength. Though the prison sapped his energy, Percival felt hope for escape surge when Arturus rose to greet him. They embraced as if they hadn't seen each other in 10 years.

A like span of time lay between Arturus Longshanks' and Merlin Ambrosius's last meeting, and their embrace was no less emotional, if more cordial, even distant. Arturus was the grandson of Merlin's best childhood friend, and the connection set up a different dynamic. Merlin was more like a grand-uncle, a quasi-relative Arturus only saw at weddings and funerals, though Merlin was officially Arturus' chief science adviser. In reality, Merlin lived in a rarefied world of research focused on understanding and repairing the Viridian Great Machine, which lay inside a mountain in the far west of Viridiae. Arturus rarely saw Merlin.

"You did what?" Arturus said, when Percival related the experience at the Lucian Academy of Science.

"It was necessary, Your Majesty," Merlin said.

"My life is far less important than repairing the Great Machine." Arturus' face turned bright red. He was angry, but he knew better than to lose his temper in a Lucian prison where guards and spies could gloat.

"My lord, I urge patience, as you've urged me many times." Percival held Arturus attention, willing the man to see that Merlin had a plan. However, he could not discuss it in the open for fear of alerting Vetrania and her cronies.

"We reminded Verus of his and Vetrania's promise to release you if we got the Grail working," Merlin said. "Verus is a little slow, but he's an honorable man. He'll make the case."

The three men heard nothing for days. Every day, Percival reminded himself of his own counsel of patience, knowing that demanding action on Vetrania's part was futile. Merlin sat in his cell next to Arturus', hardly saying a word, perhaps too tense to express worry that his gamble might have failed. Percival sensed that a clock was ticking for Merlin, and that his idea depended on a quick decision by Vetrania.

For his part, Arturus appeared to shrink a little into himself as time progressed. He never admitted that his hopes for release had risen, though Percival had seen it in his eyes, the way they lit up when Merlin arrived. When the topic of freedom came up, Arturus would close his mouth tight to shut down the conversation.

On the fourth day, Verus arrived at the prison to meet with the Viridians. They talked under a burning sun in the prison yard. No other prisoners loitered on the baked clay of the enclosure. Beneath Verus' stoic visage, Percival sensed bad news.

"Vetrania has ordered your Grail device installed in the Lucian Great Machine."

"That's good news," Merlin said.

"No, it's not, professor. The Academy argued for more tests, as you advised. She said the only test that mattered was at the Great Machine."

"Logical, if reckless." Merlin nodded, but his confidence was unconvincing.

"What about your agreement?" Percival said.

Arturus listened intently.

A scraping and clanking noise interrupted the conversation. A troop of Saepian guards entered the yard. Behind them walked Vetrania, dressed in street clothes and a combination hat and veil that hid much of her face.

When she dropped the veil, Verus stepped back and bowed.

"Your Majesty, I wasn't expecting—"

"Neither was I, but after I sent you here, I had second thoughts. I wanted to congratulate Professor Ambrosius personally."

"Thank you, madam." Merlin lifted his chin. "May I remind you of our agreement?"

"That was the second reason I came. Despite what many people think, I have a sense of honor, and a conscience. I couldn't send a messenger to tell you and the king of Viridiae that I'm going to break my word and keep you for awhile."

"What?" Percival blurted. "You promised! We trusted you. Merlin came all this way and gave you a working Grail. What more do you want?"

Arturus said, "I must protest in the strongest terms."

"Yes, of course," Vetrania said. "I've decided its more important that Merlin stay here and advise us on the installation and operation of the Great Machine, at least until it's working properly. Clearly, the Lucian scientific community" —She glanced at Verus— "is out of its depth. Unfortunately, this means you must stay as well, as an incentive for Merlin. I'm sorry."

"You're not sorry," Percival cried. "You planned this all along. You'd never let us go."

"Percival, stop," Arturus said.

But the young knight was almost in tears. "We've done everything you wanted. You have no honor, no decency, no conscience that I can see, you're a—"

"Percival! I order you to stop or I'll ask a guard to march you to your cell." Arturus grabbed Percival's wrist, as if fearing he would strike Vetrania. Percival wouldn't last three seconds in a fight with a Saepian.

Percival came to his senses, but he couldn't stop a tear from leaving an eye and dripping down his cheek. He missed home so much, he thought he would fall to pieces. His friends, Dee, his mother, all the things he loved, felt as far away as the moon.

Deflated, Merlin said, "I urge you to reconsider, madam."

"Why?"

"Your country may be at stake. Maybe your life."

"An empty threat. As for this boy, he needs to learn manners, but I'm not in the mood to teach them at the moment. Maybe later." She addressed Merlin. "You are my prisoner. I have need of your expertise. The companionship of your countrymen is my payment to you. That's an end to it."

With that, she turned on her heel and left, her Saepian guard in tow.

Red-faced, embarrassed, Verus followed his monarch out of the prison.

"We're running out of time," Merlin said.

"What do you mean?" Arturus said. "I know you've been protecting me from the truth, but it's time you told me what you've done."

"Sire, it might be better that you not know," Percival advised.

"No, I need to know."

Merlin sighed and whispered. "The Grail I put into their test chamber is a fake."

Arturus' jaw dropped. "Are you serious?"

"Remember last year, when you sent Galahad to lead an expedition to the island of Koda to find the Viridian Grail, which had disappeared? Galahad and Lancelot heard a rumor that the Grail might be in Perditon. They met with the mayor of that city, who sent them into the depths of an old landfill. They came out with what they thought was the Grail, or a Grail, but it turned out to be something less. It operated, but didn't do anything."

"I remember now," Arturus said. "It had the letters D-E-M-O on it from the old Latin alphabet."

"I'm sure that the letters are shorthand for another word, perhaps 'demonstration'. Anyhow, Galahad sent it to me, and I got it to function in my workshop. I quickly learned that it isn't a true Grail. It only behaves like one."

Percival wanted to join the conversation. "Merlin hoped to convince the Lucians it was real and trade it for you."

"I threw dice that Vetrania would send us home once they saw what they thought was a working Grail." Merlin sighed. "The gamble didn't pay off."

"How long before the Lucians catch on?" Arturus said.

"It took me a week to understand that the Perditon device wasn't a working Grail," Merlin said. "Another day or two, and Verus and his Academy will discover the same thing."

Arturus ran his fingers through his hair. "When Vetrania finds out, all our heads will be on pikes."

Percival swallowed.

Arturus paced along a thin shadow cast by the enclosure wall. Abruptly, he stopped. "I can only think of one thing to do. If it doesn't work, we're dead men."

"Tell Dardarius?" Merlin said.

"You read my mind, Merlin. It might be the excuse he's looking for."

Percival was nonplussed. "This is crazy. Sir."

Arturus put his hand on Percival's shoulder. "'Crazy' is all we have right now, my friend."

* * *

Percival barely closed his eyes that night. At any moment, he expected the prison guards or a troop of Saepians to barge into his cell and drag him off to an execution. His nightmare nearly came true the next morning when General Dardarius arrived with Cantwell and a half-dozen of his personal guard in swords and pistols. Dardarius wore a business suit, as did his nephew.

Percival, Merlin, and Arturus, in prison orange, waited at a table in an indoor common area. No other prisoners were in sight.

Arturus shook Dardarius' hand. "Thank you for coming."

"I meant it when I said I was at your disposal."

Percival kept a wary eye on Cantwell as Arturus introduced Merlin to the general.

"Guards, please leave us," Dardarius ordered.

The guards looked to Cantwell. "Uncle, they're here for your security."

"I'm sure you can protect me. Besides, Arturus gave me his word in his message that his intentions were honorable. I believe him."

Cantwell hesitated, then signaled the security detail to depart. Arturus invited everyone to sit.

Arturus made small talk with Dardarius, which irritated Percival, who saw the Lucian officers as murderers for what they did to the Viridian prisoners. A prison guard told Percival that all the captives had signed 10-year servitude contracts with various manufacturers, large farmers, and a few wealthy families. Percival wanted to lash out at Dardarius for treating soldiers who had fought hard for their country's freedom so poorly. Arturus, however, warned that any rash action would lead to everyone's death. Percival kept quiet. Merlin said little as well.

"Tell me what I can do for you," Dardarius said.

"I invited you here to offer a trade." Arturus folded his hands. "I've studied your life and career, General. I believe you care a great deal about your country and its future. Vetrania is, shall we say, a competitor?"

Percival grew alarmed. "Sire, pardon me, but surveillance."

"Don't worry, young man. I've given orders for surveillance devices to be switched off during my visit. My connections here know that disobedience would be costly to them."

Arturus waived his hand at Percival. "I'm going to trust my friend General Dardarius. He understands the delicacy of certain kinds of information."

Dardarius nodded. "Go on, sir."

"No doubt you've heard about the Viridian Grail?"

"I understand that it has been installed in the Lucian Great Machine in our eastern province. I also hear the scientists are having trouble with it."

"What kind of trouble?" Merlin said, worry creasing his forehead.

"I'm not an engineer, but it's not, well, doing what it's supposed to do."

"I can tell you why, General," Arturus said. "Before I do, I must ask if you are willing to grant a favor for this information."

"It depends on the favor."

Percival understood this as a "maybe." He wondered if Dardarius already knew the information, and hoped for confirmation.

"I'm asking that you find a way to release myself, Merlin, and Sir Percival into Viridian hands."

"You're asking me to defy my government, to break my vows of obedience and loyalty to Vetrania?"

"If that's how you see it, yes, that's what I'm asking."

"I'll respond to your request once I have the information you offer."

Again, Dardarius didn't reject the proposition outright. Percival was more convinced that ever that Dardarius suspected the truth.

"Very well," Arturus said. "The Viridian Grail is an inert device, built for show. It does nothing."

Dardarius blinked. The color left his face. Cantwell looked as if he'd been hit with the flat of a sword blade.

"Who knows this, besides you?" Dardarius said.

"No one in Lucanus, other than the people at this table," Arturus said.

Dardarius rose and paced a few steps. "You realize that once this is discovered, you'll be executed."

"Yes, General. I also know that you are looking for leverage over Vetrania. You want to be emperor."

"That is laughable." Dardarius didn't laugh, though, and neither did Cantwell. "I'm as loyal to her as Percival and Merlin are to you."

"General," Merlin said, "we know what happened with your wife. We know that you have sought revenge."

"And I know that you believe Vetrania to be driving Lucanus to ruin, even as her people begin to feel the effects of the Great Machine's failure and the changing climate."

"The Grail has nothing to do with," Dardarius hesitated, "my opinions about Vetrania's rule. There are more immediate considerations."

"Such as?"

"The Ontarii are massing on our northern border. And the tribes in the Hot Lands to the south are raiding us daily. I'm certain Lord Mordred is somehow behind this. We are stretched thin trying to cope with these threats."

"Avoid this war, General." Arturus almost pleaded. "Be ready when the truth about the Grail is revealed. Vetrania will never be weaker."

Dardarius grinned, but the gesture had little humor. "You don't understand us as well as you think you do, sir. Lucanus cannot avoid war. It is embedded within us. We fight because it is all we know."

"Then use the truth to fight for what you believe in, even if it is simply getting rid of a leader who doesn't deserve her place."

Dardarius stood in a place where he could see all the cells in the block where the three Viridians were held. Percival had never seen another prisoner, but he could occasionally hear doors open and shut with a metallic jolt that sent a shiver up his back. Watching Dardarius, he wondered if the general was imagining himself in one of the cells.

"You're asking too much, Majesty. I can't just escort you out of the Regia as if Vetrania had signed the release papers."

"I'm sure you can be creative, General Dardarius."

Dardarius and Arturus met each other's gaze. Their rapport surprised Percival. He could never imagine being other than Dardarius' enemy.

"Tribune Cantwell, please call my security team. It's time to go." Dardarius reached out a hand to Arturus. "You've given me an important opportunity, sir. Keep a watchful eye for yours."

CHAPTER 20: A CHASE THROUGH LUCANUS

Dee and Guinevere's Ontarii vessel nudged the pier below the minor Lucian port's smoking center. Charred hulks of partly submerged enemy galleys cluttered the shore. On the beach, captured legionnaires collected bloated bodies from the surf line. Queen Jarnay had ordered a punitive raid on the city as retaliation for Lucian depredations on her side of the freshwater sea. That was the public justification for the action, which was blessed by an overwhelming majority of the populace. Behind the scenes, the queen approved the raid as a favor to Lord Mordred. Jarnay agreed with Guinevere: Lucanus was a common enemy to Viridiae and Ontari:io, and joint action would check Lucian expansion.

In a secret communique to Jarnay, Mordred promised further action, and soon.

Lancelot reveled in the opportunity to see action again. Bored in Villefroide, she boarded a troop transport and attached herself to Captain Tintan's command. Borrowing a set of Ontarii armor, she strapped on Arondight and posted videos to the com net of her one-woman slaughter of surprised and terrified Lucian soldiers. The breach of security angered Ontarii military leadership, but it didn't take long for them to realize that Lancelot's self-promotion made perfect psychological warfare. Ontarii intelligence flooded Lucian media with the videos, which undercut enemy claims of little damage and few casualties from the incursion. The videos disappeared from com groups within hours, but the impact lasted for days. Lucian pundits called for an investigation, and the few independent journalists in Lucanus openly questioned Regia generals about how the most famous and dangerous Viridian knight had managed to embed herself in an Ontarii unit.

Guinevere and Dee ate a meal of bread, cheddar cheese, and wine with Lancelot at the captured city hall.

"Why haven't they counter-attacked?" Guinevere said. "Jarnay's been generous, but some of the Ontarii officers complain of under-manning. If the Lucians regroup, we're done."

"Vetrania pulled local troops to defend Lucanus' southern border," Lancelot said. "The Hot Lands' tribes are causing a lot of trouble. It seems Bors and Galahad are doing a pretty good job of stirring the pot."

"I feel like we've been too successful," Guinevere said.

"How is that possible?" Dee said.

"The Lucians were under-strength to start with and we caught them completely by surprise. They ran like scared rabbits." Lancelot tore off another chunk of bread. "They're regrouping though. That's what the drone and signals intelligence says. Ontarii units have already been evacuated from positions to the east before the Lucians counterattack."

"But we've only just got here," Dee said.

"Jarnay promised a raid, not an invasion to take and hold territory," Guinevere said. "It's worked so far, I think. Vetrania is distracted on two fronts. She's probably pulled troops off her Viridian campaign to deal with both crises."

"If that's true, Mordred will move in immediately to fill the gap. And he won't stop there. He'll attack with everything he has while the Lucians are off-balance."

"Mordred wants us to meet him while he moves east," Guinevere said.

"How are we going to get through Lucanus to Mordred? Going back the way we came through Ontari:io would take months."

"Tintan volunteered to help us," Lancelot said. "She's a good soldier. Knows her business."

"When do we leave?" Dee said.

"Tonight," Lancelot said. "The counterattack is expected to-morrow. We don't want to get caught in that storm."

Late that evening, the three Viridians rode out of the still-burning city, accompanied by Tintan and a squad of Ontarii lancers. The sky was clouded over, and with the electricity out, the darkness proved perfect cover. One of the lancers had spent a summer in the city, and he guided the party through the destruction. Often the guide had to risk showing a dim lamp to find his way. When it shown, Dee saw broken vehicles, burned-out structures, and the occasional body. She smelled them before she saw them.

By dawn, the group reached the city's outer suburbs. A ground fog rose from the fields beyond the town, and Tintan risked a brisker pace. The guide claimed that the road, built before the Dissolution, when the world fell apart, went straight through to the coast of the Peaceful Sea. Dee had a hard time believing the tale, given the choking weeds and broken concrete. By the time the sun burned off the fog, the party was alone on a landscape as flat as a griddle, with only clutches of trees and scattered, squat structures to break up the plain.

After a night spent in a gully with a gurgling stream, the party set out again. The sun rose hot, and Dee studied a circling bird overhead. It hovered for a moment, and Dee thought of the kite, which hovered over prey before striking. However, this bird was far too high for a dive onto a mouse or vole, and her heart skipped a beat.

"Lancelot, that's not a drone, is it?"

The Viridian knight shaded her eyes. "Crap. Tintan, is that one of yours?"

The Ontarii officer called for field glasses. "Nope. I think it's safe to say we've been spotted."

The drone sped to the south, as if it realized it, too, had been discovered.

"Where's the nearest Lucian garrison, Tintan?"

"On the map, it's about a day's ride."

"We can't take the chance they'll ignore us," Guinevere said.

"We don't belong out here. They'll send a search party to take a look."

Lancelot pointed to distant peaks. "What about those mountains?"

"They're out of our way, but we might be able to lose pursuers."

"Or get lost ourselves," Dee said.

"We don't have a lot of options."

Tintan ordered a slow trot toward the hills, which the guide said were badlands with no fodder for the animals and little water. At midday, Tintan ordered a stop at another stream, where the riders stuffed every pocket and bag with grass and filled their water bags to the brim.

For three days, the party managed to edge west through box canyons on nearly invisible trails. They moved day and night, resting only when they fell asleep in their saddles. Every morning, however, a dust cloud to the east gained on them, a sign of the pursuing Lucians who knew this territory as their own. Lancelot and Tintan conferred, and they explained to Guinevere discovery by the pursuers was only a matter of time.

"We have a plan, but you won't like it, my lady," Lancelot said.

"Everyone's exhausted, and the food and fodder are nearly gone. I'm ready to try anything."

Lancelot and Tintan climbed to the top of a hill and surveyed the landscape. When they returned to camp, they laid out their plans.

"We'll split into two groups. There's a narrow canyon with a stream about a half-kilometer from here. I will lead the first group through the stream. We'll make a lot of noise to make sure they follow us. Guinevere and Dee will be with me. Tintan will lead the second group of his lancers on either side of the canyon. When the Lucian enter the canyon, we'll slaughter them."

Dee lay on her blanket all night, staring at the carpet of stars in the sky. She might never seen them again after tomorrow, nor see her brother again, a thought that tortured her. She hadn't felt anything from him for months, except for flashes like daydreams. However, she never wavered from the feeling that he was alive and well, though in distress.

The morning sun cast deep shadows in the landscape, providing sharp contrasts in the sandy grays, light ochres, and rusts of the talus-sloped hills. Lancelot, Dee, Guinevere and one of the Ontarii lancers tied loose items to the animals to increase their noise. Another lancer trailed the main group to watch for Lucian pursuers. The cacophony echoed around the walls of the canyon as the party trudged through the trickle at their feet.

The mouth of the canyon loomed ahead.

"I hope Tintan is in position," Lancelot said. "If she's late, we're fucked if we're discovered too soon."

As if responding to a prophesy, the lancer at the rear shouted. Another discordant set of sounds echoed around the walls, and when the lancer turned a corner, racing up the stream bed on his horse, a half-dozen Lucian cavalry were only meters behind him.

"Run like hell!" Lancelot screamed, drawing Arondight and charging into the narrow arroyo. Guinevere, Dee, and the second lancer kept up, but the rear lancer's horse stumbled and fell. The Lucian horsemen trampled the lancer to death.

"Get through the gap. It widens out." Lancelot urged everyone through, waving Arondight like a flag. She glanced up to the canyon walls, as if wishing for Tintan to appear. Her wish came true when the Lucians slowed to pass through the gap, which was wide enough for only one horseman at a time. Tintan and her Ontarii warriors dropped out of the sky like hawks on the Lucians.

The surprised legionaries halted and backpedaled in an attempt to regroup, but oncoming Lucians behind them transformed into a wall that stopped their retreat. Tintan fired her pistol and slashed with her sword, desperate to keep the stampede from overwhelming them.

"Run Guinevere! Run Dee!" Lancelot shouted. "We'll take care of them, but you have to get away."

"No," Tintan barked. "Dee can use her power to stop this."

Dee gulped. She hadn't thought about her ability to kill or

maim at a distance. She'd only done it in the past when her brother or her dearest friends such as Lancelot was in danger. She barely knew Tintan or her lancers.

What's more, Dee didn't know if she could stop so many of the enemy. Dozens of them pressed on Lancelot and the Ontarii.

Tintan saw Dee's hesitation. "You have to help us. It's our only chance. It's our only advantage."

Dee closed her eyes, imagining the surging mass of Lucian and Ontarii bodies, blood and gore spitting onto the canyon walls. She couldn't comprehend the chaos. Lancelot was right. She and Guinevere had to save themselves.

Dee urged Guinevere away, but the queen hesitated, looking back at the hot fight. "Lancelot, I can't leave you."

Lancelot stepped away from a Lucian she had just killed. "There's more Lucians coming up the arroyo. You can't help me. Run! Now!"

Tears streamed down Guinevere's face. Dee pulled her queen away, hearing Tintan's last plea for help. The women mounted their horses and took off at a gallop on the widening floor of the canyon. The clash of swords and screams of dying soldiers faded into nothing, until Dee heard only birdsong and the whispers of wind among the hills. She blinked and wiped away her own tears.

Dee and Guinevere traveled for hours until they left the bad-lands and entered a broad, endless plain. They stopped by a copse of trees and made camp. Guinevere wanted to make a fire, but Dee objected. "Wouldn't that tell the Lucians where we are?"

"No, Lancelot took care of them. She needs the fire to know where to find us."

Dee didn't have the heart to remind Guinevere that Lancelot, Tintan and the Ontarii might be dead, having given up their lives so the Queen of Viridiae could escape. Could she have helped them? The insanity of the fighting overwhelmed her, even as she struggled to remember the details.

Despite their exhaustion, neither Dee or Guinevere could sleep. Night animals startled Dee more than once, but they didn't hear the sound of humans until around midnight. The muffled clunk of armor was unmistakable, and Dee drew her dagger.

"It's me," Lancelot said.

Guinevere leaped up and raced to her lover, kissing her sweaty, blood-spattered mouth with no regard for whose blood it might be. After a moment, they collapsed near the fire.

Dee offered Lancelot a cup of water from a nearby pond. In the flickering light, Lancelot was covered from head to toe with blood and gore. Pieces of her armor were missing, but Arondight was safe in its scabbard.

Something was different about Lancelot. Whenever Dee saw Lancelot after a tournament or a battle, she was exhilarated, even exultant, ready to boast of every kill. This time, her face showed shock, as if she'd seen something she'd ever expected, or disbelief at what she had witnessed.

"Where are Tintan and the others?" Dee said.

The question snapped Lancelot out of her reverie. "They aren't coming."

"They're dead." Guinevere lowered her head in grief. "They saved our lives."

Tintan's plea echoed again in Dee's memory.

"I've never seen warriors fight so hard as Tintan and the lancers," Lancelot said. "The Lucians must've sent a hundred legionnaires against us. We killed half before they gave up. The bodies were piled so high, they blocked the arroyo. Blood made the stream a rushing river." Lancelot exhaled. "I was on the other side of that abattoir. I saw Tintan go down. She was the last of the Ontarii. There's was nothing more I could do, so I came here to protect you."

Dee covered her face. Should she have tried harder? Maybe hurt one or two of the Lucians? She felt she could've done something to help the lost Ontarii.

Guinevere took Lancelot's hand, kissed it, and held its palm against her cheek. "Please don't make me leave you like that again."

"Not a chance. I have to get you home and safe. That's all I'm here for."

Dee thought she knew what she was "here" for. She thought it was to make art and help her queen. Now, she wasn't so sure.

CHAPTER 21:
PERCIVAL AND THE
TRUE GRAIL

The somnolent heat pressed down on Percival as he lay in the darkness of his cell. In his half-dreaming state, he turned over General Dardarius' final words to Arturus, advising the Viridians to be watchful for an opportunity. Was Dardarius teasing the prisoners? What kind of opportunity? When? In the thin hours of the early morning, the chance presented itself.

A plink woke Percival from a doze. Percival thought he heard a footfall, and he rolled out of his cot. He peered through the bars down the corridor, hearing Merlin's snoring, and Arturus' breathing, but nothing more. On the concrete floor at his feet, illuminated by moonlight, a metal object about the width and length of his forefinger reflected the pale glow. He'd seen the guards use them to open and close the cell doors, as well as the gates to the cell block. One guard explained that the codes embedded in the keys were changed every night to thwart escape attempts with stolen keys.

Sweating hard in anticipation, Percival placed the key over a panel next to the door, as he had seen the guards do, except that the panel was on the other side of the wall. Nothing happened. Percival tried to remember the panel's exact location. He had no idea if the key had to touch the panel or if he had to hold it within close proximity. He inched the key along the wall, visualizing the panel. After an eternity of searching, he heard a click.

He pushed the door, and it opened.

The metal door didn't screech or creak, as if it had just been oiled. He half expected a guard to jump at him, perhaps kill him with a sword blow, but the corridor was quiet as a grave. On previous evenings, he heard bored guards gambling in a glass-enclosed office behind the cell block. Tonight, all was silent. On hands and knees, like a cat stalking a mouse, he approached Merlin's cell door. He held the key to the panel, and the indicator light changed from green to amber. The light changed from amber to red when Percival pulled on the handle.

Percival laid a hand on Merlin's slumbering form. "Wake up! We're leaving."

Merlin snuffled and groaned, brushing away Percival's hand. The young knight shook Merlin harder and the old man opened his eyes. Percival put a finger on Merlin's mouth to keep him quiet. He pointed to the open cell door, and moved two fingers, as if a person was walking.

An instant later, Percival was in Arturus' cell. The king of Viridiae was awake, but laying still. Percival signaled Arturus to say nothing, but he showed him the key.

"This is what Dardarius promised, my lord."

Arturus nodded. Within moments, all three prisoners padded down the corridor. The key opened the cell block door. Miraculously, the tiny office for the guard was empty, except for a pine box. Merlin snatched it from its shelf and confirmed its contents: the Grail belonging to Viridiae. The False Grail had to be back at the Science Academy.

With each step, Percival imagined an alarm and the whole Lucian army pouring into the prison. But everything was happening according to somebody's plan. The Viridians, however, had no idea of their role in a larger scheme.

Percival didn't allow himself to speculate. For most of his waking moments in the prison, he had imagined several scenarios by which he might escape with Arturus and then Merlin. He had memorized the route from the cells to the gate where he and Arturus had arrived. Luckily, it was not the main gate, but in an spot hidden from the street. He felt naked, however, without any kind of weapon, save his own hands, and he knew how to kill with them. He prepared himself for an encounter with a guard, but to his amazement, he saw none. After a left turn and then a right, he spied the secondary entrance.

"What if this is a trap?" Merlin said, clutching the true Grail. "What if this is a way for Dardarius to claim credit for stopping an escape attempt and taking back what is ours?"

"There's a million scenarios, but I don't think he cares that much about the Grail and the Great Machine," Arturus said. "He wants one thing, and that is revenge."

"And to sit on the Lucian throne," Percival added.

"Indeed. We're playing some sort of part in his game, but I don't care what it might be. Let's make the most of our chance."

Percival touched the key to the entrance door panel, and after a double-click, it swung out on its own, powered by an electric motor.

Cantwell, the tribune and Dardarius' nephew, was waiting for them.

"I fucking knew it." Percival snarled like a dog. He put himself between Cantwell and Arturus. "I'll kill you if you touch us."

"Shut up, you damned fool. I'm here to guide you out of the city."

"Bullshit. You're going to hand us over to Vetrania."

"You're here on Dardarius' orders," Merlin said.

"Of course, I am. He's my clan leader. I'm bound to him. I obey him in all things."

"Bound to kill us, you mean," Percival said.

"You should've died at the River Colum." Cantwell could not conceal his contempt. "As far as I'm concerned, you are barbarians who deserve to be conquered and absorbed into Greater Lucanus. But Dardarius wants you gone. I don't know why, but that's not my problem. Do you want to leave Lucana or not?"

Arturus said. "Please lead the way."

Reluctantly, Percival broke the locked stare he'd put on Cantwell, while noting that the Lucian had unhooked the loop that held his short sword in its scabbard. Was he expecting trouble? Or was he going to disobey Dardarius and kill him, Arturus and Merlin when he got the chance? Percival had no choice but to follow Cantwell into the night.

The Lucian kept to side streets and alleys, urging his three charges to maintain a quick pace. Though Lucana presented itself as a well-scrubbed, orderly city, a model for urban design and planning, its hidden paths were as dirty and smelly as any Percival had experienced, even in Camelot. Glass and steel towers rose above them, half-lit like a holiday decoration left up too long. At ground level, rats screamed as feline predators devoured a meal. Cities were always a reflection of their population's aspirations and secret embarrassments.

Even as Percival appreciated Cantwell's effort to conceal their path, he could not understand Arturus' forbearance of the man. The king was always so solicitous, so reasonable, so willing to talk in a civilized way with people whom Percival thought were beneath him. Did Arturus not see Cantwell and all Lucians for who they were? Were they not monsters bent on pillaging their neighbors and enslaving their people? Percival understood better Merlin's attitude, that the Lucians were gullible enough to be tricked by a few flashing lights, but Arturus seemed willing to lend them trust. Percival heard that Arturus was manipulating Dardarius, but it all seemed too friendly. Percival doubted he could pull off such an act. Honest action was more honorable.

He could not look at Cantwell without thinking of the death march from the River Colum battlefield. His compatriots were little more than cattle to the tribune. Percival understood what the lamb felt like as it was led to slaughter. Would they ever know justice?

After an hour of steady walking, with an occasional burst of speed to avoid a patrolling police officer, the Lucian and the Viridians arrived at one of the dozens of sally ports in Lucana's exterior fortifications. No one guarded the inside of the port, another measure prearranged by Dardarius. Cantwell waved a key removed from a pocket in front of the identification panel, and the door, wide enough for two legionnaires, clicked open.

Before them was a ground car that could transport four passengers. The license plate displayed the Dardarian sigil. Cantwell pressed his thumb near the left-hand door and both doors on either side opened.

"This is a newly developed self-powered, intelligent vehicle," Cantwell said. "It's one of only two in General Dardarius' collection. It will take you as close to the Viridian border as it safely can."

The three Viridians glanced at each other.

"None of us drive," Arturus said.

"The intelligence device will drive you. It's been programmed with the best route."

"You mean it's been programmed with a route right into Vetrania's hands," Percival said.

Cantwell sneered. "You are the rudest, most suspicious man I've ever met. What do you take General Dardarius for?"

Percival hardly heard Cantwell. Something about the tribune enraged the young knight. He thought he'd go blind with anger, starting with the moment he first saw him on the River Colum. It grew like a boil on Percival's soul every day since, and the pain had become unbearable.

"Are you coming with us, Tribune?" Arturus said.

"No, Your Majesty. I'm instructed to send you alone."

"See, sire? It's a trap."

Cantwell ignored Percival. "No one will stop you. As far as police or military are concerned, you are General Dardarius himself, heading to the front. That's how the car's security beacon will identify you. You won't be challenged."

"It's more than we could ever have expected, Tribune. We're grateful to you and your commander."

Cantwell nodded an acknowledgment. Not quite a salute, but as much as he could manage. Cantwell did the same with Merlin, who followed Arturus into the car. Merlin held the true Grail like a baby.

Percival and Cantwell stood facing each other.

"Well?" Cantwell said.

Moving as fast as a crossbow bolt, Percival snatched Cantwell's sword from the Lucian's belt. It slid out easier than Percival expected. Before the Lucian could recover from his surprise, Percival stabbed Cantwell below the breast, cleanly slicing his heart in two. In the few seconds between the piercing and his death, Cantwell's eyes begged to ask why, but the blow had taken his breath as well. He was dead by the time his face hit the pavement.

Percival felt nothing. No exultation. No guilt. No regret. He only exhaled, as if he had held his breath for a year.

A hand grabbed his pants' waist band and pulled hard. "Percival! In the car!"

Percival dropped the sword, which clanked and bounced, its blade finally leaning against Cantwell's lifeless body. He heard a shout, but he couldn't tell if it was Arturus, or Merlin, or a Lucian who'd seen the murder and raised an alarm. His mind turned to mush, all of his will a ghost.

Percival didn't resist Arturus' pull into the car's seat. The doors closed, and Merlin tapped in the start code, according to instructions given to him by Cantwell. The car accelerated away. A mirror, showing Percival the scene to the rear, framed Cantwell's corpse like a macabre portrait.

* * *

The car followed the same evasive strategy as Cantwell. It stuck to side streets and two-lane arterials in the suburbs outside the defensive wall. Once or twice it back-tracked, giving the sense that it had seen something to avoid. Maybe pursuing police. Percival found it hard to care. He stared at his right hand, the one that had held Cantwell's sword, and laughed at the fact no blood stained it, not even a drop. No blood stained his clothes, either.

But he'd crossed a threshold, one he could never re-cross. He'd killed his share of soldiers and knights on the battlefield. He'd killed to protect his beloved country and his king. But he'd never murdered a man in cold blood. He was angry, even enraged by all he'd witnessed since the River Colum, but taking a man's sword and sticking him with it because you were having a bad time of things wasn't right. Cantwell was a war criminal, of that Percival was sure, but even war criminals faced a judge and jury, because even one exception to the law threatened protections for everyone. That's what his teachers said, and his mother, and his sister. He believed it, as well.

Then why did he kill Cantwell, even if he deserved death?

"Why did you do it, Percival?" Arturus echoed Percival's thoughts.

The intelligent car sped through fields of corn and soybeans, the outskirts of Lucana many kilometers behind them.

"Because someone had to pay for what the Lucians have done to us." Percival didn't believe his own excuse.

Arturus shook his head. "The problem with murdering someone is that you can only do it once. Cantwell was an ally."

"He hated us."

"He was a friend because Dardarius is a friend. Of a kind, at least. With Cantwell slain, obviously by one of us, Dardarius has less reason to help us escape."

"We would know by now if Dardarius had changed his mind," Merlin said. "He still sees advantage in setting us free."

"I wouldn't be surprised if this car suddenly stopped and turned around."

The car sped on, accelerating on straight sections of the lonely road, jostling its passengers. In the early glow of dawn, Percival saw a low range of mountains.

"Percival, as your friend, and your king, killing Cantwell the way you did was wrong. Even if he was a war criminal, we needed him."

Arturus spoke the words quietly, thoughtfully, which made them hurt more. After hours of feeling nothing, of seeing little except Cantwell's stricken face, Arturus' words pierced him like lances. What had happened to him? It was as if a sleeping demon emerged without warning to take over his body and strike out. Percival thought of himself as a good person, a loyal Viridian, but he had done something he never thought possible of himself. War criminal or not, Cantwell deserved better, and Percival had stolen something he could never give back.

The car sped west, and with each kilometer, the landscape became drier, and more sparsely populated. They managed to avoid anything resembling a town, only once passing through a village that appeared abandoned. Merlin complained of a full bladder and an empty stomach, but Arturus wouldn't risk stopping the vehicle, even if they figured out how. Finally, after 20 hours of non-stop travel, the car rolled to a stop and opened its doors.

The paved road had simply ended at the foot of a low mountain, one in a range that stretched roughly north and south. The road continued, but its concrete morphed into rutted gravel that deteriorated as Percival scanned ahead. Perhaps the car had rebelled before taking its chances on such a track.

"Take this." Merlin handed Percival the box with the Grail. "I've got to take a leak and a shit like you wouldn't believe." The old man hid himself in a clump of cottonwoods, grabbing a handful of leaves before squatting behind scrub.

Percival and Arturus took care of their business as well. As Merlin returned with a large grin on his face, the doors of the car closed, and it drove back the way it came.

"Fascinating technology." Merlin smacked his lips. "I wish I could've examined it in more detail."

"All we can do is start walking." Arturus gazed up the mountain and down the gravel road. "We have no food and no water."

"There's water in a creek on the other side of the cottonwood grove," Merlin said.

"We've nothing to carry it with."

"Maybe that's what Dardarius wanted," Percival said. "For us to disappear, to die of thirst in a wasteland."

"It doesn't matter at this point," Arturus said. "We're here, and he's a thousand kilometers away."

Arturus took off down the gravel track. Like Percival and Merlin, he wore a prison jumper and sandals. Within a kilometer, the unstable gravel gave way to dirt and grass, which was easier on the feet, still calloused from the trek across the desert.

The car dropped them off within an hour of sunset, and while they made good time, the temperature quickly dropped. They found a tumbledown shack full of spiders and mice, but they had nothing with which to make a fire. Percival and Arturus drew on their survival training, but a half-hour of attempts amounted to nothing. The three of them fell asleep huddled together, with nothing but torn clumps of dried grass as a makeshift blanket.

The morning brought a rain shower, which made the three men laugh. Percival found a rusted cup, and he captured rainwater sluicing off the shack's nearly see-through roof. Merlin discovered a clump of wild strawberries, and though each could only have three of the berries, the meal refreshed them. For the first time in weeks, Percival felt a sense of hope.

The road curved around the mountain, and then it ended at a wall of sand. A dune of fine dust blocked their way, and when they climbed to the top in bare feet to see if the road continued, Percival's heart sank. Laid out before them, like a vast, still sea, was a dry basin, its flat aspect broken only by charcoal-colored clumps of greasewood. It resembled the landscape of the death march, so many months ago, only more desolate.

Arturus licked his lips. "We'll wait until nightfall. It would be stupid to cross that during the day."

"Cross that?" Merlin pointed west. "We'll never make it halfway. We might as well face Vetrania's mercy."

"What do you think, Percival?"

Over the course of the day, Percival's thoughts had grown darker. His sandals fell apart and stones cut his feet. Each step was a painful burden, taking him toward an end he couldn't imagine. He had no reason to go back, and he was finding it harder to find a reason to go forward. How could he face Dee and his friends after what he had done in Lucana?

"I'll do whatever you wish of me, my lord." Percival said it mostly because he thought it was expected of him.

"Good lad. I know this is hard. We'll rest a while, and start when the moon comes up."

The darkness brought cooler temperatures, and the moon illuminated the white sand almost as brightly as the noon sun, but they had to wait hours while the ground cooled enough to walk on. The outline of the distant mountains was easy to see against the expanse of stars in the clear sky. For a moment, Percival forgot the hopelessness of their situation under the canopy of night. The Viridians walked west, at least in the direction that was their best guess, with the North Star off their right shoulder.

Walking all night, with thirst tearing at their throats like a beast, they reached the other shore of the dry sea of crystalline sand. Exhausted beyond words, Percival found a shadow under a boulder and lay his head on a low pillow of sand. He thought briefly of scorpions and spiders, snakes and rats, but he didn't care if they attacked him. He was too tired to think of anything but sleep. His companions felt much the same way, though Merlin clung to the box with the true Grail as if it were his grandchild.

A smell awakened Percival. It resembled death, but not of corpses on a battlefield. It had a thick sweetness to it, not unlike sour milk, or cheese left too long in an icebox. Percival got to his swollen feet, his joints aching as if he had aged 20 years, and discovered walls surrounding his makeshift campsite. They had stumbled into the ruins of a town.

"It must be a thousand years old, going back to the Dissolution." Merlin gazed in wonderment. "Nothing left but the formed concrete foundations of the buildings."

"Smell that?" Percival needed to make sure he wasn't imaging the stench.

Arturus wandered along a wide division between two lines of low walls, perhaps an ancient street. "Over here."

Shining in the low corner of a wall was the surface of an algae choked pond. The occasional showers that traveled through the region, like the one that blessed the travelers their first night out of the car, had left evidence of their passing in this overgrown puddle. Percival climbed over the top of the wall with one goal: a long drink of water.

"Wait, Percival, it's likely to make you sick," Arturus called, unconvincingly.

Percival ignored his sire and stumbled to the puddle's edge. Kneeling, he carefully moved the mat of algae aside to reveal a clear surface. He scooped up a taste in the palm of his hand. "It's delicious, my lord. If I'm to be sick, then at least I will not die of thirst."

Arturus and Merlin needed little convincing to join Percival.

The warm, brackish water refreshed the three men. Food became their next concern, but nothing remained in the town that resembled food storage. The civilization that had built this town had disappeared with the changing climate, and not even the Great Machines and the true Grail could save it.

With nothing to carry liquid, the Viridians waited until the sun touched the top of the mountains, drank another mouthful, and took off into the mountains again. None of them fell ill, and Percival allowed himself hope again, if only as a way to motivate himself up a slope between two peaks. Deep, unnatural cuts into the worn hills to either side suggested a road once climbed this mountain. Arturus hoped it would lead to another abandoned settlement and another cache of rainwater.

The trail ended at the edge of a chasm. Merlin examined the edge and its mirror image on the other side. He guessed that a bridge had once spanned it, but it had fallen to dust long ago. The still air allowed sound to rise from the darkness below, and Percival swore he heard the trickle of water. Arturus agreed. Because they couldn't cross the gorge, they had no choice but to climb down, perhaps to find fresh water and shelter.

With the sun at its zenith, Percival picked his way down the steep walls, stopping every few steps to find purchase in the loose stones. Merlin followed Arturus, and they traded the burden of the awkward box with the Grail. Smooth sandstone boulders blocked near every passage, but Percival managed to find a way through the maze. After an hour, Percival found a narrow, steep ledge that angled down to a shelf of round stone and gravel that might be the riverbed. He pressed his body against the dusty wall, keeping his center of gravity inward, but the footing was terrible, and he skated a meter on the ledge as if he were on an ice rink. Sharp edges sliced into the calluses on his feet.

Until now, Merlin had managed the climb like a man fifty years younger, but his age caught up with him. He froze at the top of the ledge, his knees visibly trembling. Arturus was behind him.

"Don't worry, Merlin. I have your shirt in my grasp. You won't fall."

Merlin clung to the box. "I'll never get down carrying this thing. I'm shaking so hard, I'm afraid I'll drop it."

"Percival, can you take the Grail from Merlin?"

Percival didn't want to answer. The ledge under his feet was only a few centimeters wider than the width of his foot. It had taken almost an hour to inch his way down with falling thirty or forty meters to boulders below. His body was starting to shake as well from thirst, hunger, and exhaustion.

But Merlin would never make it with that damned box under his arm. All Viridiae's hopes for its healing were contained in that package.

"Hand the Grail to me, Merlin," Percival said. "I'll get it down safely."

Merlin hesitated, then held out the box with both hands as Arturus held him steady. Percival gently took the box and wrapped his left arm around it while keeping his right hand on a hold. Closing his eyes, he willed his thudding heart to calm itself, but it wouldn't listen. Looking at his leading foot, he inched it forward. His other foot followed, and he took took more steps. He grinned to himself. "We'll make it, sire! Only a few more steps."

A slice of the ledge gave way, and Percival slipped. Instinctively, he loosened his grip on the Grail, and it fell down the sheer drop. A cry escaped Percival's throat as the box seemed to float in mid-air, but it plunged straight down, smashing on a flat boulder. The box exploded, releasing the silvery, round Grail, which fell further until it hit another stone and disintegrated as if pulverized by a hammer. The pieces disappeared into the shadows.

Percival couldn't look at his companions. A wave of shame coursed through him like a fever. A lifetime ago, he had promised Arturus he would find the true Grail and bring it back to Viridiae for Merlin to install in the Great Machine and save his country and his king. Merlin had found it, but the old sage-scientist had entrusted it to him, and five minutes later, he had destroyed it. He had utterly failed at everything, starting with his capture at the River Colum, his inability to do anything for his fellow soldiers on the death march, his impulsive murder of the tribune Cantwell. So much had depended on him, and if his country blamed its final destruction on him, he would deserve it.

"Percival! Keep going! We need to get to the river bed." Arturus' voice broke through Percival's despair. "I'll help Merlin."

Somehow, Percival managed to slither down the rest of the ledge until he reached a low shelf above the trickling water. He helped Merlin down, and the elder collapsed into a heap of exhaustion. Percival grabbed Arturus' hand, and the king's grip surprised him with its strength.

"Let's get Merlin to the stream."

Percival and Arturus lifted the semi-conscious Merlin onto their shoulders and carried him to the stream bank. Mercifully, the stream flowed in shade. They brought water in cupped hands to Merlin and washed his face to cool him. After a few minutes, the century-old scientist revived.

Percival drank deeply from the stream, but after the adrenaline of the moment wore off, a numbness much like that which he felt after killing Cantwell overcame him. He sat against a boulder worn smooth by millennia of water and stared at a swirling vortex in the stream.

"Merlin is sleeping," Arturus said. "I think he'll be fine."

Percival could not meet Arturus' gaze. "I'm sorry, my lord."

Percival's defense crumbled like the bridge that once spanned the gorge. Tears flowed freely with his sobs.

Arturus put his arms around his knight and held him like a child.

CHAPTER 22: A PAINFUL REUNION

Percival, Arturus, and Merlin rested as the shadows in the gorge deepened. Percival stayed at his spot, watching the water gurgle, letting his thoughts wander. Though they followed no pattern, they always came back to Dee, and how much he missed his twin sister. If he ever made it back to Camelot, and saw her again, he'd ask her to come with him to their mother's cottage in the King's Forest, and forget about knighthood, Grails, and war.

"Come along, Percival. Merlin is going to rest while we do some exploring."

Ever obedient, Percival responded to Arturus' prod by following him up the bank of the stream. After a few dozen meters, they found shards from the wrecked Grail device, enough to carry in their arms. They left the splintered box alone. They brought the shards to Merlin.

"Collisions between ancient electronics and sandstone don't end well," Merlin concluded.

"Is there anything you can do with these?" Arturus said.

"I had a hard enough time figuring this out when it was whole. In pieces? And only partially intact? It would be a miracle. Still —" Merlin stood and pushed a few fragments into his pockets. "—I might learn something."

"What do we do now, my lord?"

Arturus ran his hand over his dust-caked hair. "Water always leads to people. The question is upstream or downstream?" The king sighed, and he walked with the water's flow.

After climbing down the edge of a cataract, the gorge opened up to a valley that became a broad plain in the distance. The stream meandered among cottonwoods growing among reeds and tall grasses. Red-winged blackbirds perched on old cattails, while sparrows flitted among the grasses. The cool evening air invited Percival to sit and rest, despite his gnawing pit of hunger.

"I found some blackberries," Merlin said. "They're bitter, and don't eat too many."

Arturus found huckleberries and shared a handful with Percival. The sweet taste only made him hungrier, but he followed Merlin's advice.

Percival heard rustling in the grass, and he fashioned a snare from long blades of grass. Minutes later, after smashing its skull with a rock, he held a jackrabbit by the ears. Arturus managed to scrape off much of the fur and gut it with a sharp rock. Merlin concocted a fire, and the three Viridians ate their first real meal in many days.

Night fell, and a chill came over the plain. The fire provided warmth, and though Percival worried that enemies might see the light or smoke, all three men were too exhausted to care. Nonetheless, a low rumble kept Percival awake. At first, he thought it might be thunderstorms in the foothills, but the sound had a consistency that didn't match a storm's rhythm. Unable to sleep, he rose and listened, determining that the noise came from down the valley. Under a gibbous moon, he climbed a low hill to get a better view. Several kilometers away, the sky glowed. Was it a town? A Lucian camp?

All he could think of was food.

Excited, he woke up Arturus and Merlin and showed him what he'd found. Merlin urged caution, and Arturus decided on an approach before dawn. In the meantime, rest was the most important thing.

Frustrated, Percival leaned against a tree instead of following Arturus' advice. Various scenarios ran through his mind. What if they had to steal food from a market or ambush a Lucian farmer? What if they were caught before they got near the settlement? Even with Dardarius' help escaping, he couldn't protect them for long. Hundreds, maybe thousands of legionnaires were probably looking for them. Percival's defenses against his despair thinned by the hour.

The sky lightened, and Arturus urged his comrades to follow. The king's order troubled Percival. Up to this point, Arturus had asked Percival to lead the way, but today, he asked the knight to stay with the elderly Merlin. To be sure, the old man was tiring, but Arturus could easily care for him. Confidence in him was the only answer, or rather Arturus' loss of it, as Percival perceived it. Arturus always had words of comfort when Percival failed, a trait that made the young man love the man who was his sovereign. Maybe he was changing his mind about his companion. His heart heavy, Percival walked next to Merlin, readying himself for an inevitable capture and unbearable humiliation.

The approaching dawn absorbed the bright lights of the settlement, hidden behind a grove of oak trees. More and more, Percival grew convinced it was a camp, rather than a town, and he tensed, expecting a challenge at any moment. Or a crossbow bolt in his throat. Arturus waved his hand behind in a sign to halt. He kept his eyes ahead.

"Who is there? Walk no further!" The voice was unfamiliar to Percival, but the accent...

Arturus, only a few paces ahead, froze. Percival did a double-take. The language was the Common Tongue.

"I am Arturus, elected king of Viridiae."

"Yeah, and I've just been cured of VD." The female sentry laughed. "Didn't you know he was a prisoner?"

Percival startled. He couldn't see the sentry, but her accent was Viridian. He'd heard this variety on the coast before the voyage to Koda to find the true Grail. His chest tightened at the recollection.

"What I say is true." Arturus' voice was even, but firm.

"Alright then. I hope your ID chip backs you up." The sentry was skeptical. "Come forward. Slowly. Hands where I can see them."

"I have two companions."

"Tell them to stay back."

Despite the warning, Percival inched forward, eager to see the sentry for himself. Merlin leaned against Percival, who realized why the sentry didn't immediately recognize them. Their hair was matted, their beards ragged, their skin scratched and bruised, and their prison jumpers hardly more than rags. Arturus held out his right hand, and the sentry passed her tab over the flesh between thumb and forefinger.

The sentry glanced up at Arturus and blanched.

* * *

Following the procedure Percival learned as a cadet at The Keep, the stunned sentry called her sergeant, who arrived with Sir Bors. Himself shocked, he confirmed Arturus' identification, and the two men embraced. Bors fought back tears while examining Percival and Merlin's chips. The one-armed knight's embrace of Percival was no less emotional, though he shook hands with the sage-scientist rather than giving him a bear hug.

Other Viridians arrived, among them a doctor. After a cursory examination, the former prisoners rode a cart into the Viridian camp. By now, the banners, weapons and armor screamed a massive Viridian army. Percival quickly lost count of the number of tents as soldiers and knights, as well as cooks, wheelwrights, electronics specialists, and a hundred other kinds of technicians swarmed the new arrivals. Arturus stood in the slow-moving cart and waved to everyone, shaking hands and touching heads in blessing. Someone gave him a brand-new cloak embroidered with the Viridian flag, and he donned it to a rousing cheer.

They approached a pavilion topped with a large Viridian flag. Another, smaller standard of Lothia flapped beside it. Arturus asked Bors to stop the procession. The crowd instinctively opened a path to the pavilion's entrance. Percival swallowed, a tinge of fear at what might happen next.

Lord Mordred Lothia, dressed in his customary black, emerged from the massive tent. From a distance, the commander of Viridiae's armies examined the stranger, and for an instant, his mouth drooped open, as if he'd witnessed an apparition. Percival would've given anything to know Mordred's mind at that moment. Not long ago, he'd tried to depose Arturus, and now he faced the man again, under dramatically different circumstances. So many questions filled Percival's brain, he thought it would melt.

Mordred recovered his composure when Sir Galahad arrived, his face equally stunned. With uncharacteristic awkwardness, Mordred stepped toward Arturus down the lane made by the crowd. Arturus climbed down from the cart and strode toward his rival. For an instant, neither seemed to know what to do next. Then Mordred lowered himself on one knee and bowed his head. With both hands on Mordred's shoulders, Arturus lifted him up, and spoke a few words. Percival didn't hear them, but Mordred nodded and visibly relaxed. Arturus grasped Mordred's hand, and the crowd cheered again.

A woman screamed.

Everyone turned their heads, and Percival saw his twin sister, Dee. She covered her mouth, eyes brimming with tears, and she ran to the cart. Percival jumped down and caught her, not quite believing he was alive or dead and floating in an afterlife. Her embrace vouched for her reality. Her scent, her voice, her resemblance to their mother, Eleanor, underlined that he had survived a nightmare. For a moment, it seemed that every memory that he shared with his sister, their long talks in the small hours, their secret explorations of their mother's land near the King's Forest, her magical presence when she saved him from the trolls who had captured him, her power when she landed the coup de grâce on their father as he threatened to kill his son. Without his twin, he could not be whole. Perhaps that was why nothing felt right any more.

He put that aside for the moment to revel in the joy of homecoming.

The joy gave way to fatigue, and Dee enlisted a soldier to help her take Percival to her tent. She gave him water and fruit, and sent for a medic. A headache, brought on by dehydration, quelled his appetite, but the medic pronounced him sound, given his ordeal. While he lay on a cot, Dee ran a wet cloth over his face and neck. Percival asked himself again whether he had passed on to the next world, but his appetite returned, and he asked for bread and fruit.

"I have so many questions to ask," Dee said.

"I won't answer any until I'm done eating. I didn't see where Arturus and Merlin went."

"Both are with Mordred."

A shadow passed over Percival's heart at Mordred's name, but he let it pass. "Tell me your story first. Why are you here?"

Dee related a truncated version of her journey to Villefroide with Lancelot and Guinevere, the attack on the Lucian port, and the skirmish that allowed the three of them to escape. Percival decided to ask more questions about the Ontarii named Tintan at some point.

"Three days later," Dee said, "we met a Viridian patrol, and they brought us to Mordred and his army."

"Where are we?"

"We're inside Lucian territory."

The news shocked Percival. A short time ago, Viridiae was on the brink of collapse. "How?"

"Mordred's plan worked. The Lucians were over-extended. He harassed them every way he could. In the meantime, thousands and thousands of Viridians came to him and volunteered. He had trouble finding weapons for everyone. There weren't enough sergeants to train everyone, but no one seemed to care. Everyone wanted to fight."

"What about knights?"

"A few came out of retirement. Squires were promoted, even if they hadn't completed their apprenticeships. But that's not the best thing."

"Well?"

"Camelot is free! Mordred retook it when the Lucian garrison was reduced. Some of the knights who survived the River Colum were imprisoned in the citadel."

Percival had trouble absorbing Dee's story. It was if Viridiae had come alive again.

Dee continued, "Bors and Galahad convinced the southern tribes to raid Lucanus, and Mordred harassed their western outposts. When the Ontarii attacked the port, Mordred took a big force east. Beating the Lucians was easier than everyone thought. He stopped here, and the rest of the new army caught up with him two days ago."

"How many are here?"

"Somebody said twenty-thousand soldiers. Then I heard thirty thousand. More are arriving every day."

"What's Mordred's plan?"

"I haven't been invited to the strategy meetings, but there's rumors of a large Lucian army 10 or twelve kilometers east."

Percival considered the information as he finished a gulp of water. "There's going to be a big battle. Soon."

"That's what everyone says."

Percival flashed to the slaughter at the River Colum. He hadn't held a javelin or sword since then. The medic who examined him in Dee's tent said he was underweight, undernourished, and ought to spend several days in the hospital. "I should find a way to get ready."

"You're crazy. You don't have any armor, and you can barely stand. What good are you on the battlefield?"

Dee's question hurt more than she realized. It wasn't her fault. She knew nothing about his ordeal of the past weeks.

As if she'd read his mind, she said, "What is it, Perce? What happened to you?"

Percival found it harder to tell his story. Dee, along with Lancelot and Guinevere, had a mission, and they had achieved real results. His memories elicited nothing but pain. Ever since the River Colum, he had felt completely powerless. He was at the mercy of men and women who could kill him at any moment for any reason. How could he explain the horror of the death march, with friends and comrades left to rot in the dust? What words could describe the barbaric murder of the man in front of thousands of Lucians in the Regia square? These experiences festered in his heart with every moment in the prison, never knowing if he'd see home or his family.

"Perce, I know it's hard, but you have to talk to me. I'm your sister."

How did you tell your twin that you murdered a man in cold blood? That the man was despicable, but that he was helping you at the end? That you see his face, full of disbelief, every night?

"Perce, you're shaking. What's wrong?"

How did you tell your dearest friend that you had lost the Grail? That you dropped it like a child drops a ball? Even if a battle was fought, and even if Viridiae won, that you might be responsible for the end of your country, even the world?

Dee cupped Percival's face in her hands. They were soft, but strong, like their mother's. Dee wiped away Percival's tears. Her eyes brimmed with her own. "You don't have to tell me now. You're hurting. When you feel like you can talk, I'm here for you."

Percival lay his head in Dee's lap, and she stroked his hair as his body shuddered with anxiety, anger, and relief.

* * *

The sun had set when Percival awakened alone in Dee's tent. A wave of panic nearly overtook him, but when he lifted the flap, he saw Dee speaking to Lancelot. The two knights embraced and laughed to see each other.

"You're skinny as a pike," Lancelot said. "What happened to you?"

Percival gulped. "It was pretty hard."

Dee touched his arm.

"You don't have to tell me now, Percival. But I came for you. Arturus wants you and Dee in the main pavilion."

Before he fell asleep, Dee gave him a basin of water and a cloth, and Percival bathed himself as best he could. She also gave him spare clothing, and Percival made himself as presentable as he could.

In the pavilion, a gaunt but alert Arturus sat next to Mordred conferring over a map. Bors, Galahad, and Guinevere listened intently. Merlin, however, was nowhere to be seen. The scene reminded Percival of the day before the battle of River Colum. In a large tent much like this one, Arturus revealed the attempted coup against him, and he forgave Mordred, knowing that he needed his best general to have a chance against the invading Lucians. As it happened, the Lucians defeated Arturus, but Mordred was again at Arturus' side. By all accounts, the two men had forgotten the attempted coup, at least for now.

"Percival." Arturus smiled at the knight's arrival. "I've heard your sister has taken good care of you. I'm glad you've come."

Percival blushed, thinking of how he had failed his monarch over the last days and weeks. Why wasn't Arturus angry? "I'm not sure what I can offer, my lord. I feel that I have failed everyone."

"The past is behind us. We have more important things to worry about now. My Lord Mordred has accomplished amazing things while we've been away. Let him explain what we plan to do."

Percival took a seat next to Bors, who put his one hand on Percival's shoulder in greeting. Dee sat next to Percival, and her nearness helped him relax.

"Viridians, we have a chance to destroy a Lucian army and eliminate that nation's threat against our country for years, maybe decades to come." Mordred's grave affect captured Percival's attention. "Our scouts and drones have discovered the main body of Lucians about 10 kilometers to the east. It is comprised of the Sixth, Seventh, and Eleventh Legions."

These were the legions that had invaded Viridiae. The memory made Percival's chest tighten.

"General Dardarius is at their head, but Vetrania is with them. She is their true leader. They know we are here, and they are coming for us."

Mordred grinned as if he knew a dangerous secret.

"You will forgive me, my friends, if I do not tell you all I know, though I have shared everything with His Majesty. However, we plan to give the Lucians what they want. Tomorrow, we march for this point." He lay the head of a long stick on the map. "Here, the river that flows through these parts makes a long bend. The ground is flat and dry. It's nearer to us than to our enemies. We'll arrive first, and prepare. We'll wait for Dardarius and Vetrania to cross the river at this ford." He lay the stick at a point to the northeast. "It's the only fordable point for several kilometers up and down stream. After they cross, we'll attack."

Mordred explained more of his strategy, and Percival's nervousness rose. The commander was attempting to lay a trap, and it was an enormous gamble. Why was he so open about the plan? He hinted at a trick, but Percival couldn't guess what it might be.

"We have only a few hours to prepare. The orders have already gone out to our captains and sergeants."

Arturus stood. "Thank you, Lord Mordred." He wore a simple soldier's uniform. He was clean shaven, but he was still pale, and he'd lost weight as well. He managed, however, a commanding presence. "I want everyone to know, from the highest commanders to the newest page, that I have complete confidence in Lord Mordred and his plan. The fight will be hard. If we destroy the Lucians, Viridiae will be free."

A silence full of awe and anxiety followed Arturus' speech. Dee clutched Percival's hand. She had promised her brother a warhorse and armor, if he felt up to fighting. She didn't want him to go, but she was smart enough to know he'd never stay behind. For his part, Percival wasn't sure if he was ready for battle, physically or mentally, but he wouldn't risk disgrace by showing ambivalence.

Even if he did join the melee, he wasn't sure if his heart would be in it.

The meeting broke up, and Percival found himself alone outside the tent. Floodlights attracted night insects, and their chirps underlined every person's taut energy. Percival found himself near the camp's perimeter, not far from the sentry who had found him, Arturus, and Merlin the previous day.

"A little calmer out here, wouldn't you say?" Merlin stepped out of a shadow.

Percival had learned that Merlin liked a dramatic entrance. "Yes, sir. I don't know how well I'll sleep tonight."

"I haven't had a good night's sleep in decades. Age does that to some people."

Percival had trouble meeting Merlin's gaze. He couldn't forget the instant the true Grail smashed on the rocks in the gorge.

"I've been meaning to talk with you, Sir Percival."

Percival hung his head. "I'm sorry, sir. I don't know how I can fix things. With the Grail, I mean."

"As a scientist, I'm always trying to learn something, young man." Merlin cleared his throat. "I learned to be a little more careful with precious objects."

"I'd make it up, if I could."

"Percival, it wasn't your fault. It simply slipped out of your hands. It's as much my fault as yours, but blaming yourself is pointless."

Percival wanted to disagree, but he remained silent. "What will happen to Viridiae now? Will the climate warm again and destroy us?"

Merlin shrugged. "Too soon to tell. It might, if we can't find a substitute."

"What do you mean?"

Merlin let a smile take over his face. "I've tried to learn everything I can about the Great Machines. We found a false Grail in Perditon. We lost the Viridian Grail first to theft and then to the wilderness. The Lucians have a broken Grail device hidden somewhere. How many of these rare objects exist, would you say?"

Percival had no idea.

Merlin turned to the young knight. "Percival, I don't believe in destiny. Or magic. Or fate. Or any of these silly explanations for perfectly rational phenomena. But I've heard hints of another Grail. I don't know if it exists. But I know that if it does, you will be the one to find it."

Merlin bid Percival goodnight, leaving him dumbfounded. What did Merlin mean? The true Grail was lost, but another one existed? Was it a myth? Or was it just a wish?

If Percival could find it, he could erase all his mistakes, and make the world whole again.

CHAPTER 23: THE BATTLE AT THE RIVER'S BEND

The long, blue curve of the river resembled half of a bow that Dee's mother might have tied into her hair as a child. Inside the bow, waving Viridian banners and nervous soldiers spread out on the field to Dee's left. She waited with Guinevere on an outcropping of rock that formed the southern bank of the river. Camouflaged by long-needled pines and thorny shrubs, the outcropping offered a panoramic view of the entire battlefield, though Dee's palms dampened as she realized that the bucolic scene below her would soon become an outdoor abattoir.

"I wonder if the Lucians are watching too," Dee said.

"I know they are." Guinevere handed Dee her binoculars and pointed to a similar collection of flat boulders across the broad valley. The eyepiece showed tiny horses and even smaller figures. The sun glinted off their armor.

"It's almost as if they expected us to meet them here."

"Mordred is clever, but so are the Lucians. They're not ones to simply walk into a trap."

But to Dee's mind, that's exactly what they were doing. Just as Mordred predicted, lines of legionaries forded the river to her right. The river was shallow, but swift, and several Lucians stumbled as they pressed against the current. As soon as they crossed, officers on horseback ordered the warriors, armed with pila, short swords, shields, and single-shot pistols into formations that faced the Viridians.

"Look how the Lucians are deploying. It's exactly as Mordred hoped."

Dee watched the Lucians carefully, noting how they were already bunching up against the riverbank. Mordred believed that the Lucians might show their nervousness by giving themselves too little maneuvering room once they got their first soldiers across the river. At least one full legion was still waiting to cross the ford by the time the sun was within a few degrees of its zenith.

"Maybe it's time to signal Mordred," Dee suggested.

"Not yet. The Lucians are packing themselves on their end of the field like pickles in a jar."

Behind Dee, a pair of archers readied a fire arrow each. Two fire arrows loosed at the same time was the signal for the Viridian attack to begin. Dee had never seen a major battle, and now she understood why soldiers often said waiting was the most difficult part. At least when you were fighting, you didn't have time to be afraid. Dee and Guinevere wouldn't wield a pike or a sword, but they would play a crucial role upon which many lives depended.

Dee distracted herself by thinking of Percival. They had talked long into the night, with her brother speaking haltingly of his experience over the past weeks and months. Dee fought back tears, wondering how Percival managed to keep his sanity after watching so much suffering. She wasn't quite sure what to think about the murder of Cantwell, except that war took its victims whenever it chose. The loss of the Grail was a heavy blow, but Percival took heart with Merlin's hint that another Grail might be found.

Throughout their conversation, Dee had perceived Percival's burden of guilt. She told him that he was a hero for bringing back Arturus and Merlin alive, and surviving to take revenge against the Lucian invaders. He slept well until awakened by Lancelot, who gave him a new shield, a borrowed sword, a strong breastplate, and a helmet. Galahad loaned Percival a big war horse, but even as he mounted, Dee felt his unspoken self-doubt. If it caused hesitation on the battlefield, that split-second might cost him his life.

"Archers," Guinevere said, "ignite your arrows."

In a moment, the mixture of pitch and fabric was aflame.

"Loose."

The arrows flew toward the Lucian formations, landing in tufts of grass a hundred meters ahead of the leading legionaries.

A roar rose up from the Viridian army.

"Time to go, Dee."

The women and the archers mounted their horses. The archers peeled off toward their companies, while Dee and Guinevere made for the rear area and the field hospitals. By her position as a knight, Guinevere had a right to fight with the other knights, including Lancelot, but she freely admitted her lack of fighting skills. She'd be a liability, not an asset, in a battle with professional soldiers.

Dee was loath to leave Guinevere.

The tension among the surgeons and nurses was distinct in their hard faces. They understood what was coming. Many had treated survivors of the River Colum and Camelot battles. Merlin moved among them, offering encouragement. Though he was not a medical doctor, he directed the teams that managed the logistics of medicine, from sterilization of instruments to distribution of bandages.

Another roar came from the Viridian lines. This time, a peal of thunder reached the rear. Dee studied the sky, which was clear and blue.

"The knights are charging." Guinevere swallowed, steeling herself for disaster, if it came. Her husband was among the knights, as was Lancelot. "We can get a better look from the drone command and control unit."

Though Guinevere wasn't specifically allowed in the C&C tent, no one would bar the king's wife and a member of the Round Table from the scene. Inside, technicians manipulated observation craft and relayed information to commanders. On the screens, a tsunami of men and women on horseback in a broad wedge formation, their ash gray battle armor matching the plate armor on their horses, collided with the center of the Lucian line. In his plan, Mordred hoped to split the Lucian army in two. The river at their backs would act like a wall, giving them little room to maneuver.

Following close behind, the Viridian foot soldiers charged into the fray. Just as the infantry arrived, the knights pulled back, the energy of their assault expended. The foot soldiers quickly took the knights' place, their greater numbers matching the power of the knights. Viridian archers loosed volley after volley into the Lucian formations, but the legionaries lifted their curved, rectangular shields to fend off the arrows. A few of the projectiles found a mark and Dee saw two Lucians go down. Every so often, puffs of smoke marking a shot fired from a pistol punctuated the scene. Dee imagined hearing the reports, but the activity in the tent drowned out sounds from the battle.

Unlike the Viridians, most of whom were new recruits who had seen limited action, veterans led the experienced Lucians, and their lines held. A detachment of Lucian cavalry, lightly armored and more maneuverable that the Viridian knights, moved on the Viridian left flank. Officers in the C&C tent warned Mordred, who ordered a group of knights to meet the new threat. The two groups crashed head-on, and this time, Dee heard the metallic clang of spear point on plate, and the screams of wounded horses.

A moment later, Dee heard the screams of men and women. Leaving Guinevere safe with the C&C unit, Dee spotted stretchers of wounded carried to the surgeries. She hadn't seen Percival after he trotted away on his borrowed armor and horse, and she half-expected to find him on a stretcher or stumbling toward her on the shoulder of a compatriot. Percival was not among the wounded, but a feeling of helplessness nearly overcame her. The chaos of battle was more than warrior on warrior; it had spread to areas where Dee felt safe, even protected. Oddly, she didn't sense that Percival was ever in immediate danger.

Guinevere came up to Dee. "Mordred has ordered the Viridians to fall back for a new attack. We've stunned the Lucians, but they're regrouping, too."

"Where is Arturus?"

"He's with Mordred's personal guard. Mordred insisted he stay away from the fighting."

"And Lancelot?"

"She was in the first wave, but she's alive. I saw her on one of the drone feeds. Her smile was so broad, her teeth reflected the sun's glare."

Dee had seen that feral grin when Lancelot skirmished at the Ontarii border and in the fight at the badlands. On their way west, before they found the encampment, Lancelot talked about those moments. She switched off the parts of her mind that most people used to stay sane. She embraced the blood lust like many people embraced the taste of fine Napene wine. All war is a state of madness.

Dee struggled with a role for herself. She had no medical training, but she lent a hand wherever she could; holding a cloth to a feverish man's forehead, carrying a load of fresh bandages into the surgery, helping a knight take a drink from a cup. She helped a vet treat a destrier that walked in, wounded and rider-less. Another collective warriors' roar caught her attention, but it seemed less powerful, hinting of exhaustion and fear.

A bleeding soldier stumbled into the hospital area calling for more stretcher bearers. Dee jumped up and followed the soldier. Guinevere was helping a knight with a stump instead of an arm, and the queen waved Dee off. With the soldier at her side, Dee grabbed a stretcher and headed toward the lines, not knowing what to expect. She only knew that help was needed.

A light fog had risen on this part of the field, and Dee slipped in grass slick with blood. Screams of horses and wails from wounded men and women filled her ears. A sickly smell, like de-caying vegetation, made her retch. The soldier led her forward until they came to a group of prone bodies so thick Dee could not find places to put her feet without stepping on flesh. Most of the bodies were still. Many had no arms or heads. Bowels like rope spilled from bellies. Dee cried out, but the soldier urged her on.

After minutes of picking through the crowd of fallen, they came upon as group of wounded, some holding blood-soaked field dressings to arms, legs, or heads. They found a Viridian on his back, but breathing, a field dressing on his chest. Dee spread the two poles of her stretcher apart until the canvas between them was taut. With the walking wounded soldier at the unconscious man's shoulders, and Dee at his feet, they lifted him onto the stretcher. He must have weighed 100 kilograms. Her hands slippery with sweat, she lifted her end of the stretcher. She and her companion picked their way through the wounded and the dead, Dee barely keeping down her gorge. The fog thinned as she approached the hospital's triage area.

The wounded Viridian had died.

Her companion stretcher bearer urged her to go back and try again.

After an hour, the two had brought back four more: two knights and two infantry. All were alive when they went into surgery.

Dee never saw them again.

Guinevere handed Dee a flask of water, her hands stained with blood and her clothes flecked with gore. "Mordred has pushed the Lucians back to the river, but our people are thin and exhausted. The Lucians counterattacked, but we were able to hold our ground. We've lost so many, that another Lucian counterattack could change everything."

"Maybe the Lucians will see that it's time to give up."

"Dardarius is not a man to give up. Neither is Mordred. The officers say he's going to try one more attack. He's throwing in his last reserves."

Dee wasn't sure what Guinevere meant, except that it suggested defeat was possible, maybe even likely if the Lucians were strong enough to resist. "What about our friends?"

"Galahad was hurt by a pistol ball, but not seriously. Bors' horse was killed from under him, and he sprained his ankle in

the fall. He can barely walk. Lancelot is nothing short of a sorcer-
ess when it comes to survival. People are whispering that she's
killed hundreds of Lucians."

Another thunderous howl rose from the field. Mordred's third
attack had started, and within moments, someone called for
stretcher bearers. Dee and a young girl, perhaps 18, took a
stretcher into the battlefield. By now, Dee had learned to ignore
the stench and the shrieks and focus on finding wounded men
and women. But as she pressed toward the line, she lost her way
among a copse of trees, and both women stumbled into a nearly
blank landscape. Again, a light fog, like the breaths of a thousand
dead left hanging over the land, obscured their vision. Except
for a few corpses from both sides, they might have been on a
pasture on the edge of Camelot where riding horses grazed. Dee's
heart rose in her throat. The girl ran away, and Dee dropped the
stretcher.

Something like a vise pressed on Dee. The fog lifted slightly,
brushed away by a light breeze, and Dee froze. To her left, Viridians, their faces grim and determined, marched toward her. To
her right, a line of Lucians pounded the bosses of their shields
with their swords, egging on their enemy. Dee had stumbled into
no-man's land, and she was about to be squashed like a bug.

"Dee! Dindrane Rathkeale!"

Dee, her feet stuck to the ground, searched left for the voice
that called her name. The voice called out again, and Percival
pushed through the advancing Viridian ranks on Galahad's borrowed white horse. Within seconds, Lucian arrows sped toward
him, but he fended them off with his shield, and none struck his
mount.

Terror clasped Dee's throat like a murderer. The armored
Percival galloped toward her and his arm slipped underneath
her shoulder. Wincing with pain as Percival lifted her off the
ground, she dropped on his horse's rump. Instinctively, she
wrapped her arms around her brother's waist. They galloped
back to the Viridian line. It parted for them, and closed up again.

Percival wheeled his war horse around, and Dee watched the

exhausted armies smash into one another, and the sound of metal on metal, shots fired and bullets flying, and the sounds of men and women begging for their lives gave way to the muffling fog. Through the noise came an order: "Fall back!" Still on Percival's horse, Dee watched in horror as thousands of running Viridians loomed out of the mist heading straight for them.

Swept up like dust by a broom, Percival and Dee let the mass of soldiers carry them toward a low rise. Perhaps the Viridians would make a stand here. The Lucians would have to fight uphill, Percival said, and that was always difficult. Dee listened but fear hollowed out the pit of her stomach. A last stand? Would the Viridian army be destroyed on a hill next to a river she didn't even know the name of? Would she die with them?

Another voice called for the Viridians to halt and turn. The group didn't behave like a frightened mob. They obeyed the command, stopped, and formed a new line. Percival and other knights remained on horseback. They had put a few hundred meters between themselves and the Lucians, who sped toward them, sensing victory.

A detonation rent the air behind the Viridian line. It came from the other side of the rise, and for a moment, Dee thought the Lucians had surrounded them. The mist lifted, and over the hill poured hundreds, then thousands of troops on foot and horseback. Dee recognized their striped faces and plumed helmets and cheered. An entire Ontarii battalion swept down the hill like an avalanche. They poured through the Viridian lines as the men-at-arms gave way.

The Lucians, surprised, halted, and Dee heard a shouted order from a Lucian commander. It came too late. The Ontarii lancers speared hundreds of Lucians on their first pass. Follow-on riders with crossbows loosed iron-tipped bolts into arms, heads, backs, and necks. Caught completely by surprise, the panicked Lucians fled. Ontarii swords cut them down like scythes taking the autumn harvest.

The Viridians soon followed. Dee's countrymen dropped all pretense of civilization or the capacity for mercy. Every single legionnaire, wounded or whole, centurion or auxiliary, died if they encountered a Viridian soldier or knight. Butchers treated animals far better. Fountains of blood turned the blue sky purple. Dee could not tear her eyes from the slaughter.

The whirlpool of death erased the boundaries between Viridian, Ontarii, and Lucian. Though the Viridian side had the upper hand, every living thing on the field fought for survival. Percival, however, with the extra burden of Dee on his warhorse's rump, backed away from the fight.

A squad of Lucians managing to hold their discipline pursued Dee and her brother. She urged him toward the copse of trees, but his horse slipped in a muddy puddle and went down. Percival controlled its fall, but both he and his sister were thrown. In a moment, the nine legionnaires surrounded them.

"Hold on, boys. I know this man." Even as his comrades behind him died in droves, the centurion halted to take in the scene. "He's the barbarian king's aide. I saw him on the com net."

"They escaped, didn't they?" said one of the legionaries.

"You bet they did, and General Dardarius promised ten thousand denarii to the man or woman who brings him in alive."

"Twenty thousand denarii."

"Either way," said the centurion, "we're rich."

"What about the girl?"

"Worth something on the market, I'd wager."

The Lucians stepped toward Dee and her brother.

"Percival, what do we do?"

Percival stretched his arms out, as if he wanted to protect Dee.

"I don't want to kill you," Percival said to the enemy legionnaries.

Why won't he draw his sword, Dee thought.

The Lucians inched forward, growling like a pack of dogs, wary of Percival despite his apparent unwillingness to defend himself. A bank of ground fog crept over the foes like a shroud, but Dee felt a surge of energy, as if the vapor was alive. Facing certain death or capture, surrounded by a vicious enemy, she had only one choice. She closed her eyes, stretched out her arms, and held her palms out.

"Percival, come inside my reach."

He moved as she bid. She visualized a dome of energy enveloping herself and her brother, her arms and hands like antenna.

"Lucians, if you come closer, I will be forced to kill all of you."

The centurion laughed. "What are you going to do, dance me to death?"

His comrade said, "Let's have some fun, boys."

The Lucians crept closer.

Dee snapped her fingers. In an instant, all ten Lucians dropped their weapons and screeched. They held their hands to their heads. Dee imagined a vise on each legionary, squeezing their skulls, crushing their bones, pulverizing their minds like a hammer on stone. All of them dropped to the ground, passing out one by one, dying one by one.

Only a few seconds passed, but once the screaming ended, silence blanketed the battlefield. Herself in a daze, Dee let Percival lead her to his horse, which had recovered from its fall. They mounted it and rode for the Viridian camp.

Dee buried her face in her brother's back. Unlike all the other Viridians, he had held back. He watched with the same horror, his eyes filling with tears. She noticed one other thing. His armor was as clean as the moment he put it on, and his sword was in his scabbard, unused.

* * *

Arturus himself rode out into the field and put a stop to the massacre. The killing ended, but not before only a few legionaries remained alive. The Ontarii commander had an easier time controlling her troops. She pushed on to the river, where hundreds of Lucian bodies blocked the stream like a dam.

Dardarius sent a delegation under a white flag to Arturus, requesting leave to retrieve the Lucian dead. With a detachment of Viridian knights and soldiers standing by, ready for treachery, Lucian stretcher bearers and drivers of electric carts removed bodies and parts of bodies. A few hours later, the stench of burning corpses drifted onto across the river toward the Viridian camp.

Dropped off by Percival near the Viridian field hospital, Dee busied herself with tending to the wounded and caring for the dead. Images of the screaming legionaries she killed edged their way into her consciousness, but she pushed the images away, unwilling to let her emotions distract her. At a makeshift outdoor morgue, she forced herself to search bodies for anything that might identify the corpse. Some bodies were so badly trampled by men and horses that identification was impossible. She covered her mouth with a damp cloth, which reduced the smell a little, and made a mental note of everything she encountered. As an artist, she believed part of her job was to tell the truth about the cost of freedom, and she vowed her grand project, the great mural she had abandoned when Camelot was sacked, would tell this story if she was ever returned to it.

Evening came, and she could do nothing more. As the Viridians lit their own funeral pyres, she stripped off her blood-soaked clothes, splashed her face with water, and dropped exhausted onto her bedroll. Sleep, however, wouldn't come. She cried over the deaths she'd caused, angry at the legionaries who'd ignored her warnings. If only they weren't so greedy. And she couldn't stop thinking about her brother, who had become a mystery. Before she nearly lost him, he was as fierce a warrior as she had ever known.

As she lay awake, Percival came in to the tent. His tunic was as soaked as her blouse. He had spent the afternoon tending to the dead and wounded, just as she had. He removed his scabbard, its sword still sheathed, and set it aside.

"Perce, what's happened to you?"

Percival ignored her as he stripped to the waist.

Dee saw how thin he'd become. "Are you sick? Do you need something?"

He shook his head. "All I want to do is sleep."

Dee could not let her curiosity go. His manner had an edge

of fear. Something was different about the brother she loved so much. "You didn't fight, did you?"

Percival sighed. "I tried. I really did."

Like all warriors, he needed to work himself up to a froth in order to plunge into the tangle of pikes, swords, shields, pistols and make a difference for his country. But the blood lust was as elusive as silence on that field. He trotted along the back end of the melee, his trained horse confused by his hesitation, until he made a halfhearted attempt at a charge. "I rode with the knights in the first attack, but when I saw the Lucian's faces, all I saw were..." His voice trailed off.

"What did you see?"

"All the men and women I'd killed before today. A man I murdered in cold blood." He looked at his right hand, the one that wielded his weapons. "I tried to throw a javelin. I tried to pull out my sword. But my hand wouldn't do what it was told."

He'd forgotten how to hate the enemy, and that made him a liability. Dee imagined what Bors, Galahad, and the other knights thought. Did they see Percival holding back? What would Lancelot say if she knew?

Percival covered his face. Sobs escaped through his fingers. "Mordred saw me. He ordered me to fire my pistols or throw a javelin, but I couldn't."

"Why, Perce?"

"I'm not a coward, if that's what you think."

"I'd never say that, but people will talk. What you did, or didn't do, will come out."

"Maybe Mother was right. Maybe I should've studied math and science and stayed away from the knighthood."

"She's proud of you. I know this."

"Maybe I was trying to be my father in some secret way."

"He was a bully, a rapist, and a traitor. You could never be those things."

"All I know is that I couldn't do it. I couldn't kill any more. Seeing all those dead, I didn't want to be a part of it. I'm not worthy to be a knight any longer."

"That's crazy. You're the bravest man I know."

"I lost the Grail. That's how I'll be remembered. 'Sir Percival, the knight who condemned his country to death. And who couldn't fight for his country.'"

Dee had never seen her brother so bereft. In the past, even at his worst moments, he had a spark of hope that revived him and carried him to the next moment of his life. Dee could not find that spark in the tent on the night of the battle that saved Viridiae.

Percival, too, had come back from the battle, and his ordeal in Lucana, a casualty with invisible wounds.

A cough announced a visitor. Dee pulled back the flap and an unfamiliar, stern-faced knight stepped in. Outside, two men-at-arms waited. Without a polite word to Dee, or an explanation, they arrested Percival and took him away. They didn't give him time to put on his shirt.

CHAPTER 24:
DARDARIUS IS
REVENGED

Robert Dardarius jumped out of the open electric cart before it skidded to a stop. His new aide de camp, Portia, Cecily's youngest cousin, followed him up the stairs in front of the private house Vetrania had made her command post. "Sir, what shall we say to Her Majesty?"

"The truth, Tribune."

"But we have lost this engagement, sir. She won't accept that."

"I've known the Empress longer than you've been alive, Tribune. Above all, she's interested in survival."

And if I have my way, Robert thought, her days are numbered.

He found his monarch at a desk on the second floor. Behind her, a balcony overlooked the wide battlefield from the graceful curve of the river to a wall of rocky cliffs. The curtains were drawn against the view, as if Vetrania wanted to ignore what had happened.

"What have you done?" Robert said.

"Why do you not salute me before addressing me?"

"You have caused the slaughter of an entire army of good men and women."

"If you do not follow protocol, I will have you removed."

Robert took a breath. Her guard, all members of her clan, stiffened. Robert's anger consumed him, but he could not let himself lose control, not if he expected success of his ultimate plan. Mustering all his discipline, he brought his right fist to his left breast over his heart, which beat at double-time. Portia followed suit.

"Majesty," he sneered, "why did you countermand my order?"

"Because it was cowardly."

Portia drew a breath. In the short time since Robert had promoted her, she had shown herself as loyal as her cousin Adrian.

"I ordered a tactical retreat to our beachhead to give us time to regroup and bring up reinforcements. As I explained at the time, our casualty rate was higher than expected. The Viridians are inexperienced, but they fight like cornered questing beasts."

"You lost perspective, General. I watched the battle unfold from here. The Viridians are barely more than a rabble. They are peasants and menials waving swords like children. They lost at least many as we did, probably more. I decided that we should attack again immediately."

Robert disagreed. He saw the losses on both sides, but he knew his people and the Viridians. An hour of rest and his legions could've beat them, if only...

"With the greatest respect, Majesty, you ignored the intelligence on the Ontarii."

"And your intelligence was wrong. It said they were a full day away. And yet they showed up when they did. Can you explain that?"

Robert admitted he could not. Spies were rarely as reliable as videos and storytellers made them out. "Nonetheless, Majesty, if you hadn't sent the legions back, they wouldn't have met the Ontarii in a weakened state."

"Are you questioning my judgment?"

Of course I am, thought Robert. "I am suggesting, my lady, that a little patience might have saved us. An entire legion is dead or dying. Half of another legion is being butchered like sheep as we speak."

"And what is your responsibility in that disaster? You are here, not there." She pointed at the battlefield. "Like the captain of a ship, you should be there facing your fate. I have no use for failures."

"Majesty—"

Robert held up his hand to Portia. She was intelligent, but she had a quick tongue that was likely to get her in trouble someday. "I did not order the final attack. You did. If you had allowed the retreat, thousands of our warriors would be alive, eager to fight for you again."

"You are a failure, Robert. Your legions failed to hold Viridiae and Camelot. You allowed their king, their best scientist, and their best knight to slip through your grasp. It's occurred to me that you helped them escape, though no one would believe even you would commit such treason."

Robert clenched his jaw to control his rage. Of course he had orchestrated Arturus' escape, but he had never expected to pay the price of Adrian's life. By the time he discovered what had happened, the intelligent car had deposited the three men on the edge of the western desert, and he had no hope of recovering them, even if he wanted to. He gambled that the populace would blame Vetrania for the loss, just as they blamed her for falling for Merlin's trick of the faked Grail.

His gamble had paid off. Grumbles were growing louder in the Senate, toothless as it was. And media polls showed her job approval at an all-time low.

"What would you have me do now, Majesty?"

"Reorganize and attack again."

"With what? We're at half the strength we were 12 hours ago. With the Ontarii, the Viridian side has nearly three times our strength."

Vetrania pounded her fist on the desk. Portia blinked. "I need a victory. I need the Grail."

"We don't even know if the Viridians have the working Grail." Portia's intelligence reports included rumors that the Grail was lost again before Arturus stumbled onto the Viridian camp.

"Deliver me a victory. That's a direct order!"

"That would be suicide, my lady."

"If you do not obey me, I will find someone who will."

Vetrania's frustration had turned comical. All of Lucanus

knew Robert was the only general who could deliver a victory, if one could be found. Over the years, he had used promotions, prisoner sales, and old-fashioned back-slapping to make the legions his, and no one else's. They obeyed Vetrania only because he obeyed her. Her failure to understand this fact was her greatest weakness.

"They'll mutiny if you get rid of me."

"If you had any honor, you'd fall on your sword."

"If you had any sense, you'd admit defeat and take us home."

Vetrania stood, her face a fiery red. Her guard leaned away, as if she were aflame. "How dare you speak to me that way. I should have you executed on the spot for cowardice and insubordination."

Portia's hand edged toward her sword. Robert feared she might act rashly, and ruin everything.

"I beg pardon, Your Majesty," Robert said. "I worded my advice poorly. I meant that you could order a strategic retreat to prepare for ultimate annihilation of the Viridian enemy."

Vetrania either missed or ignored Robert's veiled sarcasm. Her face's color fell back to something less florid. "Your idea has merit, General."

Portia relaxed her sword arm, as did Vetrania's guards.

"Most of the Lucian survivors are already across the river, my lady," Robert said. "The Viridians and their Ontarii allies do not seem interested in pursuit, at least for now."

Vetrania smiled thickly. "Very well, General. Set an orderly retreat in motion. Mark my word 'orderly'. I won't tolerate any perception of a rout."

"Of course, my lady."

"Dismissed."

Robert glanced at Portia, and they saluted the empress together. When they climbed aboard the cart, he asked Portia to gather his commanders to plan the withdrawal. "One more thing, Tribune."

"Sir?"

"Set up another meeting with the commanders and centurions from the Dardarian clan. Ensure that the empress and the Cardeans know nothing about it."

* * *

The Lucian officers carried out Vetrania's instructions for an orderly retreat—ghost-written by Robert—to the letter. Protected by cavalry on their flanks and a rear guard of the healthiest of the survivors, the baggage train with the wounded made steady progress on the road out of the western mountains toward the capital, Lucana. Robert counted himself lucky that Arturus did not pursue him. If he had, the Viridian king might have captured or killed thousands more Lucians, perhaps even Vetrania herself. On the other hand, the Viridians had ventured far beyond their own traditional borders to find the right time and place to destroy the Lucian army. And as a tactician, Mordred proved to be more than Robert bargained for. The Lucian intelligence reports finally confirmed what Robert guessed. Mordred had orchestrated secret alliances with Lucanus' enemies through Arturus' wife Guinevere and the king's closest knights. Vetrania could never have accomplished a similar coup, even if the roles in the war were reversed. She didn't have the imagination or the drive.

Vetrania had utterly failed Lucanus.

And now came the arrests, starting in the Senate. The body served a largely ceremonial function, rubber-stamping imperial decrees, no matter how silly or oppressive. However, it also served as a relief valve for critics, who were protected by tradition from arrest and prosecution for speaking out against government policy. Vetrania ignored the tradition and ordered state security to take the most vocal senators into custody. One died during his arrest, though no one believed the statement put out by the imperial press office claiming he'd died of a heart attack.

Next came the journalists. Like the senators, at least until now, Vetrania tolerated mild criticism of her government by writers and video producers. The loss of Viridiae, Arturus, and the Grail proved too much for many commentators, and they grew emboldened by Vetrania's absence from the capital. The journalists paid with their freedom. State security agents detained them and stopped their publications or chancasts by suspending licenses or destroying equipment. Robert had little use for journalists as well, but he was a traditionalist, and he scorned Vetrania's behavior. He kept his views, however, to himself. He was waiting for the right moment.

It loomed as the broken Lucian army camped three days from the capital. As Robert read a report of a purge in the ministry of defense, Portia begged permission to see him.

"Portia, you look ill. What is it?"

"Sir, she's ordered more arrests." Portia handed Robert a tablet.

Robert studied the list. His mouth went dry. "Where did you get this?"

"One of the clerks in the empress's train is married to my nephew. He's the third man on the list."

Robert did not know the man, but he did know the family name. They were long allies of the Dardarians. The implication was clear.

"Sir, another of my relatives had close connections to Vetrania's inner circle."

"Well?"

"She's putting together a list of people whom she believes is disloyal."

Robert put his fingers together. "You're on that list?"

"No, sir. You are."

Robert swallowed hard. For weeks, he suspected Vetrania kept a list of her real and imagined enemies. Confirmation, however, gave him no comfort. He had days to live, if that many.

"Thank you for the information, Portia. I'm grateful."

"What are you going to do, sir?"

Robert breathed deep, and he feigned confidence by stretching out his legs. "For now, nothing."

Portia's eyes flared. "Sir, you might be imprisoned, or worse, any second."

"It's possible, but Vetrania is not an impulsive person. She's reliable that way. She'll wait for a good opportunity or excuse before striking."

"Meaning you'll strike first?"

Robert waved a finger and grinned. "That's treasonous talk, Tribune. I won't have it. But keep your go-bag handy, just in case."

* * *

Vetrania dithered about how she should enter her capital. Unlike Robert's triumph after conquering most of Viridiae and capturing Arturus, the mood among the populace was sullen, even resentful as the remaining legionaries awaited orders to go home. Despite Vetrania's crackdown on dissent, a few senators and cultural leaders gathered crowds on street corners and along the Avenue of Victory. The fearless ones called Vetrania incompetent and corrupt. They called on her to abdicate. When her security forces tried to arrest the troublemakers, they faced protective, angry mobs. The plebs had turned against her.

Robert watched her support disintegrate with secret joy. He never agreed publicly with the dissenters, and he even uttered a few bromides about "legitimate government" and "pushing back against chaos" to reassure her. Appreciative, in spite of her distrust, she promised to reserve the seat of honor for him at her weekly dinner for her chief officers.

In his tent, Robert changed into his evening uniform. The dinner was a semi-formal affair, and he was expected to look his best.

Portia entered the tent as a valet adjusted Robert's tunic. "I must speak with you, sir."

Robert dismissed the valet. "What is it, Tribune?"

"You asked me to pass along any news from Vetrania's inner circle."

"Go on."

Portia hesitated. "Sir, I..."

"Go on, Tribune. Don't be troubled."

"Vetrania plans to arrest you and all senior Dardarian officers tomorrow. You will be charged with treason."

Robert sighed. To fête him one night and execute him the next day was typically Vetrania. "We expected this, Tribune. Are our forces in place?"

"Yes, sir."

"And our clansmen and women in camp, do they know their roles?"

"I have met with each one, as ordered. They know their duty to the clan, and to you."

Robert adjusted his collar in the mirror. "What is your opinion, Portia?"

The tribune appeared puzzled. "I don't understand, sir. I carry out orders. My opinion is irrelevant."

"That's the answer of a cadet. I want your answer as a citizen and a soldier with a mind and a heart. What is your opinion?"

The tribune thought a moment, then drew herself to ceremonious attention. "Sir, the country needs you. Now, more than ever."

Robert let a tiny smile lift a corner of his mouth. Even if she secretly harbored doubts, it was the correct answer. Anything else and he might be the one to arrest her when the time came. He made a final adjustment to a sleeve. "I'm hungry. Time to slaughter the fatted calf."

* * *

Robert gave Vetrania credit for her attempt to impress her senior officers. The weekly dinners were normally staid affairs, but this close to the capital, she encouraged officers to invite wives, husbands, lovers, and mistresses. Her staff hung lights, creating an outdoor ballroom next to her pavilion, and musicians, also imported from Lucana, gave the evening a festive air. At evenings like this he often missed Cecily most. She was like a jewel as they greeted fellow officers and even Vetrania before the empress had her exiled and killed. Tonight, Robert would visit justice on the empress. If he failed, he was dead anyway.

The night wore on, and Robert put on his best smile, despite his incipient anxiety. He accepted a request from Vetrania for him as a dance partner. Worried that she had discovered his plan and would call him out publicly, he covered his discomfort by whirling her about the open-air ballroom with energy and dignity, saying little more than pleasantries, and grinning as if enjoying himself. She signaled her own pleasure, though dissembling was an art form at court, and Robert couldn't be one hundred percent sure of her true emotions.

He was sure of his own. Inwardly, he shuddered at her touch. The dance called for him to bring her close enough to smell her perfume. Ironically, she had no husband or lover to invite to the dinner, and Robert sensed a loneliness that he might have sympathized with, if she hadn't been the instrument of his mate's death and a threat to his own life. He struggled against the urge to put his hands around Vetrania's throat in front of all the guests and take his revenge there and then. That might satisfy his need for justice temporarily, but it would only get him half of what he wanted.

The dance ended, he bowed to the empress, and she curtsied in polite acknowledgment. She also winked at him, which took him aback. Was she flirting? Vetrania was notorious for taking a shine to a man and then discarding him like last year's shoes.

At his table, while sipping Napene wine, he noticed a change around the periphery of the ballroom. Younger Dardarian officers and a few seasoned centurions eased themselves into places just outside the perimeter. If challenged, they would say they had come to listen to the music. In truth, many were homesick, and the excuse was believable by the Cardean sentries, who also looked forward to seeing home and loved ones in the next day or two.

Most would not, a fact Robert regretted, but it was the cost of self-defense.

As the hours wore on, guests slipped away, and after a time, most of the remaining people were Dardarians or their allies. As the first tendrils of dawn snuffed the faintest stars, the master of ceremonies bid everyone a good night. Among the last guests were Robert and Vetrania, well-known as a night-owl. The general approached his monarch at the dais.

"May I escort you home, Your Majesty?" Robert eyed the two Cardean guards behind Vetrania.

Tired, but relaxed, Vetrania inclined her head. "How kind of you, General." She extended her hand, allowing Robert to steady her as she rose.

The makeshift courtyard was separated from Vetrania's pavilion by a short path. Even under the lightening sky, the ground was difficult to make out. Vetrania stopped halfway down the path, and Robert's heart rose in his throat. What was she up to now?

"I enjoyed the evening so much with you, Robert. You are a brilliant dancer."

Her use of his first name startled him. She had never used it before. He realized the correctness of his earlier conclusion: she wanted him.

"My dancing skills are nothing compared to yours, Majesty."

Vetrania grinned, reminding Robert that she was a woman, not just his empress. "I have many other skills, Robert." She drew closer to him, her intent concealed by the twilight. "Would you like to discuss them with me, in private?"

Vetrania lifted her hand to his tunic, brushing against a sensitive spot. Robert kept his face impassive as he fought to control his disgust. He also feared her fingers might find the dagger. He put his hand around her wrist, and gently pulled it away.

"Lying with you would be like lying with a snake."

Vetrania's lasciviousness change to fury. "How dare you—"

He heard grunts and the sound of bodies dragged away into the brush. Portia appeared behind the empress.

"Sir, the guards are neutralized."

"What is this?" Vetrania barked.

"You're done, my lady."

As Robert spoke, two Dardarian centurions appeared and whispered to Portia. "Sir, all is ready. Shall I give the order?"

"Order? What order?" For the first time, Vetrania showed fear.

Robert pushed her toward Portia, who grabbed the elder woman's arms.

"Do not call out, my lady, or my tribune will cut your throat."

Portia leveled a knife just above Vetrania's larynx.

"You are a disgrace to the empire, my lady. You will destroy us as surely as our enemies will, if you remain in power."

Vetrania's jaw dropped.

"In the generations since the Cardeans usurped the rightful Dardarian emperor, my great-grandfather, our country has known nothing but fear and incompetence. The people no longer tolerate the Cardean clan. The idea of your rule is anathema to any patriotic Lucian. The loss at the Battle at the River's Bend is the last straw."

Vetrania raised herself up, despite Portia's grip. "A nice speech, if dishonest. You'd make a fine politician, General, but I know better. You learned that your life was in danger, and you decided to nip the problem in the bud. It's all about survival, isn't it?"

"You're wrong, my lady."

"Don't lie to me, General. All anyone wants is to avoid the grave."

Of course, Robert thought, life was always preferable to death. But what makes life worth living? Honor in the eyes of others. Loyalty and obedience from your clan. The scales of justice balanced by any means necessary, when boundaries are crossed.

"To think I saw you as a potential consort," Vetrania said. "I have been foolish."

Vetrania's words elicited another memory of Robert's wife. They were at another dance, shortly after they met. The evening was just as beautiful as this night's, and he remembered a kiss and a desire that overwhelmed him. Stroking her cheek, he asked her if she wanted to be with him. She answered with another kiss, and from that moment, they were inseparable. Then

Vetrania took her from him.

"Release me now, and I'll forget about this, General Dardarius."

Robert removed the dagger from his tunic and stabbed Vetrania just below her sternum. He felt her heart quicken, then flutter.

With the last of her strength, Vetrania lifted her eyes to Robert.

"You may forget a slight, my lady, but I can never forget what you did to me and my family."

Without a word, the empress slumped, though Portia kept her upright. The empress's eyes were open, but blank. Portia let Vetrania's body to the ground. "We have very little time, sir." She held out a towel.

The dagger, dripping blood, rested in Robert's hand. He had taken his revenge, but it felt anti-climactic, as if he had forgotten something. Justice often took the form of a sigh, rather than a roar.

Portia took the dagger. "I'll dispose of this, sir. Shall I give the order to move against the Cardeans?"

Robert felt as if he were dreaming. In the two seconds it took to kill Vetrania, his life had changed forever. Was he ready for the burden he was about to take up? Nodding to Portia, he wiped Vetrania's blood from his hand. He doubted the stain would ever disappear.

CHAPTER 25:
PERCIVAL'S CHANCE
AT REDEMPTION

Camelot's desperate condition swamped Percival's melancholy, at least for a time. His guards, too, couldn't take their eyes off the remains of the city as it came into view. Seven of its nine towers had broken, and the two remaining towers had burned, black streaks streaming down their stones like tears. They reminded Percival of his spent hatred of the Lucians, and the bleak emotions that had trailed him home from the Battle at the River's Bend. Victory seemed a hollow thing.

After his arrest in Dee's tent, he stood before Mordred. Exhausted, but exultant, the commanding general of Arturus' armies examined the young knight with a mixture of pity and scorn. "I've received a serious complaint."

Percival raised up his head, ready for the coming accusation.

"A number of knights and men-at-arms say you refused to fight, or at least showed a hesitation beyond mere anxiety for your own safety."

Percival kept his eyes on Mordred, out of respect, not defiance.

"I confess I believe it, after what I witnessed today. You ignored my orders to engage the enemy. What do you have to say for yourself?"

Percival swallowed. "I have no answer, my lord." In truth, Percival's emotions churned like a stew, but Mordred was not the best audience for a confession.

"I have ordered you held pending an investigation into allegations against you of cowardice."

Percival expected as much. Despite his derision, however, Mordred bet on Percival's honor as a Knight of the Round Table. He put him under house arrest, which meant confinement to his shared tent with Dee. Two guards accompanied him everywhere, including the return march to Camelot with most of Arturus' army. A detachment stayed at the battlefield as insurance against a surprise reversal of the Lucian evacuation.

Unlike his time as a prisoner of the Lucians, Percival harbored no fantasies of escaping his Viridian bonds, though his hands were free and he rode a fine horse toward the destroyed capital. He shared one thing with all his compatriots: He was exhausted and he wanted to go home. Riding through the debris-strewn streets of the lower town, he saw ordinary people picking through the rubble, looking for food or bits of wood or canvas for makeshift shelters. Inside the city walls, the old neighborhoods appeared less damaged, and he found Dee's apartment building nearly intact. When he arrived, she was away at the palace with Guinevere, but the landlady welcomed him, only glancing at the two guards. Either word of his arrest hadn't reached the city, or Dee's landlady didn't care. He kept his predicament to himself.

He collapsed on the bed, his father's banged-up red helmet watching him from its place in the corner of the room. Sir Adnan deGrosse was a despicable man who raped Percival's mother, but nobody ever accused him of cowardice, at least on the battlefield. What would he think of Percival's status as a traitor to the best traditions of Viridian honor? Was Percival any better? These thoughts kept him awake, along with fears for his future, when Dee arrived home. Percival padded down the hall to the kitchen and the smell of freshly brewed tea.

Dee smiled and offered Percival a cup. He could always count on her love, no matter his circumstance.

"I knew you were home," Dee said, "when I saw your minders by the door."

"I don't need them. I don't plan on going anywhere. I'm done with adventure. It hasn't treated me very well."

"Mordred has to maintain the appearance of control, now that the war is over."

"How can you be sure?"

"I just came back from a briefing of the king and the senior leadership."

"Guinevere has put quite a bit of faith in you."

"I guessed I've earned it. That's what she keeps telling me. Anyway, the Lucians are preoccupied with internal politics at the moment."

Percival had occasionally thought of Arturus' goading of Dardarius' ambition. Had it borne fruit?

Dee brought her knees up into the living room sofa. "Vetrania was assassinated two days ago, and all the evidence points to the Dardarians, maybe Dardarius himself."

"He's taken power for himself."

"He's trying to. The next morning, a legion under Dardarian control surrounded the remnants of the force Vetrania brought to Wide Bend. They gave up without a fight when they heard Vetrania was dead. Her support in the military was paper thin."

"I supposed the people hated her too."

"Oddly enough, there were large protests. Some of them violent. She'd done her part to build up her image as a wise and just empress. Dardarius is smart enough to wait a while to take power. His allies—one of them is named Verus—is pushing through a bill in the Lucian Senate giving the imperial sceptor to Dardarius."

"He'll get what he wants, no doubt."

"He's as ruthless as Vetrania. Everyone has a feeling that the new boss will be the same as the old boss, more or less. Lucians love their backstabbing ways."

"The war is over because Dardarius has enough on his hands."

"Vetrania failed in her war aims. She didn't find a working Grail and she didn't have the resources to keep Viridiae under Lucian control. Dardarius won't repeat those mistakes."

The mention of the Grail brought to mind that awful moment

in the canyon. "They might try again someday."

"Everyone agrees on that, too."

Percival sipped his tea, the added lemon giving it a bitter kick. "Was there any talk about me?"

"No, but it felt like you were in the room, invisible. Maybe it was me. Perce, everyone is puzzled by your behavior."

Percival was still trying to sort it out for himself. "Mordred said there'd be an investigation. After that, I suppose there'll be a trial. After that..." Percival shrugged.

"I got to know a couple of lawyers before the war. Don't say anything before you talk to one."

Percival lost interest in conversation. Talk of lawyers promised complexities he couldn't handle at the moment. The tea worked its somnolent magic, and he excused himself. A quick shower, and he was in bed, asleep.

Dee shook him awake the next morning. "Wake up! You've been summoned to the palace. I'm going with you."

Percival's pensiveness didn't prevent him from putting on his best uniform. Before leaving for his deployment, he had all his clothes and a few other belongings brought to Dee's apartment. The clothes hung a little loose, but he still cut a good profile. He'd matured since the day Dame Lancelot found him starving in the King's Forest, the last survivor of yet another failed Grail expedition.

He figured he should look good if his career was about to end.

His horses were requisitioned for the war, and Dee didn't own one, so the siblings hired a public car to take them to the palace. The wealthier residents of Camelot had already started rebuilding their homes in the densely populated city, and the clear skies suggested that recovery might not take as long as most people expected.

Percival revised his prediction when he saw Government House, which hosted the Round Table, and Arturus' palace. The facades were so badly damaged, he feared how they appeared inside. His fears were realized when a footman, perfectly liveried next to pile of rubble, guided them through a temporary entrance. He hardly recognized the interior.

An usher announced Percival and Dee to Arturus, Guinevere, Mordred and other advisers and aides in a conference room. Percival remembered the room from the day Lancelot brought him to accuse Mordred of sabotaging one of the Grail expeditions. Once the war started, Mordred held sway over the kingdom, especially after Arturus was captured by the Lucians. Percival had the impression Mordred disliked returning to his previous, subordinate role.

Guinevere, for her part, was radiant, and she smiled as a sister might to Dee.

Percival bowed to Arturus. "Your Majesty, reporting as ordered."

The king raised his head from a document, and Percival noted his wan appearance. Funny, he thought, how Arturus actually looked stronger away from the palace. He may have looked stronger while in captivity. It brought home the old wisdom about the singular weight of kingship.

"I would like everyone to leave the room while I speak with Sir Percival and Miss Rathkeale," Arturus said. "That is, except for the queen."

"My lord," Mordred objected. "I believe I should be present for any interrogation, even if it is done by yourself."

Arturus was stern-faced. "Rest assured, my lord, that my questions won't jeopardize your inquiry."

Mordred hesitated, but relented. A moment later, he and the others were gone.

The sudden emptiness of the room startled Percival. In spite of its size, he couldn't help but compare it to the cells at the Lucian prison. Perhaps it was the dust that clung to everything, testament to the pounding taken by the building and its neglect by the Lucian occupiers. He waited for Arturus to speak.

"Percival, it's good to see you again. I've missed you."

The statement took Percival aback. He'd been ready for chastisement, or at least a lecture. "Your Majesty, I admit that I—"

Arturus turned away in thought. "Sharing a terrible experience often brings people together, wouldn't you agree?"

Guinevere nodded at Dee, who flushed. She'd told Percival of her experience with Lancelot and Guinevere during the embassy to Villefroide. In some ways, Dee had suffered losses similar to Percival's, but they had survived.

"I've seen how the war has changed you, my friend. Doubt and shame are now your constant companions."

Percival fought back tears. Arturus had articulated his pain.

"But as the elected king of Viridiae, I can't ignore your behavior on the battlefield. Your fellow knights and men-at-arms depended on you. Despite your actions supporting the wounded and rescuing your sister from danger, winning the battle was the most important thing if we were to save our country."

Percival felt a judgment and sentence coming.

"Of course, my comments and observations are unofficial and off-the-record, but Mordred will pursue these charges until he gets a conviction on something. You can count on that."

"I shall resign my commission, my lord, and submit to whatever punishment is appropriate."

Arturus raised his hand. "I wish you wouldn't do that, Percival. Resign, that is."

"Majesty?"

A door opened, and Merlin entered the room. He shook Percival's hand and kissed Dee's. He looked as fit as ever, and if he harbored any resentment against Percival for losing the Grail he'd rescued from the Lucians, he didn't show it. He took a spot behind Guinevere.

"Percival," Arturus said, "I expect Mordred to deliver his report in the next few days. As commander-in-chief, I will decide what should be done with you, according to the law. I've learned that even in cases of cowardice in the face of the enemy, the law allows for restitution."

"My lord, I don't understand."

Dee, however, took Percival's hand, as if she knew.

"Merlin, will you explain?"

"Or course, Your Majesty. Sir Percival, I've found another

Grail."

Percival sucked in a breath.

"You might remember, that I mentioned rumors of another Grail device." Merlin's excitement grew. "In the last 24 hours, I've received proof of its existence. It's far to the south, deep in the Hot Lands."

Arturus said, "This is our last chance to repair our Great Machine and restore the climate. Percival, I want you to find it and bring it back. If you succeed, the slate against you will be wiped clean. You have my solemn promise. What do you say?"

Percival could hardly believe it. He came to the palace expecting to be taken to the dungeon in the citadel to await trial and start a long prison sentence. But Arturus had offered him a way to redeem himself, not only for the loss of the Viridian Grail and what he'd done at Wide Bend, but for the murder of Adrian, which weighed on him just as heavy.

"My lord, Merlin, my lady, I'm so grateful. I don't know what else to say."

"I recommend you take your sister," Guinevere said. "You'll never find a stronger friend or ally."

Percival glanced at his sister, and he felt their bond tighten like those that hold nations together.

"I accept this quest, my lord. Thank you."

"I, too, my lord," Dee said.

Guinevere beamed.

"Then I wish you both the best of luck. Merlin will provide the particulars." Arturus gestured to the usher, who invited Percival to follow.

Percival hesitated. "I won't fail you, sir. Nothing will stop me or Dee."

"I'm certain of it, Sir Percival. I wouldn't have chosen you if I had any doubt."

In a matter of a second, Percival felt the weight of the world shift on his shoulders. He had exchanged one burden for another. While the first had pressed him down, the second, new burden, lifted him up. He had a new mission, and a new purpose.

He could make amends for his errors, and make the world a better place. All he had to do was succeed.

EPILOG

Dee gave up her study of Merlin's background documents on the Hot Lands Grail when her eyes could no longer focus. She admired his scholarship, but many questions remained. He could not even guarantee that the Grail existed; Only a journey to the likely location far down the coast of the Peaceful Sea would reveal the truth. For his part, Percival spent his days finding horses and equipment for their expedition, not an easy task in a city short of animals, food and forage.

She lay Merlin's tablet on the table and took up her own, which was filled with sketches and ideas from her time with the Ontarii. Ever since she'd returned to Camelot, she longed to return to Mordred's commission in the Great Audience Hall. Percival's arrival and the new mission to find the Grail had postponed the work again, but as the sun drifted below the edge of Camelot's broken walls, she decided to visit the canvas.

With her new status as Guinevere's most trusted friend and aide, she found admittance to the palace easy, despite the heavy military presence. Workmen and engineers had departed for the day, leaving the air dusty and the halls partially blocked by carts and boxes of tools. Picking her way through the mess, Dee passed under the basilica's main arch, its doors askew. Before the war, processions of officials filed through the doors, making their way down a central aisle to the ancient throne of Arturus Strong-Arm, Arturus III's ancestor and founder of the nation.

Examining the walls and the vaulted ceiling, Dee felt she had entered another world. By some miracle, the old frescoes and the sculptural details at the tops of the columns marking each side aisle had survived. As if time reversed itself, she imagined the moment when she first heard Mordred offer her the commission to create a great mural, and her decision to tell a story of Viridiae's past and future. She remembered days behind draped scaffolds programming the light tapestry emitters and seeing the outlines of her vision taking shape. The scaffolds were gone, and her equipment safely stored, but her fingers tingled with the desire to execute her ideas again.

She also remembered the moment she had taken Mordred for her lover and her doubt on whether she had made the right choice. In the months since she and Guinevere had departed for Villefroide, the ardor had faded to ash, and she had hardly spoken to Mordred since her return to Camelot. He didn't look her up, but matters of state no doubt kept him away. He was clearly unhappy returning to his old role, but she didn't know whether he might find another way to push Arturus aside. His mother, Morgause, had remained in Camelot, and she was never far from her son's side. Though Dee found him desirable, she didn't mourn the loss of a potentially deeper connection.

The one thread that remained of their relationship was her commission. Dee assumed the contract was still valid, but even if Mordred withdrew his support, Guinevere would step in, if Dee asked. Dee admired Guinevere's intelligence and ambition, though questions persisted about the queen's true goals. She'd fought hard in her own way for Viridiae, but did she fight ultimately for Arturus, or herself? Dee never pressed Guinevere on the issue, fearing that her suspicions might prove correct, even if Guinevere denied that she desired Arturus' throne.

Each day brought news of Lucana's further descent into chaos, and Dee feared a similar ordeal awaited Camelot. For now, the city was licking its wounds along with the rest of the country. Dee and Percival would soon depart on their quest, which might turn out fruitless. While they were away, could Camelot break down into Lucian-like factions, and the sides tear at each other's throats?

Dee preferred not to speculate. Instead, she stood before her canvas, a broad wall coated by a special material that enhanced the colors and tiny animations that made light tapestries so compelling. Even without her emitters, she could see in her mind's eye the sketches and cartoons that formed the outline of the work. As before, the faces on the figures were fuzzy, but they would resolve in time. She'd have to make significant revisions, though. For example, she'd made no space for the spectacular faces and costumes of the Ontarii, especially that of Queen Jarnay. Dee would have to find a way to portray the Battle of the River's Bend as well.

Dee grinned at a last thought. Throughout history, artists had inserted themselves into these kinds of works with a modest self-portrait. It took a massive ego to create monumental art, and though Dee was not so arrogant as some, she decided a simple artist's signature wasn't enough. Once she returned from the Hot Lands, she'd come up with a clever idea, assuming she survived the trip.

SPECIAL PREVIEW: THE WEEPING WAY

***Chapter 1 of* Return to the Green Land, *Book 3 of* The Future History of the Grail**

Sir Percival Rathkeale steadied himself for another gamble. He weighed the odds of victory or defeat as he and his friends approached Camelot's western gate. For the third time, he was leaving the city on a journey with a greater chance of failure than success. He didn't know if he or his companions would return. If he returned empty-handed, his country would pass away. This was the final roll of the dice.

The footfalls of his horse echoed in the half-empty streets. Early morning sparrows flitted among piles of stone and broken lumber remaining from the Lucian occupation. He glanced over his shoulder, brushing away strands of his flaming red hair. Trailing him were retainers on horses leading pack animals heavy with supplies. Percival expected the expedition to take months.

"What's troubling you, Percival?" Sir Galahad du Lac-Corbenic rode beside him on a dapple-gray destrier. Galahad's trademark white cloak flowed over the horse's rump. "Have you forgotten something?"

"I miss my sister, Dee."

Percival's twin sister was back at the palace, probably working in the Great Audience Hall, the place where King Arturus III received important visitors and conducted public ceremonies. The king had asked Dee—short for Dindrane—to accompany Percival on the journey to Cassanti, a port city deep in the Hot Lands. At first, she agreed, but a day later, she asked him to come to the Dark Unicorn, a pub popular with students at Camelot University.

"I'm not going with you, Perce." She said this without meeting her brother's eye.

"Why not, Dee? I need you. How am I supposed to find the Grail without you?"

"You can easily find the Grail without me. Galahad knows almost as much about the Grail as Merlin. He found the False Grail. Maybe it was useless, but he found it."

"Dee, I've been on two Grail quests. One to the eastern deserts. One to Koda. Both failed. I think things would've gone better if you were with me. If I don't succeed this time—"

"That's ridiculous. I'm no expert on the Grail or the Great Machine."

"When we came to Camelot, you went to university. I went to The Keep. Until then, we did everything together at home on Mother's property. We helped each other with chores, with homework. We'd comfort each other during storms. We even, well, killed our father together."

Dee winced at the memory. "I did it to save you and me. I'm not proud of it."

"How do you know I won't need you to save me again?"

"You saved me at the Battle of the River's Bend. I'd say we're even."

"Family doesn't work like that. No one's keeping a tally."

Dee shifted in her seat. "The truth is, Perce, I want to stay in Camelot to finish my mural in the Great Audience Hall. That's my Grail, the thing I want to achieve. At first, it was just a job Mordred gave me, but now it's taken on a life of its own. I belong in front of a light tapestry telling stories with lasers and mirrors, not getting saddle sores a thousand kilometers from anywhere."

That ended the conversation. Percival was so angry and upset that he didn't speak to Dee for days. She never reached out to him; maybe she was just as angry. Arturus could not order Dee to accompany Percival. Instead, the king asked Galahad to join the expedition.

"I know I'm a poor substitute for your sister, Percival," Galahad said on the street near the western gate.

Behind Galahad, on a strong pony, rode 11-year-old Penny Corbenic, though no one knew her true surname. Galahad found her wandering the streets of Perditon as he and Lancelot traced a Grail rumor. She was now his page.

Percival shook his head at Galahad, whom he'd got to know on the Grail quest to Koda. Galahad had a bright scar on his neck from the Battle of River's Bend. "No, my friend. I'm glad you're here. And Penny as well."

Percival waved and grinned at Penny, a pretty girl whom Galahad praised as clever and quick.

She returned the smile with her own, the kind that had street knowledge behind it. In Perditon, Penny sold bulbs of water and fresh batteries to travelers, while avoiding enforcers in the corrupt city government.

As a condition for joining the expedition, Galahad insisted Penny go along. But Percival thought she might attract trouble. Though he had a plan for reaching Cassanti, no one knew the hazards of the journey in detail. No Viridian had been to the city in hundreds of years. The roads might be infested with bandits, trolls, or herds of basilisks, for all Percival knew. Penny might get hurt. She was also a liability. She would be an easy target for kidnappers or slavers reportedly operating between the border and Aurelia, the first major city on the Peaceful Sea south of Camelot. Percival planned to stop there before heading to Cassanti further on.

On the streets of Camelot, a few people watched Percival's party, unimpressed. When his first expedition left for the desert nearly two years in the past, hundreds cheered or waved handkerchiefs to wish him good luck. Now they appeared sullen and resentful. Dozens queued up on a bread line. Schools were refugee centers. Tents hugged houses and apartment buildings broken by the war.

On the news chans and com boards, people argued that the money spent on the expedition was better spent on housing refugees and rebuilding Camelot. The Lucians had destroyed grain silos and burned crops, but the failing climate had also hurt harvests. Maybe Merlin could find another solution to the climate problem. Percival sympathized with those demanding help, but he disagreed with them. Yes, all of the Grail expeditions so far had failed in one way or another. But Camelot's knights had to follow any hint of a working Grail to fix the Great Machine. That was the best way out of the crisis.

Even so, Percival's confidence wore thin. "Are we doing the right thing, Galahad? People are hungry. The money we're spending could feed thousands."

"You know what's at stake, Percival. Nothing less than survival."

He didn't need to be reminded. "That's not really an answer, my friend."

"How would history judge us if we didn't try?"

"People say we're following ghosts and fairies. They think Arturus has gone mad after nearly losing everything to Lucanus. They're turning to Lord Mordred."

Mordred, Prince of Lothia, did nothing to dissuade people from singing his praises. He was still in Arturus' government, so he couldn't speak publicly about his grievances with the king. Instead, he wheedled toadies at the Round Table and sycophants on the news chans and the com boards to press his case. Viridiae had a deep history of freedom of expression, but even Percival wondered if the stand-ins for Mordred didn't commit a petty kind of treason by promoting the prince as a candidate for monarch should Arturus suffer an early death. They winked, in a manner of speaking, when they said this. It made Percival's blood boil.

"Not everyone loves Mordred," Galahad said. "He's a great general, but he thinks too much of himself. His kind of arrogance may win victories sometimes, but it also courts disaster. Losing a bet on him could cost you your life."

Percival hoped he'd never suffer the same fault as Mordred. He wanted only one thing: the find the Grail and bring it home. Percival checked himself. He realized he wanted something else: Lina.

They'd met briefly before the war. She'd worked at the art gallery where Dee had her first important show of her light tapestries. Blond-haired and gray-eyed, Lina was sweeping the gallery's floor when he first saw her. He'd thought about her a few times during the journey to Koda and in his cell in Lucana.

When he returned to Camelot, he learned the she and Dee had become close friends. When he met Lina again, the spark turned into a flame. Within a few days, they'd spent all their spare time together, even as he scrambled to pull together the expedition. Percival reached into his tunic and removed his com reader. He scrolled through a few texts until he came to Lina's.

I'll think of you every day. I know you'll succeed. I'll wait for you.

Only 14 words, but each of them were like diamonds. If he survived, Percival thought, he'd find a way to preserve them forever.

"News?" Galahad said. "You're staring at your com as if you got the last message you'll ever receive."

Percival tucked the device back in his pocket. "What if we don't come back, Galahad? Will people remember us? Will they think about us?"

"People generally forget failures, except glorious failures."

The gated portal through Camelot's outer defensive walls came into view. Before the Lucians reached the city during the war, tens of thousands of refugees had fled through the gate, which led to Camelot's suburbs and forested hills beyond. Over the decades since its construction, water collected between the stones and dripped down, creating the illusion of tears. Camelot's residents called it the Weeping Way.

As if offering reassurance, a temple to Gaia stood to one side of the gate. Percival's mother, Eleanor, a secular woman who home-schooled her children, taught Percival and Dee to value facts and reasoning. She treated religion as an annoying curiosity. Percival, however, had seen first-hand the power of the unseen. His sister had inherited an ability to kill at a distance with nothing more than her will. Was it strictly an unexplained natural phenomenon? Or was it supernatural? He didn't know, but he knew enough to respect a possibility: Gaia, the Mother of All Life, was real, even if you couldn't touch or see her.

"Let's take a break before we leave." Percival dismounted and climbed the steps into the temple, which the Lucians had left untouched. Both cultures honored the Mother, though they argued over which honored her more devoutly. They hadn't fought any wars over religion, at least not yet. Percival didn't expect his companions to follow him inside, but they did. They meant it as a gesture of loyalty, which he appreciated, and it reminded him of his responsibilities.

Their gear and animals were safe outside without a guard. That would change once they left the city.

Percival passed through a circular colonnade into a room protected by a dome with an oculus at its apex. Sunlight streamed through floor-to-ceiling windows, highlighting dust floating in the air. Fresh flowers from the People's Preserve filled vases attached to the walls. A bronze brazier with a small fire burned in the center of the temple. The fire was the only plasma fire allowed by Viridian law. Burning wood or incense released carbon dioxide into the atmosphere, breaking an ancient taboo, but the fire tradition was as old as humanity and believers insisted on it. The temple could hold fifty or sixty people. On the solstices, priests and priestesses led all-day ceremonies. On this day, the only devotees were Percival and his party.

Percival took a seat on a stone bench. He liked the peace he felt below the wooden vault. Two-dimensional paintings on the temple walls celebrated the forests, mountains, and wild coasts of Viridiae. They showed why some people preferred calling their country "the Green Land." Small twittering birds flitted among the rafters. People said the birds carried messages to Gaia.

Galahad, dressed in a dark green tunic and trousers the color of loamy earth, approached the brazier. He drew his sword, the weapon singing against the metal of his scabbard. He dropped reverently to one knee, bowed his head, and held his weapon before him. Penny looked on, wonder in her eyes. After a few breaths, Galahad stood and stepped back, deep in thought.

Outside at the temple gate, when the party remounted their animals, Percival said, "Were you praying in there, Galahad?"

"I don't really understand what people mean by prayer, but I thought about our quest and how Viridiae is depending on us. I offered my service to Gaia and our country. There are things larger than ourselves. Do you think I was silly?"

Percival didn't think so. Although he didn't feel the need for a ritual gesture, a thousand thoughts filled his mind. He worried about his ability to fulfill his task, especially without his sister. Twice he'd lost the Viridian Grail, the only thing that could save his country from a slow death. He lost it on Koda and on the trek back from Lucana. The odds were he'd fail again.

He longed to atone for what he'd done in the war. He'd murdered a man out of hatred and frustration. How do you repay the taking of a life? He'd also lost his nerve at River's Bend, when every fighting man in Viridiae challenged an army bent on destroying Camelot. He was needed, but he ignored the call. Arturus had given him a chance to redeem himself by finding what people started calling the "Last Grail," but Percival wondered if redemption was possible.

Remounting their horses, Percival and the expedition rose slowly toward the Weeping Way. Recent rains had recharged the cracks between the stones. They passed under the gate's wide arch, and drops of water hit Percival's checks and dribbled down his neck. It was easy to believe the walls of Camelot shed tears of farewell and wished godspeed.

AUTHOR'S NOTE

Thank you so much for reading *War for the Green Land*, the second book in my fantasy trilogy, *The Future History of the Grail*. Like many young boys, I thrilled at the King Arthur stories, starting with T.H. White's *The Once and Future King*, published in 1958, the year before I was born. I also loved any movie with Arthurian themes. I'll never forget watching John Boorman's 1981 classic *Excalibur* at a theatre in Seattle's Northgate Mall in 1981. Frankly, I found these versions of Arthur, Guinevere, Lancelot, and all the other Arthurian personalities far more compelling than other rising interpretations of medieval fantasy, such as Dungeons & Dragons. The inventions of Geoffrey of Monmouth, Sir Thomas Malory, and various French and German storytellers are timeless, universal and cross-cultural, available to any modern storyteller willing to take them on.

Today's challenge is finding a new approach to the characters. I've written science fiction novels that take place in a relatively near future affected by climate change, which is one of my major themes. I believe humanity faces an existential threat from a warming climate, and I wanted to speculate on how people might adapt in the next century or two. For this new project, I wondered how could I combine the Arthurian legends with the reality of an unfolding environmental disaster. Most modern interpretations of the Arthurian stories place them in a historical past or a more-or-less realistic present. I decided to project my Arthurian characters into the future, a thousand years, to be exact. To my knowledge, very few writers have tried this. I'll leave it to you to decide whether I was successful.

Figuring out the problems with this strategy took some research. Of course, I watched *Excalibur* again. I also picked up a few volumes from Powell's Books in Portland, Ore. The books included *Arthurian Myth & Legend: An A-Z of People and Places*, a reference I went to again and again. I also purchased John Matthews' *The Arthurian Tradition* and *The Grail Tradition*, which provided invaluable structural and plot help, as well as explaining the original spiritual meaning of the Grail legend. *Life in a Medieval Village*, by Frances and Joseph Gies, provided some ideas about setting. A video lecture series by Prof. Dorsey Armstrong of Purdue University was priceless in helping me understand the Arthurian narrative tradition. The series is part of the Great Courses, which I accessed through the Seattle Public Library. And then there are countless online articles and websites. A good list of sites is available at the Best of Legends. I found the lyrics for the traditional songs used in chapter 14 of *Fall of the Green Land* and chapter 21 of *Return of the Green Land* at the Traditional Music Library. I also took inspiration for the characters and culture of the Lucians from Shakespeare's *Julius Caesar* and the HBO series *Rome*. And what would writers on deadline do without Wikipedia?

Of course, I had enormous help with the project along the way. Editor Melanie Austin helped with structure and characters. My wife Edith Follansbee proved again that I have a habit of forgetting to insert certain words, thinking that people won't notice them if they've gone missing. My friends at South Seattle Fiction Writers read early drafts. More friends at Two-Hour Transport in Seattle suffered through readings of my works-in-progress. Numerous friends and relatives volunteered as beta readers, not knowing what they were getting into. Thank you all!

I'd like to hear your feedback. Please take a moment to review my book on Amazon, Goodreads, or your favorite book review site. You can follow me on Facebook (@AuthorJGFollansbee), Twitter (@Joe_Follansbee), and Instagram (@jgfollansbee). You can also follow me on my personal blog. Tell your friends!

The three novels in the *Future History of the Grail* are intended to be read in sequence. *Fall of the Green Land* is followed by *War for the Green Land* and finally by *Return of the Green Land*. Of course, you can read them in whatever sequence you like, as long as you read them.

Thanks again!

– Joe Follansbee, Summer 2020

MORE BOOKS BY J.G. FOLLANSBEE

Tales From a Warming Planet
The Mother Earth Insurgency
Carbon Run
City of Ice and Dreams
Restoration

The Fyddeye Guides
The Fyddeye Guide to America's Maritime History
The Fyddeye Guide to America's Lighthouses

Young Adult Historical Fiction
Bet: Stowaway Daughter

Maritime History
Shipbuilders, Sea Captains, and Fishermen: The Story of the Schooner Wawona
Blowing Out the Stink: Life on a Lumber and Cod Schooner, 1897-1947

ABOUT THE AUTHOR

J.G. Follansbee is an award-winning writer of thrillers, fantasy and science fiction novels and short stories with climate change themes. An author of maritime history and travel guides, he has published articles in newspapers, regional and national magazines, and regional and national radio networks, including National Public Radio. He's also worked in the high-tech and non-profit worlds. He lives in Seattle and blogs at https://jgfollansbee.com/blog/.